Love

Way Back When
Duet, Book 1

ASHLEE ROSE

Ashlee Rose
Copyright © 2021 Ashlee Rose

First Edition

The author has asserted their moral right under the Copyright, Designs and Patents Act, 1988, to be identified as the author of this work.

All rights reserved. No part of this publication may be reproduced, copied, stored in a retrieval system, or transmitted, in any form by or by any means, without the prior written consent of the copyright holder, nor be otherwise circulated in any form of binding or cover other than that in which it is published and without a similar condition being imposed on the subsequent purchaser.

This is a work of fiction. Names, characters, businesses, places, events and incidents are either the products of the authors imagination or used in a fictitious manner. Any resemblance to actual persons, living or dead, or actual events is purely coincidental.

Cover design: Irish Ink
Formatting: Irish Ink
Editing: Liji Editing
Proof Reading: Lea Joan

Two souls are sometimes created together and in love before they're even born.

– F. Scott Fitzgerald

Other Books by Ashlee Rose

Entwined in You Series:

Something New
Something to Lose
Something Everlasting

Before Her
Without Her
Forever Her

Standalones:

Unwanted
Promise Me
Savage Love
Tortured Hero

Novellas:

Welcome to Rosemont

All available on Amazon Kindle Unlimited
Only suitable for 18+ due to nature of the books.

Chapter One

I sighed as I straightened the tie in my fitted, white-collared shirt. *How the hell was it Monday already?* The weekends flew. Not that I had done much, I was lost in assignments that needed to be in this week. I didn't like rushing and putting minimal effort into my work, this was my one attempt to make what I wanted out of my life. Don't get me wrong, my life could be worse. I am surrounded by wonderful friends, a loving mum and a hard-working dad who has given us a life that you could only dream of. I have it all.

But it doesn't mean I want to live in Daddy's pockets for the rest of my life. I want a purpose, I want to live and not merely exist in this sad, materialistic, rich world.

"Peyton, darling," I heard my mum call up the stairs, pulling me from my thoughts.

I give myself a last glance in the mirror, pulling my pleated, navy-check skirt down so it sat just above my knees. I knew my dad would be mad if my skirt sat any higher than it should be. Grabbing my bag, I walked out the door, flicking my waist-length chocolate-brown hair over my shoulder.

I plastered a smile across my face as I skipped down the stairs and moved into the kitchen. My breakfast of granola, yoghurt and fruit was waiting for me, along with a pint of water.

"Morning, beautiful." My mum smiled as she handed me a spoon and I took my seat at the breakfast bar.

"Morning, Mum." My eyes glistening as I looked at her, I admired my mum so much. She was such a strong and beautiful woman. Her glossy brown hair sitting shoulder length, always impeccably dressed and her make-up flawless. Not that she needed it.

"Did you get your assignment done?" she asked, as she pottered around the––already––clean kitchen, busying herself.

"I did, thank God. Just glad to have got it out the way with a few days to spare." I nodded as I swallowed a mouthful of my breakfast. I liked to be organised and not rush when it came to my school work. My anxiety was too bad to leave things to the last minute all the time.

Her eyes darted over her shoulder as my dad stepped into the room. They looked at each other with such love and admiration.

"Morning, princess." His lips pressed to the top of my head as he kissed me, and then he moved over towards my mum.

"Morning, Dad," I chimed through a mouthful of granola. I can only wish for a love like theirs when I am older.

"Another day closer to joining my law firm." He winked, a small smile creeping onto his face, his lips turning at the corner on one side.

"Yeah..." My voice trailed off as I rolled my eyes behind his back. I couldn't hide the flatness to my tone.

I watched as he kissed my mum on the cheek then flicked the coffee machine on to make his usual, rank, black coffee. I turned my nose up. Coffee was bad enough with milk, let alone without it.

My dad wanted his precious daughter to follow in his footsteps, to work for him and eventually take over his law firm. Up until a few months ago, I wanted that too, but I always felt deep down that this wasn't the path I was due to go down.

I knew what my dream was. And I wasn't going to give up until I was living it.

I just needed to get through the last year of high school, then when I was eighteen, I would be in university, another step closer to freedom.

I was only young, but I knew what I wanted. I was brought up very level-headed and strong-willed, and maybe a streak of stubbornness ran through me, but I liked that. I wouldn't be walked over, and no one pushed me around.

I was independent.

—

I sat in the car; my earphones nestled in my ears as I played *'Paramore'* from my phone. I smiled when I saw Poppy standing there, waving as my mum pulled up to the drop-off zone of our pretentious private school. Augustine Grammar School wasn't just a prestigious private school, no, it was one of the best in the country and one of the reasons why my parents sent me here. It was because this is where they went. They would never leave New Remsley. We lived in a small town called Blossom Creek, and everyone knew everyone. We were away from the hustle and bustle of the city, but not far enough that it would affect my dad's work. His offices were based in London, but he liked to come home to something a little more rural.

One thing I was certain of... I wanted out of New Remsley as soon as possible.

"Bye, Mum." I held my hand up, opening the door to her Land Rover Discovery and hopping out, grabbing my bag from the footwell.

"Bye, darling, have a good day! I'll see you at two thirty!" she called out as she drove out of the black ironed gates.

"Morning, bitch tits." Poppy laughed as she stood next to me, linking her arm through mine. Poppy had been my best friend since pre-school. I couldn't do this thing called life without her. Her caramel-blonde hair sat long down her back and was always in waves. Her deep green eyes sat big on her beautiful heart-shaped face.

"Morning to you too." I laughed, stopping on the path to pull my socks back up around my knees.

"Only joking." Poppy, nudging into me as we began to walk again. "Ready for another glorious Monday?" She rolled her eyes as we walked towards our classroom, her arm still firmly linked through mine.

"So ready," I whined before laughing, my eyes scanning down the long, bright hallway.

"Not long and we will be out of here. I hate that we have to stay here until we are eighteen, if we went to a mainstream school, we would be out and into the big wide world now, but no, we have to stay here and have a college-like experience while still roaming the halls with the twelve-year-olds," Poppy moaned as we approached our lockers, flicking her hair over her shoulder.

"I know, it doesn't make sense, but at least we are still together. Who knows what will happen when we get our university places?" I shrugged as I unlocked my locker, going through my bag and discarding some of my heavier books. I didn't need to lug them around with me, and we had so many books.

"We will stay together, boo, I have a good feeling," she sung, fisting book after book into her locker.

"I hope so, I don't want to go into the big wide world without you," I admitted, closing the locker and throwing my bag back over my shoulder.

"You won't, ever. I promise." She wrapped her arm around my shoulder and pulled me in close for a hug. It was true. I don't know what I would do without her. We never argued and have never fallen out. Well, apart from that time when we didn't see eye-to-eye on what Salvatore brother we preferred. I was team Stefan; she was team Damon.

Poppy was more rebellious than me, and I felt sometimes that I lived vicariously through her wild antics. Her mum and dad were solely business people, hardly ever home, so she had her house to herself most of the time. The only thing I did that was rebellious was get my nose pierced one weekend without my dad's permission. My mother allowed it, but she kept that on the QT. She acted as if she didn't know that I had done it when my dad lost his head over it.

But apart from that, I am your model daughter and student.

The perfect one.

Angelic.

—

The morning flew pretty quickly. We had Spanish, Latin and English literature this morning, then after

LOVE ALWAYS, PEYTON

lunch, we have Maths and English. I hate maths. It drags.

I find Poppy hovering outside our lockers as she waits for me before we head to the canteen.

"Eurgh, how is it only twelve?" She rolls her eyes, linking her arm through mine as we walk through the halls.

"I don't think it's been that bad." I shrug my shoulders. I don't mind schoolwork.

"You wouldn't, you actually like learning, I––on the other hand––am more of a free spirit," she sings, her hand flying to the air as her fingers spread, facing the ceiling.

"That you are." I laugh. Her head snaps to face me, her long blonde hair swishing before her lips curl into a smile.

Once lunch was finished, we sat in our usual spot, the third bench on the green that overlooked the playing fields.

"So, guess who met a boy at the weekend?" Poppy drawls out as she eats her red twizzle sweets.

"Did you!?" I gasp, grabbing a twizzle from the packet that sits on the bench and helping myself.

"Uh-huh, and I found out he goes to the all-boys school, Tyran Prep!" She couldn't contain the excitement in her voice. Tyran Prep was in the same school family as Augustine's.

"Oh my God," I whispered as if he could hear me. "He

is literally just through those bushes!" My voice is louder now, my intrigued eyes moving into the distance that separates us from them.

"Yup." She sighs, her eyes moving to the bushes. "So close, yet so far..." Her voice trails off before her head spins back round to face me. She looked giddy, her eyes glistening, her cheeks blushing a soft pink.

"How did you meet?" I was a hopeless romantic, I loved hearing love stories and dreaming of the fairy tale. My elbow propped on the table, my chin resting in my hand as my ice-blues focused on her.

"I was walking Champ over the woods behind mine, and Champ spooked." She shook her head, as if she couldn't believe that he would do something like that. "I mean, come on, a massive Rhodesian Ridgeback and he spooks over a rustle of the leaves." She rolls her eyes so far in the back of her head, I worried for a second that they would get stuck there before her green eyes met mine again.

"Anyway, so there I am, running through the woods, calling Champ, when I bumped into Stefan. Our eyes locked, our heart rates raced..." She looks off into the distance and lets out a blissful sigh, her shoulders sagging momentarily before her attention is back on me. "So, we found Champ, he walked me home and then we had the most panty-wetting, hot-as-fuck sex. Honestly, Peyton..." Her voice trailed off as she mouthed 'Oh my God'..'

I scrunched my nose up. I knew Poppy was sexually active, she had been for the last few months, but it always made me feel a little uncomfortable.

"Don't screw your nose up at me, prude!" She acted as if I had hurt her feelings, the palm of her hand slapping down on the bench, her eyes widening. "Just because you haven't had an orgasm yet... I'm going to buy you a vibrator, a little battery-operated friend." She nodded her head up and down quickly. "That will sort you out."

"I don't want a vibrator!" I say, a little louder than I would have liked, my eyes moving to the group of girls that were sitting in ear shot of our conversation, one giving me the side eye and an evil-as-fuck look.

Poppy held her stomach as she leant back, her head falling back as she laughed.

"Idiot." I scowled at her.

"Oh, stop it, you'll thank me once you know how it feels." She winked at me, reaching for her bottle of water and taking a big mouthful before fisting it back into her bag.

I shook my head, my eyes drifting over to the hedge that separated us from the red-blooded males before turning my attention back to her.

"So, are you going to see Stefan again?" I asked, a little upbeat as I ignored the unknown feelings that were running deep inside of me.

"Yup, going to see him Wednesday night, at mine, of

course. Joys of being home alone most of the time." Her smile was small, forced. I knew she hated being alone, I knew she put up a front when it came to her parents. They worked hard, they gave her everything she ever wanted, but if she could choose, she would always choose them to be with her.

She was lonely.

I was lucky that she only lived across the street, literally a three-minute walk, so she was never too far from me.

"Did you wanna come over to me tonight or tomorrow?" I asked. "Mum can sort you out some dinner." I knew my dad wouldn't be best pleased with it being a school night, but I didn't want her to be alone for another night.

"Yeah, okay, let me just text my mum..." She sniggered, pulling her phone out of the inside pocket of her blazer. "Oh right, yeah, they don't give a shit. Tell ya mum I want her home-made mac and cheese." She winked as she stood from the bench. "Come on, let's get this shit over with. Two more lessons then we are free for a few hours before having to start it all over again."

I kept mute, picking my bag up and discarding the sweet wrapper and my own bottle into the bin on our way.

I worried for Poppy. I knew she could handle herself, but she seemed to be getting herself mixed up with a few different boys at the moment. I just hope Stefan is the one to level her out, to keep her feet firmly anchored to the ground. She needed to feel some sort of home, and she had no organisation when it came to her life.

She needed some stability, but how could she when this is all she knew? Boys flitting in and out of her life, just like her parents do.

Chapter Two

I was glad when our English lesson was nearing the end. Maths was over, we literally had the last twenty minutes, and then we were out. I sat, tapping the end of my pen on my notebook, my eyes fixated on the teacher. Mrs Tides. She was pretty alright as teachers go. She must have been mid-forties, but she was always open. You could talk to her if you needed to. My mind was elsewhere when I heard her mention pen pals.

What were we? Ten? Sniggering to myself, my eyes moved to Poppy as she smirked at me, her eyes moving back to the teacher. She was thinking the same as me.

"Starting today, we are moving into the Augustine pen pal programme. You will write a letter each week to your pen pal, they will write back. It's said whoever you get paired up with will be your soul mate..." Mrs Tides eyebrows raised, she thought this was a load of bull. I heard Poppy laugh, a few other girls erupting into laughter and low chatter amongst themselves.

"Whether you believe it or not, it's happening. It's a

bit of fun, something a little different." She nodded as she sat at her desk, opening the drawer that sat under it and pulling out a list.

"I'm sorry, Miss, but if you think this is how you meet your soul mate, I think you're a little deluded," Poppy piped up, Tara next to her giggling at Poppy's words.

"Did I say I believed in it Poppy?" Tides eyes burned into Poppy's, her brows sitting so high on her face she looked like she'd had a bad Botox experience. I shook my head, my pen tapping on my notebook again.

"No." Poppy rubbed her lips into a thin line. "Sorry, Miss." Her eyes dropped to her lap.

"Like I said, whether you want to believe it or not, I really don't care. It has to be done. I will be given the other person's nickname, then you can choose to be open with them or stay as your nickname. You won't know who you are paired up with, same for the other class that are doing it. It's up to you if you want to be honest or spin them a web of lies..." Her eyes scanned the room. "But I suggest you be honest, because *if* this is true and these pen pals of yours end up being your soulmates, you wouldn't want to be dishonest with them, would you?" Her brows raised again, her eyes now narrowing on Poppy. "This is an Augustine tradition that has spanned over many, many years. I don't know of anyone who has found their soul mate, but friends of my friends who came to this school did." Tides shrugged her shoulders up as she scanned through her list. "Okay, let's get started. Write your nickname and pass it to me, I will then give you the nickname of your pen pal, then you are dismissed."

The hopeless romantic in me wanted to believe there was some truth in this, but the other part of me wanted it to be nothing other than an old myth. Just a little bit of fun.

I sat, trying to think of a nickname, a small smile playing across my lips as I jotted down *Dimples.*

It was easy enough. It suited me; I did get small dimples when I smiled. I didn't want to waste too much time thinking of a nickname when I would tell them my name at some point.

I could see Poppy laughing to herself, and I just knew she was coming up with a stupid nickname.

Mrs Tides walked around, collecting our pieces of paper. I don't know why but I felt nervous, and my hand trembled a little as I held it out for her to take from me. She gave me a wink, her eyes casting down to the paper and smiling at me before she stopped at Poppy's desk.

"I can't wait to see what you've written Poppy." Her voice echoed around the room as she took the paper from her. Poppy was the class clown. She never took anything seriously, she always wanted to make people laugh.

"Poppy!" Mrs Tides exclaimed as she rolled her eyes. "You cannot call yourself *Shithead.*"

"It's not shithead, Miss, it's pronounced Shi-Ted." Poppy ran her tongue across her top lip as she batted her eyes to me then quickly moved them back to Miss Tides.

"I can't." Tides dropped the name onto her notebook, shaking her head in utter disbelief. Tides continued walking around the room as she collected everyone's nicknames, sitting at her desk for a moment as she matched up our nicknames to our real names, scanning through to make sure she had everything she needed to give us our pen pal names.

"Do you believe in this bullshit?" Poppy leant over from her desk; her voice lowered so Tides didn't hear her.

"I would like to, but then that's a little too simple, isn't it?" I admitted, my brows furrowing as I sat up with my back straight.

"Yup, and let's be honest... life doesn't work that way, does it?" Poppy raised one eyebrow before sitting back in her seat.

"Nope," I breathed out, muttering under my breath. I wasn't sure if Poppy had actually heard my response or not.

I didn't want to admit to Poppy that I had a slither of hope running through me that this could actually happen. That the person I matched up with would be my soulmate. Could you imagine? What an epic love story.

Tides walked between the desks and placed clear folders with wads of lined paper, pens, ribbons, stamps and envelopes. Everything you would need for your pen pal journey.

My heart was drumming in my chest, my fingers twisting the nose stud that sat against my skin. I felt nervous and apprehensive. I was overthinking everything, my mind running away with everything. I hated it.

Tides stood in front of my desk, placing the clear folder down before making her way over to where Poppy was sat.

My fingers fiddled with the zipper of the folder, my eyes scanning the room as people were revealing their pen pal's nicknames.

Poppy wasted no time, diving straight in and pulling out her bit of paper with her name on.

"What's the name?" I asked. I could hear the laughs bubbling out of her.

"McDreamy." She howled before placing it back in her folder. I couldn't help my own laugh escaping. What sort of name was McDreamy?

"Come on, stop stalling. It's only a nick name." She laughed.

My fingers delved into the folder, pulling the bit of paper out and reading the nickname in my head... *Casanova.*

"What is it?" Poppy was perched on the edge of her chair as she leaned over.

I turned it around for her to see, which only caused

LOVE ALWAYS, PEYTON

another loud laugh to erupt around the room.

"Casanova?" She continued to laugh, her fingers wiping the stray tears that had managed to escape.

"How original..." I rolled my eyes, stuffing the name back into the folder and throwing it into my backpack. *Bloody Casanova.*

"Okay class, you are dismissed. I will see you tomorrow. Your letters need to be back here by Thursday so they can reach Tyran Prep for Friday morning," Miss Tides called out.

I see Poppy's eyes widen; this would put the shits up her if she knew that someone else had Stefan.

"Fuck, what if someone gets Stefan?" she asked, speaking my thoughts out loud.

"It might not even be his class." I tried to reassure her, not that it would work. Poppy was like a dog with a bone, never letting anything drop whether it was right or wrong, true or false.

"There is only one class per age group. Of course, it would have to be Tyran Prep," she growled as she pulled her bag onto her shoulder. "Shitty pen pal bollocks," she cussed as she stormed out the room.

I shook my head softly from side to side as I followed her out to our lockers.

"Why have you got to see the bad in everything? You never know, it could be Stefan you have. At least you've actually met him. I've got bloody Casanova! No doubt some stuck up, pretty rich boy who thinks his shit doesn't stink and sinks himself in-between a different girl's legs every night," I rushed out, my own frustration spilling out of me now, my cheeks flushing just thinking about it.

"Nothing wrong with that, doll, just think of the experience he carries with him. His fingers and tongue will blow your mind." She winked at me as she slammed the locker shut. Trust her to have to make a comment.

"I'll come tomorrow night... Is that okay? I'm gonna go home and start writing this letter to McDreamy, don't really wanna spend all week doing it." Poppy shrugged as she turned on her heel and walked down the hallway to the doors at the front of the school.

"Yeah, no worries, and yeah, I thought same, just get it done for tonight... Wonder why they didn't let us email them? Why have we got to write them?" I sighed as we stepped outside in the afternoon sunshine, the warmth beating down on our faces.

"Because emails would be too easy. At least this way, they know we are actually going to have to do some work... clever bastards." She nudged me as she walked towards my mum's car. "Okay to grab a lift?" she asked me, already hovering by the back door.

"Of course." I smiled. "You never have to ask." Opening the door for her, I then stepped around the back of the car, dumping my bag in the footwell as I slipped in the front.

LOVE ALWAYS, PEYTON

"How was your day, girls?" my mum asked, her eyes on Poppy's before she looked to see if it was safe to pull out.

"Same old, Mrs Fallon, what about you?" Poppy said, sitting forward, her head popping in-between the head rests.

My mum laughed. "Same old, Poppy." Her eyes were bright. "Please, call me Cassie, how many times have I had to tell you…"

Poppy winked, clucking her tongue to the roof of her mouth as she pointed her index and middle finger towards my mum, as if it was a gun she was shooting. "Gotcha."

I sighed.

"Mum, did you do the pen pal programme when you went to Augustine's?" I asked, my brows raising as I turned to face her, my body twisting towards her as I did.

"Ah, yes! The pen pals." A smile appeared on her face. "We did. Why? Have you got your names today?" she asked excitedly, her fingers tightening around the steering wheel as she fidgeted in her seat.

"Yup." I sighed, I couldn't hide the apprehension in my voice. My heart fluttered in my chest at Mrs Tides' words regarding the soul mates.

"What's wrong? It's exciting." She wiggled in her seat.

"It is, but the whole soulmate thing… do you believe in it?" I couldn't help but ask.

"Oh definitely, I was paired with your father. He was a bit of a dick at first." She laughed, and my eyes widened. I had never heard my mum say dick before, especially not about my dad. "But..." she continued. "Once I got to know him; I didn't want to be without him. I didn't believe it at first, I thought it was just some crap they were spinning us, but it worked out for me." I went to speak but she carried on. "But it doesn't work for everyone. Auntie Meryl ended up with her best friend's pen pal and vice versa. But then again, how can they work out who your soul mate is? It's all done randomly. Just a bit of fun and an old Blossom Town myth. Anyway, what's your soulmates name?"

"Nickname, we only know the nicknames at the moment." I tapped my finger on the bare skin of my thigh.

"Yeah, honey, we were given nicknames too. Come on, tell me." She slowed as we approached Poppy's house. My mum's face faltered, her perfectly shaped brows pinching together before she smoothed them back out again.

"Casanova." I rolled my eyes hard in the back of my head.

"Oh no." My mum gasped. "What a name..." She shook her head, her attention lost as she turned to face Poppy in the back. "Poppy, darling, what about yours?" she asked.

"McDreamy." Poppy winked. "How hot is that?

"So... hot?" My mum eyed me, her lips parting slightly, a confused look smothering her face.

I shrugged, and my mum shrugged back at me as Poppy opened the back door.

"Oh, Mum, is it okay for Poppy to come for dinner tomorrow?" I rushed out before Poppy disappeared.

"Of course! Always welcome, my darling, you never have to be invited, you know that!" my mum said loudly so Poppy could hear.

"Wicked! See you tomorrow, Mrs F! Bye, bitch tits, I'll call you in a bit, we can plan what we are going to write to our *'Soulmates',*" she said loudly, air quoting soulmates.

My mum sat and waited to make sure she was in safely, Champ greeting her at the door.

"I do feel for her, her parents need to put her first." My mum's voice broke slightly.

"I know, me too. It's a big old house to be rattling about on your own, isn't it?"

"It is. Maybe we should move her in with us for a while? Break up the days and nights. I know she's got that big dog there with her, but I don't like the fact that she is a seventeen-year-old girl on her own most of the time. Her mum and dad are either away with work or working early mornings and late nights. It's not on." My mum huffed as she indicated, pulling into our driveway and waiting for the large oak gates to open. Once she could, she drove through them, parking the car outside the garage and walking up to the house with me.

I kicked my shoes off, holding on to my bag as I stood at the bottom of the stairs. "I'm just gonna get changed and look through this folder," I muttered as I began climbing the stairs.

"Not a problem, angel, dinner will be done in an hour," she said as she tidied my shoes away. "Oh, and, Peyton, don't stress about this whole soulmate pen pal thing... it's just a little fun... okay?" she called out as I made it halfway up the stairs.

"I know, Mum." I turned, smiling down at her.

"Good." She nodded before disappearing.

She knew me too well; she knew this was going to bother me. Eat away at me. My every thought would now be consumed with this and my brain would be working overtime.

I stripped down, folding my skirt and blazer up and placing my tie on top of the neat pile. I threw my white shirt in the laundry basket in the corner of my room, and pulled a loose tee over my slim body and some shorts up my legs. I fell onto my bed, leaning on my front as I grabbed the clear folder. I couldn't stop my heart flutters, the butterflies swarming in my stomach. This is what was bugging me, the fact that in this folder could be the start of my new beginning with a soulmate that I didn't know existed. I wondered whether they were told the same as us?

I reached across and pulled the lined paper out, then reached down and grabbed one of my textbooks so I had something hard to lean on.

I propped my head on my hand, my elbow resting on the duvet of my bed as I tapped the pen on the lined paper. I didn't even know where to start.

Why did the Augustine girls have to start? Why couldn't the Tyran boys start the letter chain?

I rolled on my back, my hand resting on my stomach. This was ridiculous. I could feel the anxiety bubbling away deep inside of my stomach, churning with the unknown.

I sat up, grabbing my mobile off of my nightstand, dialling Poppy's number.

"Bitch tits!" she called down the phone.

"Help me out, have you started writing yet?" I whined as I rolled back on my belly, tilting my head to hold my phone in place as I picked my pen up again.

"Yeah, halfway through the letter. To be honest, it's a load of shit but it's something. What about you?"

"Nope, still staring at the page." I groaned, letting my head fall onto the paper, a thud filling my quiet room.

"Stop over thinking it, you are obsessing. Ignore everything else and just write the bloody words. It doesn't have to be perfect, just a little introduction." I heard the sigh leave her. I knew my constant obsessing and overthinking annoyed her, and it annoyed me too. But she understood me, she was always straight and honest with me, and that's what I needed.

"Okay..." I trailed off, lifting my head and pushing myself up so I was sitting cross-legged on my bed. "Thanks," I muttered.

"No problem, see ya tomorrow. Peace!" she shouted down the phone before hanging up.

"Bye," I whispered to myself, dropping my phone to the bed.

She was right. I just needed to write and stop focusing on the whole 'soulmate' aspect. It's just a rumour, a myth. My mum and dad got lucky. Well, not even lucky, just right place, right time. Plus, things were different then. You didn't have social media and mobile phones to distract them from their relationship. I shake the intrusive thoughts away, plugging my earphones into the bottom of my phone and blasting my playlist, *'The Used'* filling my ears.

~~Dear Casanova,~~

Casanova,

Before we begin, can I just say how cliché your nickname is? Casanova? Are you really like him or did you just think it would be a fun name *to use?*

As you know, my nickname is Dimples. Not really that hard to work out why. But, if you need to know, it's because I have small dimples when I smile.

What do you like doing? With a nickname like Casanova, I can probably guess...

Tell me something no one else knows about you... I'll start...

I don't want to work for my dad's law firm. I want to follow my own dream.

There. Said it.

Feels nice to actually write it down instead of carrying it around with me. Like an anchor pulling me down, a chain around my neck.

One last thing... do you believe that we are meant to be soulmates? Or do you think it is just a myth too? I'm not sure what to think.

Write back,
Love,
Dimples x

After reading the letter back over and over, I stuffed it into the envelope, sealing it and simply writing *Casanova* on the front before shoving it into my bag. Just as I went for the door, my mum appeared, telling me dinner was ready. Smiling and closing the door behind me, I followed her down the stairs, surprised to see my dad sitting at the dinner table.

He was never here for dinner. My brows pulled together, my eyes on him.

"Daddy?" My voice was laced with confusion

"Princess, you okay?" he asked as I stepped closer to him, his lips pressing to my cheek before I took my seat next to him.

"I am." I nodded as I waited for my mum to sit down

so we could eat.

"How was school?" he asked as he cut into his steak, his eyes staying on me. I felt like he had an ulterior motive or was it that he actually wanted to have dinner with us tonight?

"It was good, busy, but I am working hard." I gave him a small smile as I tucked into my dinner. My mum sat quietly at the top of the table. Her lips pursed as she cut into her food.

"Good girl, that's what I like to hear. Not long and you'll be by my side, heading up Fallon Law." He nudged my arm with his elbow, winking at me.

"Mmhmm," I hummed with a mouthful of steak in my mouth. Good excuse to not have to answer him.

"So, your mother told me about the pen pal programme. Are you excited?"

"A bit, I feel nervous." A small laugh bubbled out of me, my fingers tightening around my cutlery.

"Don't be nervous, just see it as another bit of homework. Don't read too much into it." He looked from me to my mum and smiled with such admiration and love. "Not everyone is lucky enough to meet their soulmate at seventeen, isn't that right, sweetheart?"

"It is," she agreed with him. "But remember not to focus too much on the soulmate part." She smiled at me, but her eyes seemed dull. Maybe my own anxieties were rubbing off on her? Or maybe she just didn't want to make a bigger deal out of it?

"No, definitely not, just focus on writing your letters and making a friend." My dad nodded, agreeing with my mum.

"I won't. I just want to get the letters done. I don't even know how long the programme runs for. Miss Tides didn't say."

"From memory, I think it is about three months... I could be wrong though." My mum shrugged.

Great.

"Why are you home early?" I turned my attention to my dad; I didn't want to talk about the pen pals anymore. I needed something to distract my thoughts.

"Why not?" He stopped chewing as he looked at me.

"Why not?" I mimicked him in a childish manner, throwing my shoulders up and continuing to eat my dinner.

"Can't a man come home early so he can eat dinner with his family?" My dad smirked at me. I smiled back,

"Sure" nodding my head.

The rest of our dinner was pretty quiet. I went to help my mum tidy up, but my dad wouldn't allow me to and said he would help her.

I excused myself to my bedroom for the night, flicking Netflix on and losing myself in *Vampire Diaries* for the third time.

I felt exhausted all of a sudden.

My phone beeped, and reaching over, I saw Poppy's name flash up.

Manage to get it written? I feel excited now, do you? P x

I smiled. It made me happy that she felt that way.

Yup, got it finished. Not really much, but I suppose until we start writing, I'm not going to know what to talk about. Not sure about excited, apprehensive maybe? I'm going to sleep, see you tomorrow <3 x

Just as I went to put my phone back, it beeped again.

Night, bitch tits, loves ya <3

I laughed, shaking my head and silencing my phone.

I felt wiped. I flicked the tele off and closed my eyes, dreaming of how I imagined him to look. A blonde-haired, green-eyed Casanova.

Chapter Three

I woke feeling heavy headed and groggy, the dreams that plagued me of my mysterious pen pal made for a very restless sleep. I wanted to get to school as soon as, so I could rid myself of this letter that I felt was burning a hole in my bag.

I showered quickly and threw on my clean uniform before rushing downstairs and shovelling my toast into my mouth.

"Mum, can we go? I have study class this morning," I lied.

Her eyes scanned my face for some sort of expression, but I gave nothing away. I had already text Poppy to let her know that we would be picking her up early. I didn't want to go into school alone. I knew people, I had a few friends but none like Poppy. She was my best friend and had been since pre-school. She always had my back, and I always had hers. That's just the way we were. We always stuck together. A team. Just the two of us.

Mum didn't question me as I picked the bag up from

the floor and darted down the driveway, waiting for her to unlock the car. The spring air still felt cold of a morning, but it wasn't cold enough for a coat. Once the car was unlocked, I hopped in, slamming the door behind me.

I couldn't calm these nerves, I felt so anxious and could feel it swarming in my stomach. I just wanted to get to school and get this day over with. I was hoping I would look forward to these letters in the future, but at the moment, they filled me with dread and anxiety.

If I was this anxious now, what would I feel like when he had actually responded, and I had to read his letter? What if he didn't actually respond? Oh my God, could you imagine the humiliation I would feel? I felt my chest tighten, my throat closing as I tried to swallow the large lump back down.

"Are you okay?" my mum asked, her eyes flitting from the road to me and then back to the road.

"I'm fine," I snapped at her. I didn't want to talk about it with her. I spoke to her about most things, but I didn't want to keep going over the same shit. They would just re-assure me that I was overreacting and that I didn't have to see this whole pen pal thing as a big deal. There was no truth to this whole soulmate situation regarding the pen pal programme, it was just a myth. That's what I had to keep telling myself. I didn't like the unknown, and I hated being unprepared for anything. It just didn't work for me. Some people could be blasé about things, but not me. I was regimented, something I got from my dad. It was drummed into me at an early age. To always have structure in all aspects of my life. I was a planner.

I listened to the light chatter amongst my mum and Poppy after we picked her up this morning, I wanted to join in, but I was worried that as soon as I did, I would cave and tell them what was going on in my head. I preferred to argue with my sub conscious than air my thoughts aloud.

I was relieved when we pulled up outside the school. I leant across, giving my mum a kiss on the cheek before hopping out of the car. Poppy ran around the back to catch up with me as I put my head down and headed for the hallway.

"Wait up! Jesus Christ!" Poppy called, grabbing the top of my arm and pulling me back to face her, stilling my legs.

"What's got your knickers in a twist?" Her brows pinched, her eyes darting back and forth to mine.

"Nothing!" I snapped at her, my voice blunt and to the point as I walked towards the classroom, relieved to see it empty as I dumped the letter to my pen pal in the tray at the end of Mrs Tides' desk. I instantly felt like a weight had been lifted from my tired shoulders. The shackles of my anxiety loosening a little.

Poppy stood in the doorway, her eyes trailing up and

down my body as I stepped towards her. Her face was stern, her eyes narrowing on mine as I got closer to her.

"Sorry," I muttered, pushing past her and standing against the wall on the other side of the classroom, my head tipping back.

"Sorry for what?" Poppy stood in front of me. I could see she was pissed off, and rightly so. I just spoke to her like a piece of shit.

"Just for me being an anxious mess." I shook my head softly from side to side a little, disappointed in myself.

"Peyton..." Her voice was quiet, her eyes softening slightly. "You haven't got to apologise, I knew this had been getting to you, but I don't quite understand why. Why are you getting yourself so worked up over this?" Her brows pinched again, her arms folding across her chest as she leant up against the door frame.

Her voice stayed hushed as the school halls started to fill.

"I don't know, okay!?" I snapped at her before I realised how I just spoke to her. "I don't know..." I whispered, the guilt instantly consuming me. I rolled my eyes, averting them to the floor, kicking the toe of my shoe on the tiled ground.

"You're too in your head, worrying about this whole soulmate situation." She groaned, rubbing both hands at her temples, her eyes closing.

"I know…" I admitted. "But I can't help it. I just sit there and think, how can your soulmate be someone your school sets you up with through a few poxy letters?" Even saying the words out loud made me realise how ridiculous it actually was.

"That's exactly it! How can the school play match makers and define your soul mate? They can't! It's impossible!" Her voice was louder now, her hands moving down from her temples, her back still against the door frame. "Please, Pey, listen to what I just said. It. Is. *Impossible.* It's just a bit of fun, a silly little past time. Just enjoy it, it lasts a few months and then it'll be over." She wrapped her arms around me and hugged me. "You never know, Casanova might pop ya cherry and show you why he's called Casanova." She let me go and shrugged her shoulders up, laughing at her own comment. I could always rely on Poppy to come out with a crude comment to bring me out of my own head.

I blushed, her eyes focusing on me, her smile growing on her face.

"Shut up." I groaned, tightening my grip on the strap of my backpack. "Can we just drop the conversation now? I feel better now I have dropped the letter off, and I feel better after your little pep talk." I nudged her as I passed her, walking to our science lesson.

"Of course, Dimples." She laughed again, linking her arm in mine as we walked side by side to class. I never told her enough, but I was so grateful to have her in my life.

—

I had never been so relieved for the day to be over. Poppy was coming over to ours tonight, and as promised, my mum was doing her macaroni cheese.

Mum was sitting outside the school like always, and I was grateful that I was in a better mood than I was this morning.

"Hey, girls," my mum called out as we slipped into her Land Rover.

"Hey, Mum." I smiled at her, leaning across and kissing her on the cheek. "Sorry about my mood this morning, just got myself worked up," I admitted, feeling instantly better that I had apologised.

"Darling, you don't need to apologise, you had a rough morning. We all have them." She smiled at me before pulling away and onto the road, heading towards the house.

We could easily walk home, but she always insisted that she dropped me and picked me up, and occasionally Poppy too. She just struggles to let go. I get it. I'm sure I will be the same when I have kids. *If* I have kids. The thought scares me, daunting me.

Before I could think any more of my random thoughts, we were outside our home. Poppy was out the car first, already running for the front door. My heart warmed but then cracked soon after. I felt sorry for her. I was glad that she had us though, a safe place for her. Always.

As soon as we were in the door, we headed for my bedroom.

"Girls, dinner will be in an hour," my mum called as she walked towards the kitchen. I nodded, thinking she could see me.

Poppy took no time making herself at home and diving onto my bed, grabbing the control and flicking the television on. My room was calming, in light creams and pinks. Cream satin bed covers lay over my queen-size bed, a bed canopy sitting in ivory as it cascaded at the sides. I had my show cushions that went in the ottoman as well as my bolster cushions. I had huge, ornate wardrobes in a designated dressing area that led to an en-suite that was completely white and bright, customised with dusty pink towels and bathmat.

"I'm just gonna get changed, do you want some clothes?" I asked as I threw my stuffy blazer on the ottoman at the end of the bed.

"Nah, I'm good." Poppy turned her head to face me, smiling before her eyes averted back to the television.

"Cool," I muttered, but I was just talking to the room as she was too engrossed in what she was watching. Grabbing my black lounge suit, I padded into the bathroom. I splashed my face with water, patting my skin dry and pulling my long brown hair into a messy bun.

I walked back into my room to see Poppy laying on her back, her head hanging off the bed, her fingers dancing over her phone screen. I rolled my eyes before flopping down next to her, making her phone fall onto her chest.

"Douche!" She slapped my arm as she rolled on her front then side-eyed me before her eyes averted back to her phone screen.

"Who you texting? *Stefan?*" I said his name in a whiney, high-pitched tone.

"Don't be jealous, bitch tits, you never know, he might know who your Casanova is," she teased, licking her top lip as she faced me, giving me a wink.

"Stop it." My tone was clipped as I warned her, rolling on my side and resting my head on my hand.

"Why? All I have to do is ask him and he will tell me." She giggled as she carried on texting, the smile plastered on her face.

"Don't," I whined at her as I kicked her leg with mine, making her shift and roll slightly.

"Fiiiiiiiine." She dragged the word out, shaking her head.

"How are things with Stefan anyway?" I asked as I rolled on my front. I couldn't help the pinch of jealousy that panged through me.

"Really good, he is coming to mine tomorrow…" She

bit her bottom lip, her cheeks glowing a slight pink.

"Oh course, yeah, for your hot sex," I teased her.

"You know it, girl."

"Dirt bag." I giggled, which caused her to laugh.

"You wait until you finally give your 'V' plates up, you'll know why I love it so much."

"Mmm, we will see." I shook my head, sitting up and crossing my legs. I looked over at my sad little phone, sitting there, not getting any attention. I scoffed.

"I can get Casanova's number." She answered my quiet thoughts.

"He doesn't even know who Casanova is!" I snapped at her, my eyes burning into the side of her head.

"I bet he does. I know that he is McDreamy." Her smile grew, and she wiggled her shoulders.

"No way!" I gasped, my jaw lax, my lips parted, my eyes widened.

"Yup! I am starting to think this whole *soulmate* myth might actually be real." Her voice was full of hope.

And there they were again. The damn butterflies. Only, I wish they were butterflies instead of anxiety ripping though me.

"I thought you didn't believe in the soulmate thing? I thought you agreed that it was just a bit of fun?" My voice was panicked, slight hysteria lacing it.

"I do... well, I did." She rushed the words out as if they tasted bitter on her tongue, her eyes widening as they searched my face.

"So now, because of Stefan, you think it's real?" I couldn't even hide the shock in my voice. I didn't want to.

"I don't know, okay? Is it so wrong that maybe, just maybe, I want to believe it is real so I might actually have a chance of happiness and someone who wants to be with me instead of rushing out to work and staying late for as long as they can?" Her voice was raised, her eyes glistening as she fought back tears. I couldn't even muster the words to answer her, but I didn't have to worry, because she continued.

"No, no, it's fine, Peyton. How dare I have a slither of hope that I may actually get the guy and the happily ever after." She threw her phone on the bed, standing up, crossing her arms across her chest and turning her back to me.

"Poppy... I... I'm sorry." My bottom lip quivered. I didn't want to fight with Poppy. We never fought.

"Just let me have five, will you?" she snapped, walking towards the bathroom and slamming the door behind her.

I felt awful. And so I should. Too consumed and wrapped up in my own anxiety that I attacked her.

I pulled my knees to my chest; my head turned and watched the door for Poppy to come out. I had fucked up. Massively.

How dare I diminish her little bit of hope, her

happiness.

It had been longer than five, but I was grateful to see Poppy walk back towards me.

"Pey... I..." She knotted her fingers before I lunged myself at her.

"Don't, don't. This is on me. I'm sorry. I really am," I choked as I wrapped my arms around her. "Forgive me?" I asked.

I felt her body relax, her shoulders sagging.

"I will always forgive you; you didn't do anything wrong," she muttered into my shoulder.

"I did. You deserve everything in this life, Poppy, you deserve your happiness with Stefan."

She pulled away, smiling at me, wiping the stray tear that was running down her cheek, palming it away quickly.

Our little moment was interrupted when my mum stood in the doorway to tell us dinner was done.

We exchanged smiles and made our way downstairs for Poppy's favourite dinner. My mum had gone all out for her. And that made my heart burst with joy.

My dad joined us ten minutes into our dinner, making light chatter with Poppy. They always got on so well.

"So, Poppy, me and Jason were talking and we were wondering whether you would like a room here? You know, for when being home alone is a little too much." I could see my mum felt awkward even suggesting this, and my fork fell to my plate before I quickly picked it back up again. My eyes moved to Poppy; I wasn't sure what she was thinking. Her face was unreadable.

I moved my eyes to my mum, hers on mine before they shifted to my dad's then back to Poppy's.

"Wow… I… Erm…" She sat back in the high-backed velvet chair, scratching her head then shuffling forward again.

"It was just a thought, sorry, I… well… maybe I didn't think this through…" My mum stammered slightly, her hand reaching for her wine as she glugged it down.

"No, oh, Cassie, no, honestly, I am just shocked and a little overwhelmed if I am being honest. Of course I would, but Champ would have to come… I can't leave him," Poppy rushed. "Are you sure though? I don't want to intrude… I've been okay for the last year with them popping in and out…" I heard the crack in her voice. This bothered her so much more than she let on. She is seventeen, she shouldn't be being left alone for days on end to fend for herself.

"Of course Champ can come. Just let me know when you want to stay and I will help you back with some of your bits." My mum smiled at her, instantly relaxing in her chair as she began to eat again, my dad smiling at her before his eyes dropped to his plate.

We continued dinner in light chatter before me and

Poppy excused ourselves. Poppy had already asked my mum if she could spend the evening, and of course, my mum said yes.

"Can I jump in the shower?" she asked as she clung onto the pyjamas I had given her.

"Of course, you don't need to ask." I smiled at her as I sat on the bed, flicking through the programme list before settling on *'Friends.'*

Poppy didn't say anything else, just slipped behind the bathroom door, closing it behind her. Her phone beeped a couple of times while she was showering, my eyes quickly looking and seeing Stefan's name on the screen. I was happy that she had found him, but it also worried me. I didn't want her getting strung along by him, or anyone else for that matter.

The bathroom door clicked, and Poppy stood there in my pyjamas, her hair wet before she sat on the bed next to me. "What shall I do with my clothes?" she asked.

Before I could answer, my mum swung the door open. "I'll take it, Poppy where are yours?" she asked as her eyes scanned the room.

"Skirt and shirt are already in the wash basket." I smiled at her, my eyes warming as I looked at her. She was so beautiful, kind and caring. I was in awe of her.

"Perfect, I'll have them washed, dried and back in the room before bedtime." She smiled as she closed the door behind her.

"Why is she washing them on a Tuesday?" Poppy asked, her brows pinging up slightly.

"I don't know, this is what she is like." I let out a little laugh, shrugging my shoulders.

"Well, at least she gives a shit about ya, I suppose." I heard the sigh leave her before she fell back on the bed, grabbing her phone and smiling when she saw Stefan's texts.

"So, you still having him over tomorrow?" I asked.

"Yeah, I think so. He wants to take me out on a date at the weekend, just cinema, but still... how sweet is that?" she gushed, her eyes not leaving her phone screen.

"Very sweet, you gonna go?"

"Of course, unless there was anything you wanted to do?" Her voice was a little hesitant.

"No, no, I've got studying to do," I admitted, my eyes flitting down to my linked fingers. "Go on your date." My eyes met hers as I beamed.

"You will have this soon." She pulled me to her.

"Mmm, maybe." I giggled.

"No, not maybe. You will. He is coming... in the name of Casanova." She laughed as she pushed me away.

"Stop it, he is just a pen pal." I rolled my eyes at her.

"I know, I know, but just have an open mind... I know I have changed my tune since earlier, but what are the odds of me getting Stefan? The boy has my heart already. I know I am only seventeen, but what an epic love story to tell the grandkids one day of how me and their grandad met." She swooned, her hand over her chest.

"Erm, hello, who are you and what have you done with my best friend?" I teased.

"She's still here, boo, still here." She smiled.

I got under the covers of my bed, Poppy lying next to me as she continued to text Stefan into the night, while I laid and lost myself in *'Friends'* until my eyes fell heavy and I gave into sleep.

Chapter Four

The rest of the week went pretty quickly. I pushed thoughts of Casanova to the back of my mind and threw myself into my work. I was so determined to pass my exams at the beginning of the summer term, it would mean I was one step closer to my dream. This last year left of school, then onto university. That's when I would have to tell my dad, shatter his heart and break his hopes and dreams.

We had one day to get through then it was the weekend. Not that I had any plans, but Poppy had her big date and I said I would help her get ready before I got back into my studying.

She had made a big online order using her mum's credit card, and she wanted to try her outfits on.

One thing about having extremely rich parents, they didn't care how much you spent.

Poppy sneaked up behind me, linking her arm through mine as we made our way to English. I felt the nerves crash through me; I was pretty sure today was the day that we received our replies. My heart was hammering in my chest.

"Excited?" Poppy whispered in my ear as we walked side by side, like we always did.

"No! Are you?" I scowled as I pulled my head away from her, she was too close.

"A little. I wanna know what McDreamy has written." She sighed blissfully, her mind elsewhere.

"You talk all the time, what could he have possibly written that you don't already know?" I laughed.

"Not a clue, but it's still exciting," she chimed, letting my arm go as we got to the classroom. I couldn't help my wandering eyes that moved to the filled tray on Mrs Tides desk.

I ran my clammy palms down my skirt. I needed to get a grip.

It was going to be fine. Of course, it was.

I sat in my seat, Poppy just across from me. Her eyes were glistening, a smile so big gracing her pretty face.

"Good morning class," Tides called out as she stood from her desk, the light chatter amongst class friends starting to dwindle. "Settle down, let's get started, shall we?"

The lesson was spent going through Romeo and Juliet which we would be taking in our end of term exam. I knew the story by heart. It was the most tragic love story, and it doesn't matter how many times I have watched the films and read Shakespeare's work, it still broke my heart and hurt as if it was the first time.

We had five minutes until the bell sounded, letting us know that our day was over, when Tides grabbed the basket with the letters in.

"Okay, you have all had a letter back. I am excited for you all! Your first write back." She beamed. "Letters need to be back by Tuesday, please. If you don't get them back in time then your letter won't be sent, it's that simple." Her eyes narrowed on a couple of the girls at the back.

She started making her way down the aisles between the desks, handing the letters out one by one.

I took a deep breath, holding it as I tried to slow my erratic heart. *It's fine. See the fun in it,* I was telling myself over and over again.

Tides stopped at my desk, handing me the sealed white letter. My trembling fingers took it from her, flipping it over and seeing my nickname scribbled on the front.

Dimples.

I wanted to tear it open right here and now, but then again, I didn't want to. I thought it would be best to wait until I got home to read it. It felt thick, maybe he had written an essay?

Poppy wasted no time in ripping her letter open, her

smile growing as she read on.

I couldn't stop watching her, my own smile growing as I saw how happy she was. I just hoped it lasted.

I just hoped Stefan wasn't a fuck boy.

I wanted to meet him so bad, but I didn't want to push it. I wanted her to tell me when she was ready for it.

The bell rang which caused a stampede out of the class. Everyone felt the same on a Friday. We all wanted out.

I walked quickly, stopping at my locker and filling my bag up with all my textbooks. I wanted to make sure I had them all. Last thing I wanted was to not be able to study because I left a book at school.

Poppy was at my side in an instant.

"Have you read your letter yet?" she asked, her fingers wrapped around her own letter.

"Nope, not yet! Going to wait until I am home." I shut my locker and lifted my bag. Shit. It's so heavy.

"How was your letter from Stefan?" My voice was slightly strained as I started making my way towards the exit, the hallways empty now.

"Amazing, he is just so sweet. I can't wait for our date tomorrow. Am I okay to stay at yours tonight? I'll go home, get showered and grab my clothes for tomorrow."

"Of course, you know you don't need to ask. My mum has your room all set up and ready for you now."

"Okay, cool, we can have a pizza and film night," she

chimed, pushing the fire exit bar on the double mahogany doors.

This school was so old, but it was a pretty school.

If you didn't know, you would never know it was a school.

It looked like a castle, a small castle but never-the-less, a castle.

The ceilings were high and the over-the-top décor just screamed of how prestigious this building actually was.

The hallways were pretty basic, not much to see apart from walls and walls of lockers.

I breathed in the fresh spring air, filling my lungs before climbing into my mum's waiting car.

"Hello, darlings." She air-kissed both of us, turned her radio down and pulled away.

"Cassie, are you okay to drop me home? I'll walk over later." Poppy's head appeared in-between the front head rests.

"That's fine, darling, what do you want for dinner tonight?" she asked me, but I knew she was asking Poppy.

"Erm, I thought maybe we could get a takeaway pizza? You know, Friday night treat." I smirked.

"Perfect! Your father wants a Chinese tonight, so we are going to go down to the Golden Bridge for dinner, so that works better for me. I don't have to worry as much." She laughed, stopping outside Poppy's.

"Do you wanna come in with me? I could do with some help bringing my clothes over, plus I need someone to walk Champ over with me."

"Yeah, of course," I chirped, opening my door and leaving my bag in the footwell. "Mum, would you mind taking that in with you? Just leave it by the front door. It's heavy so be careful," I warned softly, my eyes twinkling at her as a smile graced my face.

"I'm sure I will be okay." She winked at me. I closed the door and watched as she pulled away.

"Did you bring your letter?" Poppy asked as we waited for the gates of her driveway to open.

"Nope, left it in my bag," I muttered, and I was grateful I did.

"Argh, we could have read it!" she whined as she squeezed through the small gap between the gates. I followed.

"We could have, but we can't." I shrugged, smirking behind her back.

She unlocked the door, disabling the alarm before walking to the utility room at the back where Champ was.

Our houses were pretty similar in size, just the décor was different. Poppy's parents were very eccentric, had to have anything that made a statement. They paid the best designers in our area to fully kit out the house from top to bottom.

Her house was immaculate, but I suppose when

you're seventeen, you don't use the eight bedrooms, two reception rooms, the lounge, the dining room, the kitchen and the cinema room. You only need the one bathroom out of the six, one of the bedrooms, and obviously she used the kitchen for food... I think. My mum runs her food over when she knows that she is here on her own, to save her having to do it.

I was pulled from my inner thoughts when Champ came bounding down the long hallway towards me.

"Hey Champ!" I made a fuss of him as his tail blew a breeze onto my legs.

Poppy came walking down after him, flicking her long blonde hair over her shoulder as she walked past and started the climb up the stairs.

I followed, and of course, Champ did too.

"When have your parents next got their three days off?" I asked.

"Monday. I can't wait. I've missed them," she admitted.

"Yeah, I bet, not too long to wait."

"Nope. I love that they are so work orientated but it would be nice if they loved spending time with me more than their jobs. They are renowned surgeons, they're needed all over the country and I get that, I get that they need to go where the work is. But they also have a teen daughter that could do with her parents a little more." Her eyes filled with tears, brimming, but she soon shut the emotion off.

"I know..." I whispered as we walked into her large bedroom.

"It's just hard," she admitted, her eyes dropping to the floor.

I stepped towards her, throwing myself at her and wrapping her in my arms.

"I can't even imagine..." I sighed. I couldn't. I wouldn't be able to do what she does.

"I am so lucky to have you and your mum, and your dad, I suppose. I know he isn't around much either, but he is still so lovely to me." She pulled away, smiling. "Anyway, enough about me and my sob story. Let's get my clothes packed and sort the clothes for the weekend. I am so excited about Saturday." Her voice was high as she spoke about her date, as if her moment of sadness never happened.

"I'm excited for you," I said, falling onto the bed, Champ jumping up and laying his big head on my lap.

"Maybe we can double date one day?" she said quickly, spinning on her heel and giving me her mischievous look, then poking her tongue out.

"Oh, maybe... we will see." I laughed nervously, tucking my brown hair behind my ear.

"Come on!" Poppy said, throwing her blazer at me and Champ. I threw my hands up to catch it. "I'm sure McDreamy has a friend." She laughed.

"I'm sure he has many friends, let me think about it." I sighed.

She stood for a moment, silence surrounding us.

"Okay, have you thought about it?"

I couldn't help the loud laugh that left me. "No, I haven't!" I said while still giggling.

"Okay, well, I am going to decide for you. Yes, you are going to come on a double date in a couple of weeks, I'll get Stefan to sort it out with one of his friends. Any preference on hair colour, eye colour?" she said as her eyes were pinned to her phone, her fingers skating across the screen.

"Tall, dark and handsome." Sarcasm laced my voice, a small smirk edging onto my lips.

"Oooo, original." Her eyes rolled, her head dropping back.

"I don't bloody know! Surprise me," I said nonchalantly, waving my hand in the air. I really didn't care, I wasn't interested in finding a boyfriend, or going on a double date. I merely did it to shut her up.

"It's on." Poppy winked at me, grabbing some clothes and throwing them in a bag before pulling loads of new clothes off the rail in her huge walk-in wardrobe. I couldn't help but furrow my brow at the thought of a double date with a stranger.

"Okay," she said, breathless after a few minutes. "I'm ready." She nods, her hands on her hips as she looks at the pile of clothes that lay over the bed.

"Are you?" I asked, a little uncertain. My brows raising at the amount of clothes she had pulled out.

"Yup," she replied. "Now, let's get this downstairs and get Champ ready..." She trailed off, grabbing a big handful of clothes and disappearing out of the room, Champ following her. I grabbed the rest of the clothes and made my way towards the stairs. It was a good job I knew the layout of her house, otherwise I would've fallen down and possibly broken my neck. Poppy was standing by the door, holding Champ and her clothes. I didn't know how she was doing it.

We struggled out of the door, locking it behind us and walking towards my house. She nattered the whole way about Stefan and how she couldn't wait for her date tomorrow. I just wanted to get home and rid myself of these heavy clothes. I am sure I had the bigger pile, but I couldn't complain, she did have Champ.

Once she had bundled everything into my wardrobe and Champ was settled downstairs with my mum, she flopped on the bed.

"God, I feel exhausted." She yawned, stretching her arms above her head.

"Me too, it's been a long week, don't you think?"

"Yeah, it really has. I don't think it has helped because I have been looking forward to tomorrow for what feels like foreverrrrr." She dragged *forever* out, just to emphasise to me how long she felt like she had been waiting.

"Yeah, possibly. What's my reason for a long week?" I laughed as I sat up on the bed, crossing my legs under me.

"Your letter from Casanova." She winked as she moved slightly. My eyes widened as she darted off the bed as quickly as she could, grabbing the letter out of my bag and holding it above her head.

"Poppy," I warned, standing in front of her, my eyes burning into hers.

"What?" she asked dumbfounded, the letter still above her head.

"Give it to me," I whined, standing on my tip toes, trying to reach it. It was useless, I couldn't reach.

Damn it.

She was only a bit taller than me, and it was annoying me that I couldn't get it.

"Poppy, please." I could feel myself getting agitated. I knew she wouldn't read it, but she was winding me up with how she was teasing me.

Her lips curled into a smile before she began to laugh, dropping her arm and shoving the letter into my needy hands.

"Chill, woman, of course I was going to give it to you... lighten up, will you?" she teased, nudging me as she strolled back to the bed and resumed her position.

"Sorry," I mumbled, spinning on my heel and facing her before my eyes fell to the letter in my hands.

It was crumpled slightly, and my brow creased at the imperfect letter.

"You going to open it?" she asked, her brows raising as she sat up, crossing her legs under her.

"Yeah, but would you mind if I read it on my own?" My voice was quiet, hesitant.

"Course not, I'll go down and see to Champ. What pizza do you fancy? I'll order it while I'm down there," she asked as she stepped towards my bedroom door, holding onto the doorframe.

"Anything, I'm not fussy." I shrugged my shoulders and smiled at her.

"Okay, volcano hot it is." She winked before walking out the door.

"ANYTHING BUT THAT!" I shouted out after her, but I feared she didn't hear me.

I climbed onto the bed, crossing my legs underneath me as I burned holes into the letter with my eyes.

Sighing deeply, I ran my finger under the flap of the envelope, pulling the letter out and unfolding it.

My heart leapt in my chest as soon as I saw his writing.

Dimples,

How nice to meet you, sort of.

First off, my name, Casanova, is not cliché.
I am the original.
The one and only.
But in answer to your question of am I like him? You'll never know, I guess... seeing as these letters are merely pen pal letters.

I bet you look cute with your little dimples, dimples.

What do I like doing? I like seeing my friends, I like playing football, I like playing the guitar. What about you? What do you like?

Why don't you want to work for your

father's law firm? It's a solid and secure job. We all need security in life.

But thank you for telling me something no one else knows.

What do you want to do instead?

Okay, my turn. Something that no one else knows... I'm not really like Casanova. I promise. It's just a name. I couldn't think of anything, so my friend came up with that one. Plus, I have to keep up some sort of reputation, if you know what I mean. I can't have people really knowing that I am a sensitive little flower now, can I? ;)

I bet now you are thinking you have been paired up with a man whore, aren't you?

I'm not one of those either.

LOVE ALWAYS, PEYTON

I promise.

Oh, look, another promise.

What do you like to do in your spare time? It's hard between studying and school to find much spare time, don't you think?

What are your dreams, dimples? Tell me, I want to know them all...

~~Love~~, (forgot we are not on the love part yet, are we?)

Casanova.

P.S – truthfully? I don't think the myth is real...

I smiled as I folded the letter back up, placing it back into its envelope. I sat for a moment, thinking of his letter.

He seemed kind, and I was sort of grateful to think that he wasn't like a real-life Casanova. But then again, he doesn't know me, I don't know him. He could spin me a web of lies for all I know.

But I was glad he seemed nice and not chauvinistic.

I wonder whether he knows Stefan?

Should I ask?

I stood from the bed, walking into my walk-in wardrobe and grabbing an empty pink box. I opened the lid, placing the letter inside and popping it back up onto the shelf above my clothes.

That's where I would store them. To keep them safe.

I would like to try and keep them all, something to show the kids, if I ever have any one day. I made my way downstairs; I could hear Poppy and my mum laughing.

Walking into the kitchen, I saw Poppy sitting on the worktop, my mum standing next to her as both of their eyes moved to me.

Our kitchen was open-plan, all creams and marbles. The dining room table sat over the other side, in front of a huge bay window that overlooked the front of the house. My mum had pretty cream curtains sitting either side, but they were just for show. You never shut the curtains. Dark oak flooring ran throughout the downstairs of the house. I loved the colour scheme. Warm, inviting, cosy.

"You okay, darling? How was the letter?" my mum asked as she moved away from Poppy and poured me a glass of water.

"Yeah, okay, not too much. Just answered my questions mainly, thought I would write back this weekend, so it's done." I smiled. I don't know why I felt so nervous.

"That's good, did you find out his name yet?" Poppy asked.

"Nope, but then, I haven't revealed mine yet. Gonna keep it as nicknames for a while yet, see how things go." I took a mouthful of water, placing my cup on the worktop next to me.

"Exactly." My mum nodded as she pottered about, cleaning the sides down. "Poppy mentioned about a possible double date. That would be good."

"Yeah, maybe."

"I think it'll do you the world of good, darling, not for dating reasons as such, it would just be nice for you to go out, meet some new people." She spun to face me; a silly smile plastered over her face.

"I like Poppy, that's about it." I shrug, my face showing how not interested I am in this conversation.

Poppy winks at me, pats her heart then brings her fingers to her lips and blows it my way.

"Thank you, boo. That's all we need, just us two." She giggles, jumping off the worktop and coming to stand next to me, wrapping her arm around my shoulders.

"Well, until you fall madly in love with Stefan and

trade hanging out with me for him." I side eye her. It was a snide comment, but it was also the truth.

"Noooo, that'll never happen." She shakes her head from side to side fiercely.

"Mmmhmm, it always does." I nod. It was the truth and the stab in my stomach reminded me just how soon it was going to happen.

"Well, if it does and you are still single, you can third wheel with us all the time."

"Oh, lovely, thank you. Just what Stefan wants. Get a girlfriend and you get a free best friend tag along." I roll my eyes, shaking my head from side to side, keeping my voice light-hearted.

"Orrrrrr..." She smirked. "You could come on the double date, fall in love with his mate and we can all be like those older couples that have been friends since school. Bit like your mum and what's her face next door." Poppy moves her thumb behind her, moving it backwards, pointing to our next-door neighbour.

"June," my mum pipes up. "June and Steve." She smiles.

"There we go, you could be another June and Steve." Poppy pats me on the back before moving away from me.

"Brilliant." My voice is laced with sarcasm.

The room falls silent for a moment before my mum steps towards me, her hands on the tops of my arms, her eyes burning into me but her beautiful smile still firmly painted across her lips.

"Are you sure you will both be okay whilst me and Daddy are out?" my mum asks me as if I am a child who cannot cope with her mum not being close.

"Yes, Mum, we will be fine. Plus, we have Champ." I beam, reassuring her.

"Oh of course, Champ. Beautiful dog." She sighs happily. "Okay, well, I need to go and start getting ready. I'll call you up if I need any help, darlings." Her voice is soft as she walks towards the grand staircase.

"Pizza is ordered," Poppy says as she sits at the dining room table.

"Did you really go for the volcano?" I ask, sitting down next to her.

"Of course I didn't, went for a Hawaiian. That okay with you?"

"Yup, I'm good with that."

"So, the letter… was there any flirting?" She puts her arms down on the table, leaning in closer to me and lowering her voice.

"No!" I shook my head, a little taken back. "No flirting, just pleasantries." I smiled. "He seems nice, but it's easy to be who you want when you're hidden behind paper and a pen," I admit, twirling a bit of my brown hair around my finger.

"I bet he is nice. So, he didn't give his name up?"

"Nope, like I said, I think it'll be better this way anyway. Just stick to nicknames, and if things do progress, then I can find out his name at that point." I shrug.

"Makes sense." She sits back, picking at her nails. "Can I sort a double date out for next weekend?" She swoops straight back in with the burning question.

I sit and think for a moment. Would a double date really be that bad? I did need to loosen up a little, and Poppy would never leave me to just be with Stefan the whole time... well... I hoped she wouldn't. No, no, she wouldn't.

And also, it would be nice to have some eye candy and someone else to talk to.

I take a deep breath and smile. "Go on then, why not?" I laugh and Poppy squeals with excitement, throwing herself at me.

A pang shoots through me and I am not sure if it's excitement or regret. Before I could even think about it, Poppy grabs my hand and drags me upstairs and back into the bedroom, Champ following behind us.

"Let's do outfits!" Poppy squeals.

"How about we eat first? Otherwise you could end up with pizza grease all over your clothes." I raise my brow at her.

"Gah! You're right. What was I thinking? Sorry, I just get so carried away. And I am super excited to have gotten

LOVE ALWAYS, PEYTON

you to agree to a double date." She smirks at me.

Champ's ears prick up before a low growl leaves him.

"Pizza must be here!" Poppy claps her hands before running down the stairs, Champ rushing past her as she opens the front door. I followed in a bit of a daze, the double date anxiety whirling deep inside.

"Champ! Heal!" she commands, Champ sitting by her side as she takes the pizza off of the nervous guy and throws him the cash before slamming the door in his face.

She skips through to the kitchen, placing the pizza box on the side and flipping the lid. I can hear my stomach growl as the smell of the pizza wafts through the kitchen.

I step over, grabbing a slice and taking a mouthful, groaning in appreciation.

"Oh my god, this is so good," Poppy says with a mouthful of grease.

"It is." I nod as I grab another slice.

Once we have eaten and cleaned up after ourselves, we head back up to the room.

"We may have to put dress up on hold, I have a food baby." Poppy lays back on the bed, patting her bloated belly.

"Yeah, I agree." I groan, rubbing my own food-baby-belly.

I felt exhausted all of a sudden, bloated and full. I just wanted to curl up and get under my covers.

I reluctantly pulled myself from bed, walked into the

en-suite and stepped under the shower. I needed to wash my hair, but I just didn't have the energy to do it tonight. After the quickest shower ever, I dried myself off and pulled on my biggest and comfiest pyjamas. I needed an elasticated waist.

My hair was pulled in a messy bun as I padded out to the bedroom to see Poppy star-fished on the bed, gently snoring. I let out a small laugh as I knelt on the bed, turning the tele off and gently rolling her over. I loved her, but I wanted my bed also. She was still clutching her phone, which I gently prised out of her hands and plugged into my charger in the wall. Just as I settled into bed, I remembered Champ would need to go out and the doors needed to be locked. I groaned, making my way downstairs. Champ was lying by the front door, his tail wagging as he saw me approach.

"Hey, Champ," I cooed quietly as he followed me towards to back garden. Our house sat on a couple of acres, I was just hoping he didn't pick up a scent and run off down the bottom.

I slid the bifold doors across, Champ bolting past me and running into the darkness.

I sighed as I sat down, my legs hanging over the door threshold as I waited for Champ to come back.

I couldn't stop my mind drifting away, thinking of our double date. I hoped Stefan brought someone nice for me, I would hate for my first ever date to be with a complete dick.

Poppy wouldn't allow it, I hoped.

Champ surprised me by bounding back towards me, jumping through the open door and padding down the hallway to where he was laying by the front entrance. I locked the back up, then switched the lights off before checking the front door once more.

My parents shouldn't be too late, but I didn't want to risk leaving it unlocked. We lived in a beautiful area where crime was low, but still, I locked the door.

I was half expecting Champ to follow me up, but as I got halfway up the stairs, he was still by the front door. He yawned before bowing his head down and tucking his nose under his front legs. I smiled, my hand holding onto the banister.

"Night, Champ," I said quietly before I made my way to bed.

Chapter Five

I was startled by a loud tapping nose. I rolled over, panicked when I saw Poppy lying next to me, still in a peaceful slumber. I reached over for my phone to check the time; it was one a.m. I felt like I had been asleep for only a few moments, when in reality, it had been a few hours. I flicked my lamp on, rubbing the sleep out of my eyes as Poppy groaned. I looked around the room utterly confused. Was I imagining it? A dream maybe? Just as I was about to switch the lamp back off, I heard the tapping noise again. My eyes followed the noise, it was coming from my bedroom window. My heart started racing, my breathing harsh.

"Poppy! Poppy, wake up." I turned, nudging her.

"Go away," she moaned as she tugged the duvet over her head.

"Poppy! Stop it, someone is outside!" My voice was urgent but quiet as I nudged her again.

"What do you mean someone is outside?!" She sat bolt upright in the bed, her eyes narrowing on the window.

She did not like being woken up.

She looked so pissed.

She threw the covers back in temper, stomping over to the large sash window and sliding it up, the warm breeze blowing through the light, sheer curtains dancing in the gentle wind.

"Stefan!?" she squealed.

"Hey, beautiful, you coming down?" I heard the deep voice echoing in the darkness.

Poppy didn't say anything, she just slammed the window down and ran into the en-suite. Within minutes, she was back out, her cheeks flushed, her hair tidied and toothpaste evident on her lips.

"You aren't seriously going down there, are you?" My brows raised as I still sat in bed.

"You bet I am! Come on, he has someone down there with him." She winked, pulling her shoes on. She looked a right mess, but a beautiful one. She had leggings on, and oversized pale blue T-shirt and her blonde hair was pulled into a messy bun.

I was envious.

I, on the other hand, looked like a troll.

"Come on, Peyton, live a little," she teased as she stood there, hands on her hips.

I didn't want to, but I couldn't stop my legs from moving towards her and leaving my warm bed.

"Just give me a couple of mins…" I whispered as I stepped into the bathroom, splashing my face with cold water then brushing my teeth. I tugged my hairband out and let my long brown hair tumble around me. At least I could hide behind my hair if I wanted to.

My skin looked dewy, my ice-blue eyes were glistening and dancing in my reflection. I pinched my cheeks, trying to get a small bit of colour in them. I looked down at my plaid pyjama bottoms and oversized tee, and I debated changing, but before I could even think about it, Poppy ran into me, grabbing my hand and dragging me down towards the stairs. I was grateful to see the toothpaste gone from her lips.

I was worried that Champ would bark and wake my parents up, but he wasn't where I left him. I slipped my feet into my white trainers and unlocked the front door quietly. Our house was big and old, and everything made a noise when you didn't want it to.

Last thing I wanted was to get caught by my parents and embarrass Poppy in front of Stefan.

Poppy rushed past me, running towards Stefan and jumping into his open arms, her legs wrapping around his waist as they kissed.

I closed the front door behind me and stepped towards her, my eyes wandering to the figure standing next to Stefan.

It was hard to make them out in the dark, but the

streetlights made just enough light for us to be able to see a little.

Once Poppy and Stefan had finished their PDA, he put her down, grabbing her hand and tugging her toward the gates at the bottom of my drive. I was a little hesitant, standing there, my hand rubbing the top of my left arm before I followed reluctantly.

Once down there, I could see Stefan in much better light, and he really was a handsome boy. His mousy-blonde hair was pushed away from his face but styled in a high quiff, his opal eyes wide and glistening as he looked at Poppy with so much love. His skin was pale, his lips a rosy red. He really was beautiful. He was taller than her, and broad shouldered. I couldn't help but wonder if he worked out?

"Stefan, this is Peyton." Poppy smiled at me quickly before her attention was diverted back to Stefan.

I didn't say anything, a small smile played across my lips as I held my hand up awkwardly to signal a 'hi.' I dropped my head forward, focusing on my feet, my hair falling forward and masking my face which I was grateful for.

"She's a little shy," I heard Poppy say to Stefan. "Are you going to introduce us to your friend?"

"This is Knight. He is also a little awkward and shy." Stefan laughed at my expense.

I lifted my head slightly, my blue eyes moving to look

at Stefan's friend. He was also tall, a lot taller than Stefan. He had dark brown hair, short around the sides, and long and curly on top. It sat on his forehead, but every now and again, he would push it away slightly, so it was off his face for just a moment before it fell back down again.

His hazel eyes dragged up and down my body, the blush smothering me. His tongue darted out across his bottom lip before he moved his eyes to Stefan. His hands were fisted deep in his pockets. He rocked forward on the balls of his feet which sat in black high-topped converse. He had tight black skinny jeans on that were ripped at the knees, and an oversized white tee that hung a little lower than his belt hoops. I smiled when I noticed his black leather jacket that sat over his broad frame. I couldn't help but stare.

"What you looking at?" he spat, snarling slightly, his top lip curling.

"Nothing," I squeaked, dropping my face again so I was hidden.

"Ignore him, Peyton." Stefan chuckled as he wrapped his arm around Poppy's shoulders and pulled her into him.

I huffed, I wanted to go to bed. I was dog tired.

After standing there like a spare part for what felt like forever, I stepped back and slipped away into the darkness, sitting on the steps of the house.

I could feel myself getting agitated.

I didn't want to leave Poppy out here on her own with Stefan and douchebag, but Stefan wouldn't do anything to her, would he?

Don't leave her, Peyton. My subconscious nudged me.

I rested my elbow on my knees, my hand supporting my chin as I tried to make out their bodies in the dark. I could hear Poppy laughing, Stefan and whatever the dick's name was talking.

This is why I don't want to go on the double date. For this exact reason that Poppy will get too caught up in Stefan and I'll be left standing like a loner on my own. Not that she has to stay with me all the time, she is entitled to be with Stefan, but I would rather her keep me out of it instead of inviting me because she felt sorry for me. That's all I needed. A pity date.

Poor little Peyton. Can't even talk to a boy without shying away. Well, not that said boy actually wanted to talk to me. I couldn't even look at him for whatever reason. I mean, how dare I look at him.

I furrowed my brow, anger rising inside of me.

I saw an orange light getting closer to me, and it took me a moment to register it was a cigarette hanging out of douchebag's mouth. Disgusting.

He stopped in front of me, one of his hands still in his pocket, the other removing the cancer stick from his lips.

"Want a smoke?" he asked as he blew out a ring of smoke from his perfect plump lips.

"No, I don't. Filthy habit." I screwed my nose up, shaking my head from side to side.

"Suit yaself." He shrugged, taking another drag before sitting down next to me. "Do you mind if I join you? Getting a little sick of listening to those two confess their love for each other."

"It doesn't look like I have much of a choice seeing as you have already seated yourself next to me." Agitation clear in my voice.

I scooted up and away from him, not too much, but I felt like I needed to put some distance between us.

"I don't bite." His eyes bored into me.

"I don't know you." Now it was my turn to shrug before I nibbled on my––already––short nail.

"Filthy habit," he mocked me, shaking his head, a small laugh bubbling out of him. I rolled my eyes and averted them in the direction that Poppy and Stefan were.

"Sorry about earlier, I'm a bit of a loner." The grumpy boy's voice crashed through me.

"It's fine, no need to apologise. It's not like we are friends." I scoffed as I looked at him, the porch light illuminating his face and features.

His skin was tanned, and his deep hazel eyes hypnotized me. It's like I could see swirls of caramel running through them. His cheek bones were defined, his jaw line sharp. He looked so much older than me. Maybe he was? Who knows? I wasn't going to start asking him about himself.

He was incredibly handsome, but also, I felt he was insufferable.

"Can we start again?" His voice woke me up from my daydream.

"Start what again?" I snapped as I turned away from him.

"Us, me, introducing myself. I was very rude." And in that moment, I am sure I saw a hint of a blush appear under his glorious skin.

"If you want to, doesn't bother me." I cocked my head to the side before I looked forwards and down the driveway.

A few moments of silence passed when I felt him shift closer to me. The smell of mint flowed through my nostrils as he attempted to hide the smell of smoke that still swam in his mouth.

"I'm Knight, Stefan's friend... and you are?" he asked with a stupid smirk on his face, only one side of his lip lifting as he held his hand out.

"Peyton." I couldn't help the smile that danced across my lips, taking his hand in mine and shaking firmly.

"Nice to meet you, Peyton, I know I've said it once already, but I am sorry for earlier..." His voice trailed off for a moment. "Also, the smoking... it's very rare, I normally have one when I'm stressed..." He winked before his brows pinched together then smoothed them out as his eyes were on our hands that were still sitting inside of each other's before he pulled away quickly.

He scooted back up the step and away from me again. He didn't say another word for the rest of the night, which I thought was weird, maybe he literally tolerated me for Stefan and Poppy's sake. We had only just met, we weren't friends, we would never be friends. I obviously wasn't someone he would normally hang around with and vice versa. We were just two spare parts who were somehow dragged on a late-night meeting which neither of us wanted to be on.

Knight stood up, pulling out a cigarette box and putting the tip of a cigarette in-between his lips before he flicked his lighter, the flame crackling as it met the tip of the cancer stick in his mouth. He fisted the lighter into his back pocket, his thumb and index finger holding onto the cigarette as he took a long drag and blew out the smoke into the clear skies.

He took a couple of steps forward, his head turning to look at me over his shoulder, but no words were exchanged. I just sat there, looking up at him. Our eyes were pinned to each other for a mere moment before they soon left each other's as he strolled away and down into the darkness at the bottom of the drive.

LOVE ALWAYS, PEYTON

"I'm off, Stef, this has been lame. Catch ya tomorrow, night, Pop," I heard Knight say as he climbed our gates and disappeared.

It was a few minutes after when Poppy and Stefan appeared in front of me.

"Thank you for surprising me," Poppy gushed as she pushed herself out of Stefan's arms and pressed her lips to his.

"You're most welcome, I love you," he muttered, smiling before his lips met hers again.

"I love you too, night, my king." She smirked, her hand going into his hair and roughing it up.

"So handsome," she cooed, kissing him again then turning to face me. "Come on, Pey, let's get you to bed." She winked and skipped up the steps towards the front door.

"Night, Peyton, was nice to meet you. Sorry about Knight again." I could see the remorse on Stefan's face.

"Oh, please don't apologise for your friend's rude behaviour, it's fine." I waved my hand towards him, dismissing his apology. "And night, Stefan, it was nice to meet you too." I smiled, pushing myself off of the steps and walking towards the front door.

"Night, beautiful, I'll see you tomorrow. I can't wait for our date." He spoke into Poppy's ear.

I didn't stick around to see what else was said, I slipped in the front door and stood in the hallway, waiting for Poppy to come in. I didn't want to disturb the rest of the house and especially not Champ.

Within a couple of minutes, she was inside with me. I closed the door behind her and locked it before we carried on upstairs.

I could tell she wanted to talk, but I was utterly exhausted.

I climbed into bed, pulling the covers up under my chin. "Pop, I know you want to speak, but it's three a.m. and I am so tired. Can we talk tomorrow morning?" I ask, yawning, my eyes falling heavy.

"Of course, night, boo."

"Night," I managed before I fell into a Knight-filled nightmare.

Chapter Six

I woke, rolling over to see Poppy sitting up, bright eyed and bushy tailed. Her legs were crossed under her as she was tapping away on her phone. I rolled over to face the window, reaching for my phone to check the time. Nine a.m.

I felt groggy, and snappy. I didn't sleep well, a hazel-eyed demon taunted me in my dreams.

"Morning, boo," Poppy chimed as she leaned over me, kissing me on the cheek.

"Morning." My voice was flat, my eyes staring at my lonely phone.

"What's wrong?" Her voice was higher, and I could hear the concern lacing it.

"Nothing, I just didn't sleep well," I admitted, throwing my phone on the bed and rolling on my back. I still felt agitated. Knight agitated me and I had only had a brief meeting with him.

"Someone on your mind?" She over exaggerates her wink, nudging me with her elbow.

"Ew, no!" I shook my head fast from side to side. I didn't want her getting any silly ideas that me and Knight were ever going to happen.

"Stop it, Knight is a dream boat." She huffed, falling back on my bed.

"You date him then." I shrugged my shoulders up. A pang of jealousy shot through me.

"No! Stefan is my McDreamy." She giggled before pulling herself up and hopping out the bed. "Talking of McDreamy, it's time for me to get showered. He will be here at noon, so I need to make sure I look all pretty for him."

"You always look pretty, no need to change." I smiled weakly, my eyes narrowing on her slightly. I didn't want her to think she needed to better herself for Stefan, or anyone for that matter.

"Ah, thank you, doll." She winked, turning on her heel and disappearing into my wardrobe, hunting though her clothes.

"I'll go get us some tea and breakfast; I'll be back by the time you're out the shower." I hummed as I walked to the door and disappeared downstairs.

"Morning." My face broke into a smile as I saw my mum and dad sitting in the snug, cradling a hot cup of coffee.

"Don't talk to me!" My mum dropped her head, holding it with her hand.

"Your mum is feeling a little delicate," my dad grumbled before breaking into a laugh.

"Oh no..." My voice trailed off, laughing with my dad.

"It was the cheap wine, okay?" she defended herself.

"Cassie, when have you ever drunk cheap wine? The bottles you were drinking were fifty a pop... and that's before you asked them to break out their boxed champagne." He roared, holding his belly as he laughed harder now.

"Oh, deary me." I giggled, flicking the kettle on. "I was going to see if you would make us breakfast, Mum, but I'm sure I can manage." I nibbled on my bottom lip as I watched my mum, her head still sitting in her hand.

I really wanted to laugh, but I kept it in.

Once the tea was made, I lifted the glass lid of the cake stand and pinched a couple of butter croissants then walked to the stairs, moving carefully, not wanting to spill the tea.

My mum would never let us eat upstairs, but I was making the most of it while she was hungover.

Poppy was sitting on the bed in her towel, her hair wrapped up as her eyes lit up when she saw the tea and croissants.

"Thank you, I am so hungry." She mewed as she took them from me.

"Me too, we stretched our stomachs with the pizza we ate last night." I rolled my eyes. "Sorry it's not much,

Mum is hungover so just had to go with what we had." I laughed.

"No, she isn't?"

"Yup, blaming it on cheap wine." My lips curled into a smile as I tried to stifle the laugh that felt like it was going to erupt at any second.

"Stop it." Poppy's head fell back and she let out a loud laugh which caused me to laugh with her.

"Seriously." I cried tears of laughter.

After a few minutes, we had calmed down, and Poppy ran her fingers under her eyes. "Mate, your mum makes me die. I can't wait until we can go out drinking with her."

"Don't, she isn't a fun drunk. She is annoying." I scowl.

"Oh stop, it'll be fun. Wait until our eighteenth, we can get silly drunk. I can't wait," Poppy exclaimed excitedly.

"It doesn't seem fun; you should see the state of my mum." A laugh bubbled out of me again.

"She's older though, apparently the older you get the worse your hangovers are." Poppy shrugged her shoulders, taking a mouthful of her tea.

"Delish." She licked her lips then took a bite out of the flaky, buttery croissant.

I was already done with mine, I was ravenous.

I sat, sipping my tea while Poppy finished.

"How you feeling about today?" I asked. I was feeling a little better than I had early this morning.

"I'm excited, my first date. I have never been taken on a date before."

"I am excited for you, Stefan seemed really nice last night." I tilted my head to the side and smiled at her.

"He is really nice... I am lucky." She nodded, licking the butter off her fingers.

"You deserve it, hun." And I meant it.

"So do you, your knight in shining armour will come soon." Her smile was small, weak even.

"Eurgh, I don't ever wanna hear the word or name Knight again." I shook my head. "He wasn't pleasant."

"You know what they say though, horrible boys... it means they like you." She winked.

"That's the biggest load of bull I have ever heard. There is no excuse for boys being like that, or men for that matter." I could feel the anger bubbling away inside of me. There was never an excuse for someone to act like that towards a girl. It was never okay.

"Alright, calm down."

"I'm sorry, I just don't believe it. Girls shouldn't be told that––"

"Okay, fine, you're right." She sounded defeated for a moment.

The silence was thick around us, the tension growing by the minute.

"You decided what you're going to wear?" I asked before taking a sip of my tea. I loved a cuppa, and this one was delicious.

"Not a clue, weather is meant to be warm, but you know what spring is like in the UK." She rolled her eyes.

"Mm, why not a little summer dress with a cardi over your shoulders?"

"Maybe, I have so many options, so we can play dress up in a little while. We can play real life barbie."

"I can't wait!" I clapped my hands together. "I'm gonna jump in the shower, need to wash my hair… won't be long." I smiled as I stood from the bed and walked into the shower.

I didn't spend ages in there, I didn't want to keep Poppy waiting. I knew she was a little anxious, and I know she wants to look perfect for him.

And we would make her perfect.

To be honest, she was already perfect. She was a natural beauty.

I padded back into the room; my towel wrapped around my petite frame.

I stopped at the wardrobe, grabbing a pair of skinny high-waisted jeans and a white cropped tee. I slipped my underwear on and pulled my tee over my head. I shimmied into my jeans, doing the button up. Gazing at myself in the mirror, I was happy with the way I looked.

Poppy was still sitting on the bed in a towel, her hair

still wrapped up.

"You ready?" I asked.

I needed to dry my hair, but I would do it in-between getting her ready.

"Yup, lemme get my undies on." She moaned as she stood from the bed, dropping the towel and disappearing into the bathroom.

She didn't give two fucks.

We were best friends, but I still knew where the line was. But no, not Poppy. She didn't see the line; the line was invisible to her.

I scoffed a laugh, shaking my head in disbelief as I walked to my large dressing table, opening the drawers and pulling out all my makeup. Half of this I didn't have a clue how to use, but I knew the basics.

She reappeared within minutes in her underwear, her long blonde hair damp and wavy.

"Right, let's do this." She clapped her hands together, rubbing them before she started grabbing all of her clothes out and throwing them on the bed.

"You look cute by the way," Poppy said before turning her attention to the bundle of clothes on the bed.

"Er, thanks." My brows pinched, my eyes focusing on the clothes. "Right, what are you feeling?" I asked.

"I don't know." She tipped her head back, softly shaking her body as if she was frustrated.

"What are you doing? Do you know?"

"Nope, surprise." She shrugs her shoulders.

"Right, so we need something versatile. So maybe not a dress, just in case it is something a little sportier or something." I giggled.

"Mate, he better not have done something like bloody rock climbing." She sighed, reaching for her phone under the mountain of clothes.

"Text him and ask what shoes you need to wear, then we can have some sort of idea."

"How about you text him off your phone and ask him where we are going?" Her eyes widen as she gives me her best puppy dog eyes.

"But... it's a bit weird, isn't it?" I asked, a little nervous

"Of course it isn't." She shook her head, walking around the bed, grabbing my phone and tapping the screen.

She stepped towards me, handing me my phone. "There, you have my Stefan's number. You are only to text him to talk about me, my birthday and Christmas presents." She winked, flicking her hair off her shoulder. "Oh and valentines and anniversaries."

"Mmhmm." I rolled my eyes at her.

I stared down at the screen, my thumbs hovering over the keys on the screen. "What do you want me to ask?"

"Ask where we are going, then tell me." She perched

her bum on the edge of my bed.

"I'm not telling you! It's a surprise."

"Fine!" She slapped her hand down beside her. "Just ask where we are going then give me some hints." She smiled sweetly, batting her eyelashes at me.

"Fine."

My thumbs danced over the keys as I started my text.

Hey, Stefan, sorry for the random message, it's Peyton. You know, Poppy's friend. Erm, she is struggling with what to wear and I was wondering if you could give me a little clue on what you are doing? Just so I can help her choose something. You know, in case you are taking her rock climbing, she doesn't want to be in a dress.
Thanks.

I internally groaned as I hit send, I was so awkward.

I stood, tapping the back of my phone as I waited.

"Anything yet?" Poppy asked.

"Nope."

"Boys." She shook her head from side to side in a disapproving manner.

Literally, no sooner than the words left her mouth, my phone vibrated.

It was him.

"He's replied," I muttered.

"And?"

"Give me a minute," I snapped.

Hey, Pey,

You okay? Sorry again about Knight yesterday, next time you see him, I'll make sure he apologises and is kind.

Tell her to stop worrying her pretty little head about it. No rock climbing ;)

I am taking her on a picnic, so she can wear a dress if she wishes… but don't tell her. I want it to be a surprise.

Just one quick thing, what's her favourite sandwich filler?

Stefan

I smiled. He was so sweet.

"Are you gonna tell me what he said or just gawk at your phone, smiling?" she teased, letting out a small giggle.

"No need to worry about rock climbing, all is fine. It's the perfect date." I looked up from my phone, smiling at her.

I quickly text back saying her favourite sandwich filling was cheese, tomato and salad cream, with a layer of plain crisp in the middle. Little weirdo.

"Okay, so now can you help me find the perfect outfit for the perfect date?" she asked as she stood up.

"Of course I can, let's go." I beamed at her, I was happy to help.

Half an hour passed and we were no closer to her finding an outfit. She was getting frustrated, and so was I. I had studying I wanted to do, and I wanted to get my letter written to Casanova.

"I give up." She sighed, throwing herself into the pile of clothes.

I stepped towards her, grabbing her arm and pulling her up to her feet.

"We will find something, stop being pessimistic."

"Everything looks disgusting on me." She groaned. "I feel fat in everything."

"Pfft, I have seen more fat on a chip. Now, stop groaning. You would look lovely in a black bin bag." My voice cracks and breaks into a laugh

"Thanks for the optimism, but I still feel rank." She poked her tongue out, screwing her face up.

"Stop it, right, let me see..." I trailed my voice off as I rummaged through her clothes. "No wonder you can't find anything when you have them here in a heap." I shook my head before grabbing a pair of light blue jeans and a Bardot cropped top with frilly sleeved arms.

I shoved them into her hands. "Now, go try that one."

My hands moved to my hips as I tapped my foot while I waited for her to put the outfit on.

Once she had it on, I clasped my hands together, smiling at her.

"Poppy, you look beautiful."

"Do you think? What shoes would I wear? And can I wear a cardigan with it?" she asked me, her head tilted as she looked at her reflection.

"Your black patent doc martens, or high-top converse?" I suggested as I sat cross legged on the bed. "Which are more comfortable?"

"Docs." She turned to face me. "I think."

"Put them on, let me see." I watched as she disappeared into the wardrobe, and I reached behind me and grabbed my phone to text Stefan.

She looks amazing. You're a lucky guy.

She walks back in the room, falling to the floor and slipping her feet into her boots before standing up and giving me a twirl.

"Perfect, you look so good." I beamed, clapping my hands in excitement.

"Are you sure?" Her brows crinkled, a deep frown line setting in, her lips pouting.

"Yes!" I pushed myself off the bed, grabbing her shoulders and turning her around to face the mirror.

"Look at yourself, you look amazing. Trust me, Stefan isn't gonna know what to do with himself." I smiled at her in the mirror.

"Thank you, Pey." She smiled, turning around to face me and hugging me.

"Always." I hugged her before pulling back, my hands now gripping the top of her arms. "Let's sort your hair and makeup out." I grab her hand and drag her to follow me.

"Lead the way, pretty lady."

—

Once she is waved off and walking down the road with Stefan, I shut the door and let out a deep sigh. I hope she has a lovely time.

I walk into the kitchen to see Mum still looking a little worse for wear.

"Still feeling rough?" I asked as I grabbed a cold glass bottle of water out of the fridge.

I heard a noise come from her that was barely audible.

"Good talk," I muttered before taking a mouthful of my water. "Go and have a bath, and drink some water, you'll feel better than just moping around."

I heard her groan. Shaking my head, I wandered back upstairs to tidy the shit tip that was my room.

After an hour, my room was relatively clean. I

checked my phone, disappointment searing through me that Poppy hadn't text me. But then again, why would she?

I thought about texting her but decided against it. I didn't want to bother her on her date with Stefan.

I sat in the middle of the floor, looking around my room. I needed to study, but I just couldn't be bothered, and all of a sudden, I felt exhausted. It had just gone two p.m., and the thought of an afternoon nap seemed so appealing. I pushed up off the floor, pulling back the duvet and climbing into my bed. Before I could think about it anymore, I was gone.

Chapter Seven

I woke with a jolt, the feeling of someone's eyes on me. It took me a moment to register that it was Knight in my head again. I was frustrated that I let him into my dreams, I didn't know why he was there. It was the same dream, his hazel eyes finding mine. His glare was heated, his gaze not leaving mine.

He made me feel uneasy, but for some reason, I wanted to get to know him that little bit better.

I wonder if I could––somehow––let slip to Poppy for Stefan to bring Knight along for our double date next week.

I will probably regret it, but for the minute, I wanted to see him again. I wanted to see if he made me feel anything else other than rage.

I looked at the time, it was only three-thirty. But that nap was needed, and I felt more refreshed and not as agitated as I did before.

I climbed out of bed, walking into the walk-in wardrobe and grabbing my school bag. I walked back into my room, sitting on my bed and pulling out my English book. I wanted to get my Romeo and Juliet paper finished and turned in on Monday.

My phone beeped and distracted me from my textbooks. I reached over and smiled to see that Poppy was on her way back. It was four-thirty. I decided to ditch the books and continue tonight or tomorrow morning once Poppy was back home. Well, I was assuming she was heading home tomorrow, seeing as her mum and dad were going to be back.

I left my textbooks scattered over my bed, the heart-breaking story of Romeo and Juliet swimming through my thoughts.

I padded back into the walk-in wardrobe and reached for the pink box on the top of the shelf in my wardrobes. I brought it into my bedroom and lifted the lid off. My fingers ran over the envelope before I pulled it out and laid down on the bed. I sat and stared at it for a moment, then picked it up and read the two pages again.

Casanova,

God, even writing the name gives me the ick.

So, you like doing all the usual boy stuff

then? Are you a big sport junkie? Or not really? Oh wow, the guitar. Do you compose your own songs? I am useless with instruments; I couldn't even play the recorder. How pitiful. I would love to play the guitar, something about it just seems so appealing.

I like reading, I used to horse ride, but as always, life gets in the way, and I had to grow up a little. Fun hobbies got replaced with studying and essays. The role model student, as my father likes to remind me daily.

It's never ending, so no, in-between studying and school there isn't much time left to do what I would like, I suppose.

I like to hang with my friend, she is more like a sister really. But I am worried that soon I will lose her to her new boyfriend. You know what happens when girls and boys meet, their *friends slowly but surely get replaced.*

~~Do you have a girlfriend?~~
How rude of me, sorry.

I internally curse myself, debating screwing the whole letter up and starting again, but a small part of me wanted to know if he had a girlfriend. I pick my pen up and start to write again.

I have just never really been interested in law, and I know it's job security and I will be looked after and very wealthy, but how can you do a job you don't love? Life is so short, why waste it being unhappy?

I want to be a nurse or midwife. I want to look after sick and premature babies. I am learning to knit at the moment, I want to start sending blankets into the local hospital for them.

I know you'll probably laugh at that, but

that's what I feel like I am meant to do.

My dreams? To be happy. To find an epic love, a love to consume me and live happily ever after.

Ha, how cliché ... and I had the cheek to say your name was cliché when I come out with the dream of most girls.

I would love to travel, see the world with my partner by my side.

I don't have many goals, I just want a happy life.

But life doesn't always go the way you hope and dream, does it?

What are your dreams, Casanova?

Love,

Dimples x

I read the letter twice. I felt like I had indulged a little too much but then it felt good to get it all out. Only Poppy knows what I want to do... well, and now Casanova.

I heard Poppy singing as she walked up the stairs and I quickly stuffed my letter into its envelope before pushing it into the inside pocket of my backpack just as she pushed the door open hard, her hands on her chest, her lashes fluttering as she looked at the ceiling.

"I am in love, and I don't care what anyone thinks!" she sings.

"Good date I take it?" I giggled as I slid off the bed.

"Amazing, perfect... Oh, Pey, he is just..." She swoons. "He is just amazing." A blissful sigh passes her lips as she drops her bag and sits on the bed.

"Where did you go?" I ask innocently, even though I already know.

"He took me on this amazing picnic in Rosewood Park. Sitting amongst the wildflowers under the big cherry blossom tree. The lake just a stone's throw away. It was idyllic. The perfect first date."

"Sounds amazing," I admit, clearing the textbooks up and shoving them in my bag.

"Did he get a kiss?" I tease as I fall down next to her, looking at the ceiling as she falls back next to me, grabbing my hand and squeezing.

"Oh, he did, he got a full tongue-locking snog." She sniggers as she rolls on her side, laughing.

"Gross." I screw my nose up at her and laugh.

"Oh, Peyton, stop it!" She playfully slaps my arm. "Honestly, wait until you have your first kiss. Oh, it'll be amazing. It's even better knowing that I am going to be with Stefan forever. We are going to grow old and wrinkly together." She rolls over on her back and sighs. "I honestly never got it when people said that they were head over heels in love. Like movie love, it just seems so unrealistic, but now I get it. He has come in like a bulldozer and floored me."

"I'm happy for you." A smile graces my lips, but I feel it is slightly forced. Poppy picks up on it, her head turning fast as her eyes settle on my mouth.

"Pey…" she whispers. "You'll find your person. It's rare that you find love at seventeen… Heck, let's be honest, I may feel like I have found the one, but Stefan––or even the universe––could have completely different plans for me, for us. But as this moment stands now, he is the one. I know he is. My heart knows he is as well."

"I know he is too; I did from the moment I laid eyes on him. You were made for each other. A match made in heaven." This time the smile that plays across my lips is real, because I do know that they're soulmates. And not because they were paired up in the letters, but because of the aura's that radiated from them when they met each other. Their souls knew they were soulmates before they did.

I felt my nerves rippling through me as I thought about asking Poppy to see if Stefan would bring Knight next week.

Our conversation had fallen flat, and she was busy texting Stefan. I laid for a moment, debating how to start the convo, but either way, I just wanted to rush it out. I wanted to say it and be done. I didn't want her thinking there was a hidden motive behind it, I just wanted to see if I still felt as pissed off with him as I did last night. And the fact that he is plaguing my dreams is annoying me.

"Pop," I started, my head turning to face her, her smile big as she text Stefan.

"Uh-huh," she automatically answered without taking her eyes from her phone.

"I was wondering whether, if at all possible, obviously..." I knotted my fingers together then tapped them on my stomach.

"Spit it out." She laughed, her eyes finally moving to me as she dropped her phone by her side.

"Can you ask Stefan to bring Knight next week?" I rushed the words out so quickly I didn't even understand what I had just said.

"Mumble much? Hardly got a word of that." She rolled her eyes as she turned on her side, her head sitting in her hand as she propped herself up on her elbow.

"Fancy saying it a little slower?" She smirked.

I rolled my eyes.

I knew full well she knew what I said.

She just wanted to prove a point and make me say it again.

"I said... can you ask Stefan to bring Knight next weekend?" I felt the blush creep on my face.

"Wow, really?" Her nose scrunched up.

"Yes, really." My tone was clipped.

"I didn't think you liked him? Or do you and you just don't want to admit it?"

"No! I don't like him, but I don't know, I keep dreaming about him and I am agitated that I can't get him off my mind. And well, he pissed me off so much last night that I want to see whether I still feel rage when I see him or if––you know––I feel something else..." I trailed off. I sounded so pathetic and needy.

"Now, let's be honest with each other, you want to see if you feel fanny flutters?" She burst into a laugh.

"Oh my God, no, what is wrong with you? Stupid girl" I laughed with her, swatting her hard which only made her laugh more.

"Okay, okay." She held her hands up before they flew to her stomach as she calmed herself down. "I will mention it to Stefan." She held her thumb up to me.

"And, Pop, make sure you do mention it as such, don't go in all guns blazing and telling him I want him to bring Knight." I shook my head.

"I won't. He already had someone lined up, someone called David. What a boring name... David. But I will tell him to call off the search party and just see if Knight is up for it." She smiled.

Oh my God, what if Knight doesn't want to come? He did say it was lame last night. Shit. I opened my mouth ready to tell her that David may be the better option when she started talking.

"Already text him, done and dusted. I'm sure Knight will come. I think he secretly digs you anyway. Apparently, he was asking about you, well, that's what Stefan said. He is a dreamboat, so I would want him on a date too." She smirked.

"Don't be greedy," I warned.

"I'm not, I have Stefan. Stefan is more than enough." She rolled onto her front. "Enough about boys, am I okay to crash here again tonight? I'll sleep in my own room tonight though."

"Of course, and you haven't got to. You're not that much of a bed hog, plus you don't snore." I shrugged as I sat up, turning my head over my shoulder and smiling at her.

"Perfect, thanks."

"Always. I'm gonna go and see how my mum is, see if she is feeling better. I need food." I groaned as I walked towards my bedroom door. "Want anything?" I asked as

Poppy was back on her phone.

"Just a drink, if you wouldn't mind?"

"Yup," I muttered as I stepped over the door.

"Oh, Knight is coming next weekend. All sorted," she called out as I disappeared down the hallway and towards the stairs.

The swarm of butterflies began, the nerves and anticipation crashing through me.

I felt a pang of excitement shoot through me, but it was soon replaced with anxiety.

I just hoped I wouldn't regret it. I hoped he would be kind and actually a little fun this time, but it wasn't just him. I was a misery guts too.

I made a mental note to be more upbeat, to show him what I am really like. That I wasn't some uptight, spoiled little rich girl.

It didn't help because I was woken up, I was groggy. So in my defence, I had every right to be grumpy.

But I promised myself I would be happier this weekend. Whatever we were doing.

And all of a sudden, I wanted this week over.

Chapter Eight

The week dragged. Of course it did. It didn't help that I never received a letter back from Casanova. The thoughts whirled in my head. *What if I had overstepped the mark with my letter? I shouldn't have asked if he had a girlfriend.* I was gutted. Everyone else was handed their letters, small smiles gracing their faces and then Mrs Tides stood in front of my desk, her eyes full of pity as she shook her head from side to side.

Part of me wanted to believe he had just forgotten, or maybe he missed the cut off point? But either way, it still hurt.

I was excited about my date today, even more so because I never heard back from Casanova, but I was also nervous. What if he was horrible like he was before? Poppy was due over any minute. I hadn't seen her much this week due to her mum and dad being home, but they were flying out again this morning for a local charity that needed their help. They were heroes.

I had been raiding through my wardrobe for most of

last night and this morning.

I just didn't know what I wanted to wear, I wanted to look nice for Knight, of course I did, but I didn't want him to think I dressed up for his benefit. The sound of the hangers sliding across the clothes rail was annoying me. Footsteps distracted me when I saw my mother walking into the walk-in wardrobe.

"Found anything?" she asked quietly as her eyes scanned my clothes.

"Nope." My voice was defeated. I slapped my hand down onto my thigh, my head tipping back.

"I know I want to wear my cherry red Doc boots, but I don't know what with." I shrugged my shoulders.

"Okay, let me have a look." My mum pushed past me and pulled the clothes along the rail.

Poppy came bursting through the door, skipping and whistling.

"What's up?" she shouted as she walked into the wardrobe, throwing a peace sign towards me and my mum.

My head turned to her, she looked amazing.

She was wearing high-waisted shorts, a cropped white tee and her patent black doc martens.

"You look hot." I winked at her.

"Why thank you, and you look..." Her eyes moved up and down my body, her brow pinching. "Well, you look like you." She laughed.

"Stop it, I can't find anything to wear." I sighed.

"What about this?" my mum asked, holding up a ripped-knee pair of black skinny jeans and a plain, thick strapped vest top.

"It's a bit boring, isn't it?" I asked, scrunching my nose up as much as I could before grabbing them from her hand.

"Just go and put it all on." My mum shook her head. I didn't respond, just stomped into the bathroom and ignored the quiet chatter that I could hear between both of them.

Once I had my jeans on, I tucked my black vest into them. The weather had really picked up and a heatwave was set for this weekend. Once I looked at myself, I actually quite liked the look of my outfit. I always worry about wearing vest tops, I have a big bust for a young girl. I am always conscious. But luckily, this vest top sits quite high, so my boobs aren't spilling out over the top.

I ran my fingers through the ends of my straight hair and stepped back out into my bedroom.

"Darling, you look lovely." My mum smiled, and my eyes moved to Poppy.

"I like it. You look good." She held both her thumbs up.

"Sure?"

"Sure," my mum and Poppy said in unison.

"Okay," I breathed out, smoothing my hands down

my flat stomach before shaking my hands out.

"Nervous?" my mum asked as she stood for the door.

"Hell yes." I laughed. "But I am looking forward to it." I smiled.

"Good, you deserve it. Let me know when you're ready, and I'll drop you off," my mum muttered, but in the direction of Poppy.

"Drop us off where?" I asked, my head snapping to Poppy before my eyes moved to my mum. I didn't know where we were going, I hadn't been told, but then, I hadn't asked.

"Stefan's." Poppy smiled.

"Oh."

"I hope that's okay?" she asked, her head tipping down slightly, her eyes on mine.

"Yeah, fine." I cleared my throat before I sat down at the dressing table, brushing through my hair before I flicked my lashes with mascara. I dusted a light layer of bronzer across my high cheek bones, then swiped my lips with a red gloss.

I slipped into my Doc Martens, giving myself one last look before turning to Poppy. "Ready?" I asked, the nerves apparent in my voice.

"Yup!" Poppy chimed as she walked out the door. I grabbed my bag off the side with my phone and money then followed Poppy downstairs to my mum.

Once we were in the car, the nerves really kicked in.

My fingers were tapping on the armrest in-between me and Poppy. The car journey wasn't long, but for a moment, I wished it was.

"It's going to be fun," Poppy whispered as she leant towards me. She was trying to reassure me.

"I know, just a little nervous." I couldn't stop the laugh that left me.

"It's okay to be nervous, I won't leave you... unless you want me to?" She wiggled her eyebrows at her inuendo.

"Fuck's sake," I whispered under my breath, pouting and shaking my head, my lips curling slightly.

"I'll stop, I promise." She winked, her head turning to look out the window, her eyes widening. "Here we are!" she exclaimed, opening the door before we had stopped.

Stefan's house was huge. I thought mine and Poppy's were big, but Stefan's was something else.

"Have fun, girls, I will pick you up at six, okay?" my mum said, her eyes narrowing slightly.

"Yup, we will see you at six." I leant forward and kissed her on the cheek. "Love you, Mum."

"Love you too, sweetie, and remember, if you need anything or want me to come and get you then just text me, okay?"

I nodded.

I gave a weak smile before following Poppy outside.

A swarm of nausea swam through me, making me

feel a little uneasy. Poppy stopped, grabbing my hand and giving it an encouraging squeeze.

It was going to be fine. Of course it was.

I wanted this. I wanted it to be Knight. I did ask for it to be him after all.

Poppy stood outside the tall, gold painted gates. I could hear the blood pumping through my ears as she rang the intercom.

The wait for someone to answer felt like hours.

His voice crackled through the mic.

"Baby, is that you?" I heard him coo at Poppy.

"It sure is, sugar." She screwed her nose up and pretended to gag at the nickname that she called him.

"Sugar?" I whispered, a giggle bubbling out of me. It was the nerves, they were kicking in.

"Shut up," she snapped before laughing herself.

The gates clinked and slowly opened, revealing the beautiful château style house in front of us. The brickwork was grey, the roof a dark graphite. The large rectangular windows sat in grey metal frames. It made the house look cold, but it truly was stunning.

My jaw laxed slightly as we were greeted by what I could only assume was a butler.

I side eyed Poppy as she handed him her jacket, and I did the same. I felt rude. Like I said, we had money, but this place screamed filthy, stinking rich.

We both stood in the grand lobby of the house when

we saw Stefan walk down the huge staircase that sat in the middle of the room.

"Girls." He smiled at both of us then turned his attention to Poppy and winked.

"Hey, babe." She smiled back at him, embracing him as he stepped close to her, her hand still gripping mine.

If this didn't scream third wheel then I don't know what did.

"You okay, Peyton?" he asked, once he let go of Poppy, leading us up the stairs.

I had lost my voice, so I just nodded.

"Good." He smiled at me, and I felt myself melt, so God knows how bad he affected Poppy if he made me swoon by him just smiling at me.

We walked the stairs in silence, following Stefan as he turned left and continued up. My eyes travelled to the right side, and I wondered what was over that side of the house. In the middle of the stairs was a massive arched window overlooking acres and acres of landscaped gardens. Stefan stopped outside a door just a few steps away from the staircase, opening it and letting me and Poppy through first. We had to walk down a small staircase before we saw the room. It was a game room, cinema and snug, all-in-one with a pool table and a bar which had every flavour slush puppy machine you could think of. There was also a kettle and a vending machine filled with snacks and more soft drinks.

LOVE ALWAYS, PEYTON

I couldn't stop the surprised look that came across my face, Poppy's face surely mirroring mine.

It was amazing.

The ceiling was black with little firefly-like lights scattered over the ceiling, giving the illusion of a starry night.

We couldn't see it in all its glory because the lamps were on in the corners of the room. I assumed the ceiling lights only came on when it was being used as a cinema.

As my eyes scanned the room, I saw him, sitting there, watching some computer game on the tele.

He hadn't even turned around.

Poppy finally let go of my hand as Stefan held his out for her to take, which of course she did in a heartbeat. I––all of a sudden––felt very alone, my hand rubbing up and down my left arm as it sat across my chest.

I stayed still, my eyes scanning around the impressive room again.

My heart was racing, and I felt like I was sweating.

"Pey, come over here, babe," Poppy said, patting the seat next to her on the plush black leather sofa that her and Stefan were snuggled on.

I gave her a small smile, walking slowly over to her and sitting down delicately, afraid to disturb them as such.

My eyes moved to Knight, my lips parted and my breath hitched as I took his appearance in.

His big hazel eyes were fixed to the tele, his dark brown hair pushed back, but a few curls were sitting on his forehead, flopping in his eyes slightly.

He sat wearing a tight white tee which gripped his slender body. He had muscle, clearly, but it wasn't a lot.

He was wearing tight ripped skinny jeans and black high-top converse.

I would be lying if I said he didn't look hot.

Because he did.

"Knight, stop being a rude prick and say hello to Peyton and Poppy, will ya?" Stefan said, throwing one of the cushions that he was leaning on at Knight and hitting him in the side of the head.

But still his eyes didn't leave the screen. He just held his hand up, gesturing a hello.

"You're such a dick." Stefan laughed, dropping his eyes from Knight and shaking his head. He lifted his chin, looking at me and mouthing the word 'sorry'. I gave him a small smile and shrugged my shoulders a little.

"No biggie," I whispered as I fiddled with my fingers.

I continued to sit in silence while Poppy and Stefan chatted amongst themselves. They tried to include me, but the conversation just fell flat. I made it awkward. I stood from the sofa, and no one realised, but then why would they?

Dickhead Knight acted as if I didn't exist, which made me think he was forced into this double date by

Stefan. My thoughts whirled on what Poppy may have texted him and said to make Knight agree to this. Poppy and Stefan were so loved up and lost in each other, they wouldn't have realised if I was there or not.

I walked towards the bar area, looking at the different flavoured slushes and decided on a cherry one.

I grabbed the slush cup, nibbling my lip as I pulled the handle down, watching the thick iced drink fill my cup.

Once filled, I picked a straw, sticking it into the ice and taking a sip. Mmm, it was delicious.

I sighed, placing it on the bar top and reaching for my phone out of my bag.

My fingers hovered over my mum's telephone number, my eyes batting up and staring at Poppy and Stefan then moving over to where Knight was sitting.

I clicked dial and held the phone to my ear.

"Darling, is everything okay?" my mum's voice was worried.

"It's all okay, I was just wondering whether you could come and…" I couldn't finish my sentence when I felt fingers wrapping around my wrist that was holding the phone.

Knight's hazel eyes were on mine, holding my gaze.

"Don't go," he whispered.

"Peyton, baby, are you okay?" my mum asked, and I could hear her grabbing her keys.

"I'm fine, sorry, Mum. I felt a little unwell, but I am okay now. Sorry for worrying you." My voice was hushed as I answered.

"You sure?" my mum's voice was rushed.

"Yes," I whispered, pulling the phone from my ear and cutting it off, my eyes not leaving his.

I pulled my wrist from his grip, and he stepped towards me, glaring down at me as he towered over me.

"Want to know me now, do you?" My voice was hushed. I felt like it was shaking but it didn't sound like it.

"Maybe..." He smirked. "Or maybe the game just got boring and I wanted a new plaything." Winking at me, he stood his ground.

"I'm not your plaything," I scoffed, stepping back and away from him.

"Aren't you?" He looked a little shocked, both his brows rising. "Are you sure?" His hand reached up and tucked a stray strand of brown hair behind my ear. I sucked in my breath before I held it.

I didn't want to move.

"No," I whispered as I held his gaze.

"That's a shame, Peyton." His breath was on mine as he ran his tongue across his bottom lip.

"Peyton, you okay?" Poppy shouted over, making Knight stand up straight, pushing his hair out of his face as he stepped away from me.

"Yeah," I called out, my eyes not leaving him as he

stared at me. Our gaze was heated, and I could feel the way his stare was penetrating through me. My heartbeat quickened, my palms clammy and the butterflies swarming in my stomach. I just didn't know if it was nerves or excitement.

"I like your boots." He smiled before turning on his heel and stepping away from me. He took a couple of steps then stopped, looking over his shoulder as his eyes trailed up and down my body. "You coming, Cherry?" He smirked.

I couldn't help the silly smile that crossed my face as I began to follow him.

"Cute dimples." His voice was smooth as he winked at me, his eyes widening for a second before he composed himself quickly. He held his hand out for me as he led me back to the seating area. I gladly took it, I felt like I was betraying myself, but I couldn't stop.

I couldn't still my heart. The butterflies fluttered in my stomach. The heat swarmed through me.

Was this what it was like to have a crush?

Chapter Nine

Stefan had ordered pizzas to be brought into us as we all sat and watched *Mrs Doubtfire*. I loved this film, it always made me laugh.

Once the food was eaten, Stefan and Poppy excused themselves, leaving the room for a while.

I felt a little annoyed that she just upped and left, but then, she was allowed some alone time.

Me and Knight sat in silence, a seat space between us. I tried to stop the anxiousness filling me, but I couldn't. I just sat and picked at the skin around my fingernails.

I could feel the awkwardness in the air, and at that moment, I just wanted to go home. I didn't move my eyes from my fingers. I could feel him looking at me, the intensity of his gaze burning into me.

I had to fight the urge to look at him.

"You're very shy, aren't you?" he muttered as I felt the sofa dip as he adjusted himself to face me.

I broke my stare, tilting my head towards him

slightly and giving him a small smile. "A little," I admitted, my voice barely audible.

"Why is that?" he continued.

I shrugged. *What sort of question was that?*

"You lure me in." He smirked, scoffing.

"I do?" My eyes widened at his words.

"Mmhmm, I want to get to know you. You have these walls built up around you."

"So do you," I snapped back, a little harsher than intended.

"I know." His voice was quiet but unbothered by my comment. "But I will allow people in. Whereas you... I don't think you will, and if you do, you'll make me work for it."

"Who said I wanted to let you in?" I countered back at him.

"Oh, I see how it is." A throaty laugh bubbled out of him. "Let me get to know you, we will probably be seeing a lot more of each other if these two love birds are anything to go by." He tilted his head to where they were sitting before they left, his left arm resting over the back of the sofa, his body twisted towards me with his leg tucked under the other.

"That's true." I nodded, my eyes back on my black painted nails.

"So, tell me about you, Peyton." His gaze was back on me, heated.

My breath hitched, the smirk playing across his lips made me realise he heard it too.

"I'm just me," I mumbled.

"That's a pretty shit answer." He laughed. He had a beautiful laugh.

"I'm going to be seventeen in August, baby of my year," I stammered. God, why did I find this so hard? "I feel like all I do is study... but I'm in this new pen pal programme thing at school which I am enjoying... I think." I pinched my brows together, a frown apparent on my face.

"Oh yeah? And how's that going for you?" he asked.

"What? The pen pal thing?" My eyes met his, those beautiful, caramel, hazel eyes pulled me in.

"Yeah."

"It's okay, it only started last week, so we've only spoken, well, written a couple of times." I laughed nervously.

"Yeah, same as us, we're doing it as well... obviously." He laughed with me, patting his hand on the back of the sofa.

"Of course, I forget you go to the same school as Stefan." I nod, slowly. "I know we can't talk about them as such, but how does your pen pal seem?" I couldn't help but ask, a small pang of jealously searing through me at the thought that he could be set up with his soulmate because of these letters, and I could lose out on him.

His head lifted, and he nibbled on his bottom lip. "She seems okay, I suppose, a little boring, but then like you say, we've only written a couple of times." He flashed his pearly whites.

"Yeah." I rub my lips together.

"What do you wanna do when you grow up?" he asked after a few minutes of silence.

"A nurse." I smiled, keeping my answer short and sweet. I don't know why I was so worried about our date, he seemed really nice. Maybe he was just nervous like I was and felt the need to put on some sort of front? I felt myself relax a little as he began to speak again.

I couldn't work out the expression that crossed his face before he answered me.

"That's awesome." He winked. "I could totally imagine you in a slutty nurse uniform."

I screwed my nose up. Eurgh, moment ruined.

"You're disgusting." I shook my head; disgust clear on my face and in my voice. I moved further away from him.

"What?" he snarled.

"You, making comments like that. Haven't you got a girlfriend you can annoy?" I huffed, crossing my arms across my chest.

"Unlucky for you, no." He smirked. "Or is it lucky for you?"

"Definitely unlucky."

"Come on, Peyton, you know you fancy me. It's so clear." His cockiness was taking over the sweet boy that was here mere moments ago.

"I really don't. You must be mistaken." I pushed up from the sofa, grabbing my bag off of the floor when Knight was in front of me, pushing me back against the wall behind me.

I caught my breath, stilling as my eyes widened when I looked at him.

His hard body pushed against me; his eyes focused on my parted lips.

"I want nothing more than to kiss you," he whispered.

I didn't feel scared. I felt far from scared. I was intrigued. I wanted him to kiss me, but then I didn't. I wanted my first kiss to be meaningful. Not like this, with this horrible boy.

I couldn't respond. My voice didn't want to come out.

My heart was jack-hammering in my chest as his eyes moved from my lips to my eyes.

I had to get away.

Otherwise, I would press my lips against his and be filled with regret.

I placed my hands on his chest, pushing him away when he grabbed me, pushing into me.

"Tell me you don't want me to kiss you..." His voice was low, a hum.

"I don't," I whispered.

"I don't believe you."

"The thought of my first kiss being taken by you makes me feel sick," I spat.

"Oh, Cherry... so innocent and naïve." He bit his bottom lip.

The things I was feeling were surely not normal, I shouldn't be feeling things like this.

He lowered his lips over mine, they were hovering so close.

I heard his breath hitch as my hands were back on his chest. But this time, I didn't push him away. I could feel his own heart racing beneath his T-shirt, which made me think that maybe he wasn't as cocky as he acted.

I flicked my eyes up to look at him, my breathing shallow before he pressed his lips over mine softly.

It wasn't a kiss like I had imagined. There were no tongues, no deep, meaningful kiss.

His lips barely touched mine, they grazed across them. His lips were delicate, brushing across like a feather.

He stepped back, pushing his hand through his hair and away from his face.

His cheeks were flustered before he sat back on the sofa, not looking at me again.

I closed my eyes, my back still against the wall. I grabbed my phone, texting my mum to come and get me.

It took everything in me to keep my eyes focused in front of me and not to look at the boy that just took my first kiss. I wanted to get home.

I didn't care that I hadn't told Poppy.

I just needed to get away from him.

—

Once I was home, my face clear of makeup and comfortable in my pyjamas, I slumped into my bed. Poppy had messaged saying she was spending the night with Stefan, and that was fine. I could do with a night on my own.

I switched the tele off just as my mum came in with a cup of tea, handing it to me before she perched herself on the edge of my bed, her hand pushing my hair away from my face.

"Want to talk about it?" She smiled, but I could see the worry in her eyes.

"Just... the date wasn't what I had hoped." I shrugged, a weak smile appearing on my face as my fingers wrapped around the hot cup of tea.

"What did you hope for?" Her eyes were soft, her head tilting to the left as she looked at me.

"I don't really know." I let out a scoff of a laugh. It was the truth. I didn't know what I was expecting or hoping for. Maybe I wanted what Poppy had with Stefan for their first date?

LOVE ALWAYS, PEYTON

"Darling, you have to kiss a few frogs before you find your prince." She winked, taking my hand in hers as I gripped the cup handle with my spare hand.

"I know, one day…" I laughed, my shoulders feeling a little lighter. I didn't want to feel like this at the age of seventeen.

"Anyway, moving on from smelly boys." She poked her tongue out, whispering. "We've got your birthday to arrange, and also, prom." She clapped her hands excitedly together.

"Ah, prom." I rolled my eyes. "I don't really wanna go," I admitted, my eyes dropping as I looked at my cup of tea.

"Why not? You have always wanted to go to prom." I could see the shock on her face, her eyes widening as she took in what I said before they narrowed on me as if she didn't believe what I had just said.

"I just don't." My tone was short, but I didn't really know what else to say. The thought of going to prom on my own with Poppy, who would no doubt take Stefan, was just too unbearable.

"Okay." My mum sighed, stepping from the bed and walking towards me. She bent down, placing a kiss on the top of my head.

"Try and get an early night, you look exhausted." She smiled before walking to the door. "I love you, darling."

"I love you too."

I finished my tea, placing it on my bedside unit then reached across to turn my lamp off. I grabbed my phone and looked at the screen. It had just gone nine and I felt utterly wiped.

I needed to do some studying, we only had a couple of weeks until our end of year exams before we broke for summer holidays, and I was concerned that I had let Knight get in my head a little too much.

I wanted rid of him.

He was just a mistake.

He would get bored of little old me and soon move onto someone who wanted him to kiss them.

I scowled at the thought of him kissing someone else. Why? Why was this bothering me so much?

I grabbed my pillow from behind my head and covered my face, screaming into it. The pure frustration that left my body was in that scream. I needed the release.

I pulled the pillow away, dropping it to the floor and inhaling deeply, trying to fill my lungs with clean air.

My eyes fluttered shut for a moment, and I inhaled through my nose before letting my calm breath push through my lips.

I did this five times.

That's how long it took to calm my erratic heart and reckless thoughts over Knight.

Annoying, douchebag Knight.

Handsome, beautiful Knight.

I was doomed.

How the hell had I gotten addicted to the most venomous boy I had ever met?

He was a drug that I craved, and not in a good way.

The thought of how easily he could intoxicate me, scared me.

I would overdose on him, just to get one little taste.

I jumped, the beep of my phone pulling me from my thoughts. My brow furrowed when I saw an unknown number on my screen, showing me that I had a text message.

I sat up quickly, crossing my legs underneath me as I unlocked my phone, my finger hitting the message icon quickly.

My heart stilled, my eyes wide, my lips parting as my jaw fell lax.

I'm sorry. Sorry for kissing you, and sorry for being a jerk. I'm not normally like this. But you, Peyton Rose Fallon, do something to me.

I feel like I have to put on a front for you and I don't know why.

I hope you don't mind that Poppy gave me

your number and told me your middle and last name.

Seeing as I know yours, it's only right you know mine.

Knight Arlen Pierce.

And, if you would let me, I would like to take you on a date.

A proper one.

And actually, thinking about it, I'm not sorry for kissing you. At all.

Knight x

What. The. Actual. Fuck.

It took me a moment to catch the breath that left me as I read his message again.

This boy was a head-fuck.

I couldn't deal with this tonight.

I came out of my messages before turning my phone off.

I threw myself back with force, groaning as my head hit the mattress, rolling my eyes when I realised my pillow was on the floor. I reached down, grabbing it and putting it behind my head then forced my eyes shut. I needed to sleep.

I just wanted tonight over with.

Chapter Ten

I woke up with a banging headache, and just like every night before, I dreamt of Knight. I couldn't escape him.

Whether I wanted him there or not, he haunted me.

I rolled on my side, grabbing my phone and turning it on.

I wasn't surprised to not see anything from Knight. I mean, why would he text a girl that left him on read?

Once I was out the bed and dressed in my camel-coloured lounge suit, I grabbed my bag and lost myself in my textbooks. I wanted to get the last of my studying done this morning while the house was quiet. No doubt Poppy will be over within the next couple of hours, and I didn't want her distracting me from my school work.

I needed to get my grades, I needed to be able to show my father how much I could achieve and that I didn't need his name or his company for me to make it in life. I had my dream, and that's what I was focusing on.

Not silly little boys who acted up.

I had to focus on what was going to give me a better life, and it certainly was not Knight Pierce.

I felt my heart flutter at his name, my stomach flipping.

I hated that he affected me like that, I hardly knew him, yet I felt like I always had.

All these new feelings confused me; they made my head hurt every time I tried to decipher why I felt the way I did.

I shut my thoughts off, losing myself in my English coursework. That's all I needed to worry about.

—

The morning had disappeared, and I was still deep in my work when Poppy walked in. She was acting sheepish. She knew I was annoyed. I wasn't annoyed that she stayed with Stefan, she was entitled to stay with him, but I was annoyed with the situation I had gotten myself into.

I always promised myself that I wouldn't be one of these girls that let boys distract her and get into her head, yet I was becoming everything I never wanted to be. That's what was infuriating me.

"Hey, Pey." Her voice was cautious, her footsteps quiet as she slowly moved towards me. She crouched down next to me and handed me a cup of tea. I smiled.

"Thank you," I muttered, taking a mouthful and

instantly regretting it as I burned my tongue. *Brilliant.*

"You're welcome, you okay?" she asked as she sat down next to me, cross legged.

"Marvellous." Sarcasm laced my voice, my head snapping to the side to look at her.

"Yeah... I can tell." She gave me her biggest smile.

"I'm sorry, I'm not annoyed at you." My eyes sought hers. "Just frustrated," I grunted.

"What happened? Did *he* upset you?"

"Not really..." My voice trailed off, and I turned my head away from Poppy.

"Then what?"

"We kissed, sort of, not properly." My words were rushed, I felt so humiliated.

"You what?!" she squealed. "Oh my, Pey! You kissed Knight!" She wiggled the top half of her body in some weird dance while waving her hands in the air.

"Shh." I was conscious that my bedroom door was open, the hallways were large, and every little noise echoed and bounced off the walls.

"How do you feel?" Her voice was still loud and full of excitement.

"No different." I shrugged it off, wanting to show it wasn't eating me up inside.

"Bullshit!" she shouted, tipping her head back and laughing. "Ohh, it's so obvious that you both like each other."

"I don't think so, it was just a *'caught in the moment'* kind of thing."

"He is into you though, I heard him telling Stefan." Her eyebrows wiggled high.

"Well, he is wasting his time because I am not into him." My voice was blunt. "At all." My head shook from side to side. "Not even a little bit."

But that was a lie, of course it was. Because I was into him, more than I wanted to admit to myself or anyone else.

I knew his kind.

Anything for a quick leg over, and I am not that kind of girl. I want to wait until I meet the one. I always thought I would wait until marriage, but as I got older that has diminished slightly. But I definitely don't want to be seventeen and lose it to some random boy. I know it's legal, but it just doesn't appeal to me just yet.

I am not interested in sleeping around with boys.

Poppy has always been a lot more sexual than me, and that's fine.

"Oh really?" Her voice was high. I knew that tone. She didn't believe me.

"Yes, really." My eyes narrowed on her then quickly looked away and focussed on my work.

"Why are you lying to me? More importantly, why are you lying to yourself?"

"I'm not." I dismissed her, waving my hand.

"Okay, Pinocchio." I heard the deep sigh leave her. "Whatever."

She stood, kicking her boots off and diving onto my bed.

Fabulous.

I stopped for a moment, the end of my pen rubbing across my bottom lip as I thought about her words. *Could he really like me? I don't believe her. The way he acted last night, the stolen kiss he took from me.*

My heart raced at the thought, but what about Casanova? We had only just met, and I wasn't ready to give up on him, you know, just in case the whole soulmate myth was real.

Then I would have ruined it for both of us.

My mood suddenly went from bad to worse. Slamming my text book shut and throwing my pen down into the pile of papers, I stormed past Poppy and into my bathroom, making sure the door banged.

Turning the shower on as hot as it would go, I sat on the toilet, my breathing harsh.

I wish I had never met Knight Pierce.

He was getting in my head, every thought that coursed through my mind was him. Whatever I was doing, he was there with me. His intense hazel stare burned through me.

I felt him around me, all the time. Even though that was impossible.

LOVE ALWAYS, PEYTON

Ripping my clothes from my body, I stepped under the burning shower, wincing as it scalded my skin but the burning feeling soon turning to a soothing feeling. I tipped my head back, my brown hair cascading down my back and resting just above my bum. The water fell over me, relaxing me instantly. I felt the tension and weight wash away. How the hell someone could make me feel this way was ridiculous.

I needed to push him from my mind and focus on more important things.

Hopefully, after that disaster of our double date, he would leave me alone and not text me again. Even if he was saying those things to Stefan, it was most likely just so he could add another notch to his bed post.

I didn't want to get out of the shower, but I had to. I had to face Poppy and get over my strop. Reluctantly, turning the shower off, I wrung my hair out and stepped onto the bathmat. I stood for a moment and made a mental note to shut off anything I was feeling for Knight there and then.

He was just a mistake.

It'll never happen again.

Grabbing the towel off the radiator, I wrapped it around my body and reached for the other one to wrap over my hair.

I took a deep breath, opening the bathroom door and holding my head high as I stepped back into the room.

"Feeling better?" I heard Poppy pipe up from the bed, laying on her back but her head turned to the side, so she was looking at me.

"I don't want to talk about it," I huffed, ignoring her and walking through to my wardrobe and grabbing some comfy clothes.

I heard the small laugh that left her at my strop, but I just needed to compose myself before I spoke to her.

I felt humiliated, but I was humiliated with myself.

Once I was dressed, I pottered back over to Poppy and sat on the bed.

"He gets under my skin," I muttered, my eyes focussing on my feet.

"I know he does, but don't take it out on everyone around you. We are all here for you, you are new to this. He is just being a bit of dick, but if you don't want to see him again then I will make sure you don't. I will tell Stefan to keep him away."

"Thank you," I smiled at her, my eyes glossy. I felt my cheeks burn, I felt so silly for getting myself in a pickle about this.

"You're welcome, I'm sorry I ever introduced you to him." She sighed, wrapping her arm around my shoulder and pulling me to her.

"Don't apologise, you did nothing wrong. It was all him. I let him get to me and he won."

"He didn't win, there was nothing to win."

"Knight stole my first kiss." I shook my head from side to side. "I was saving it for someone special."

I know Poppy didn't care about things like this, but to me, they were important. She probably couldn't even remember her first kiss.

"I know you were, but we can just forget it happened. No one else saw it." Her shoulders shrugging up slightly.

"Mmm," I hummed. But the thing was, I didn't want to forget about it. Because it had happened. He was a thief. And if he had it his way, he would have stolen my innocence as well.

I didn't want that to happen.

"Are you going to write another letter to Casanova? Just in case your one didn't get to him last week?" She dropped her arm from my shoulder and shuffled up the bed a little.

"I did think about it," I admitted.

"I think you should."

"I don't know, he didn't write back to me. Maybe there was a reason, but I don't want to be seen or known as an eager beaver. Plus, if he can't be bothered to write me back..." I nibbled on my bottom lip. My heart hurt. "Nope. I'm not writing him another one." I blew the breath through my nose harshly. "You hungry?" I asked, changing the subject as I pushed to my feet from the bed and walked towards my bedroom door, waiting for her to respond.

"I am *always* hungry." She laughed, skipping across my large bedroom to me.

"Me too." I smiled at her, grabbing her hand and heading downstairs to find my mum.

We sat at the large dining room table as my mum plated up some toasted cheese and ham sandwiches. My stomach grumbled.

My mum was pottering about in the background, tidying up after herself.

"Oh, I have been meaning to say to you... thanks for giving Knight my number." I rolled my eyes as I took a mouthful of food.

"Yeah, sorry about that. Once I walked back into the basement and found you gone, I ran at Knight." She waved her hand in the air as she took a bite of her own sandwich that was sitting in her other hand. "Then..." She started again with a mouthful of food. "He filled me in what had happened, but I was so pissed off with him. Then, once he started explaining just how bad he felt and that he wanted to apologise, and after him pleading with me and not taking no for an answer, I finally gave in."

"Well, I left him on read," I said nonchalantly.

"I love it." Poppy sniggered. "Brutal."

"I am sure he hasn't even noticed; he probably has so many different girls on the go that he doesn't even remember little old Peyton."

"Stop it, of course he does."

"Don't be silly, I can assure you, he doesn't." Just as the blunt words left my lips, my phone vibrated on the table. And there, on my screen was a message from Knight.

I screwed my nose up, pulling my eyes from the screen. Poppy sat there, one leg bent up on the chair, the other on the floor. Her body was turned towards me, her jaw a little lax at the sight of me not reaching for my phone.

"Don't you want to check it?" I could hear the shock in her voice.

"Nope." My tone was clipped.

"Why not?"

"Because I don't want to." I shrugged, stepping away from the table and placing my plate in the dishwasher. My mum was no longer in the room, and I was grateful she wasn't. I didn't want her to worry about this, I would speak to her later, once Poppy had gone, if she was going. I never knew until later in the evening. I didn't know whether she was seeing Stefan again, going home or staying here for the night.

Poppy didn't say anything else about the text message, she just stood there, waiting for me to move so she could put her plate in the dishwasher. I stepped aside, walking the few steps back towards the table, my heart in my throat as I reached for the phone. Of course, I wanted to know what he had said, but I would do it later tonight.

I just didn't have it in me to read it now. Part of me was hoping that if I ignored him long enough, he would give up, of course he would. He is obviously still trying to prove something, trying to win me over. But he would eventually get bored of chasing me. Because I am no one. To him, I am most likely just a game.

He would give up.

I hoped.

Chapter Eleven

Poppy was home tonight, and after a lot of 'umming' and 'ahhing' she wanted to meet up with Stefan before spending the night at home with him.

I spent most of my afternoon lazing about, in my textbooks before school tomorrow. I was hoping I would get a letter back from Casanova this week and ignored the crippling anxiety that he was bored of me.

Once I had finished for the evening, I reached for my phone to see Knight's unread message. My fingers danced over the screen as I thought about reading it.

I swiped across, showing the little bin icon. I could just delete it and forget it ever happened, but then, I would always wonder what was said.

Before I could stop myself, I had already opened the message.

Pey,
I'm not going to stop.
Stop being stubborn.

Knight x

What a dick.

Coming out of the message screen and locking my phone quickly, I ran downstairs. I didn't want to be tempted to message him back. I wanted to––God I wanted to––but I couldn't.

I was not giving into the temptation.

Mum was plating dinner up and I bounced into the kitchen.

"Hey, sweet." She smiled, her head turning to look at me quickly before she faced forward and continued serving dinner.

"Hey," I muttered, taking my seat next to my father.

"You okay, sweet pea?" Dad asked as he took a mouthful of his beer.

"Yeah, all okay. Just tired," I admitted. It wasn't a lie, but it wasn't exactly the truth either.

I was tired, but I was more annoyed at Knight.

I wanted rid of him.

"Early night, need your beauty sleep." Dad winked, reaching across and grabbing my hand. "Plus, another big week of studying."

"Yup." I sucked in a breath. I needed to tell him about my nursing dream, but it just wasn't the right time.

But then, I don't think there would ever be a right time. It didn't matter when I did it, he was still going to be devastated.

I pushed the thoughts out of my head, a humming noise making me look up from my hands.

"Isn't that right, angel?" My dad's voice crashed through me. I smiled politely and nodded.

I had no clue what he was talking about.

Before I could ask, Mum served a Sunday roast with all the trimmings. Beef, Yorkshire puddings, vegetables, cauliflower cheese, parsnips, potatoes and thick gravy. My stomach grumbled. Roasts were one of my favourites.

"And for dessert, homemade rhubarb and apple crumble––your favourite." She kissed the top of my head before taking her seat next to me.

"Can't wait." I smiled.

Once we were all seated and said our thanks, we tucked into our dinner.

I was famished.

I helped my mother clean up the table and put the dishes in the dishwasher as my father excused himself to his office.

"How has your weekend been anyway, darling? Thought we could have a movie night one night this week?"

"That would be lovely, it's needed. All this studying... I need to switch off a bit." A small laugh escaped me.

"I bet, go easy though. Ignore your father." She tsked. "You're your own person. I know how much it would mean to him for you to work within the law firm, but it's not the be-all and end-all." Her arm moved around me and pulled me in as she kissed the side of my head.

"Thanks, Mum." I sniffed. I didn't want to talk about it at the moment, but it made me feel a little better.

"So... weekend good, apart from the bad date?"

"It wasn't too bad, apart from the bad date." I giggled as I leant into her. I needed a cuddle.

She opened her arms for me, pulling me in and holding me tight.

She always made everything better.

I broke away from her, and my lips curled into a smile. I stepped back, turning around and flicking the kettle on.

"Tea?" I asked as the evening settled in.

"Please," she chirped as she washed down the table.

I was so grateful for the life I had been given. I never wanted for anything, and my parents were so down to earth. My mother didn't believe in hiring people to do her chores, she was brought up to respect everyone, no matter their background. And I admired that about her. I wanted to be like her when I grew older, but damn, they were big shoes to fill.

I handed her the cup, kissing her on the cheek and wishing her goodnight before I dragged myself up to bed. I could do with calling Poppy, but I didn't want to intrude on hers and Stefan's time together.

I flicked Netflix on, placed my cup down on the bedside unit and walked towards the wardrobe. I tugged my clothes off, throwing them into the wash basket and reached for clean pjs. The evening was stuffy, the summer threatening. Slipping into black silk shorts and a cropped cotton tee, I brushed my teeth and padded back to my bedroom, climbing into my bed and losing myself in *The Vampire Diaries*. I was hoping my dreams would be filled with Damon and Stefan Salvatore. And not Knight.

I was woken to a tapping noise. I hastily looked around the room, rubbing my eyes. I groaned, the television still playing in the background. I couldn't have been asleep long because Netflix was still playing. I threw the covers back, reaching across the bed and turning my lamp on, squinting as the light hurt my eyes.

Tap. Tap.

The noise ricocheted around the room.

After a moment or two, I realised it was coming from my sash window.

Not again.

I debated going back to bed, but I knew he wouldn't stop.

Damn it. Why did Poppy ever have to bring him here?

I rolled my eyes as I stepped towards the large window over the other side of the room before I stopped.

I turned my head, looking at the time to see it was quarter past midnight.

Inhaling deeply, I strolled towards the window, undoing the silver catches and sliding the window up.

There he was.

A monster in disguise.

Knight.

His brown hair was sitting loose around his face, and it was longer than I remembered. A white tee sat over his toned body, and a leather jacket covered most of him.

"What do you want?" I hissed, both my hands still holding the window up as I leant forward, looking down at him.

He looked handsome. I hated it.

"I wanted to see you."

"Well, I don't want to see you," I snapped, pulling my head back as I went to pull the window down.

"Pey, wait!" he said, a little louder than I would have liked him to. The expression on his face said that he knew he wasn't expecting to be that loud either.

"Don't go. I just wanna see you. You haven't been responding to my messages, and well... being honest... it's driving me insane."

"Good." I couldn't help the sharpness of my tone.

The air grew thick between us, the silence deafening.

"Just come down." His voice broke, his plea sounding desperate. "Please?"

I sighed heavily, pulling the sash window down and locking it.

I stormed over to the bed, sitting on the edge for amoment while I weighed my options up.

Number one––I could go down there, let him charm me with––no doubt––his usual spiel that he gave all the girls and hear him out. I didn't actually have to listen to him.

Number two––I could ignore him.

But let's be honest, if I ignored him; he wouldn't stop. Knight Pierce isn't the sort of boy that gives up. The fact that he is here at midnight, standing outside my house and throwing stones at my window––like you see in the movies––is proof that he will stop at nothing.

Tap.

Tap.

"Fine!" I growled out, storming back over to the window, peeking around the curtain at him.

I couldn't quite make out what he was signing, but from what I could work out, if I wasn't going down, he was coming up.

I slipped my trainers on, walked to the wardrobe and grabbed an oversized jumper and pulled it over my head. I frowned. It sat just above my bum, my shorts nearly disappearing.

I debated changing, but then again, I was going to be out there for two minutes then I would be back in my bed and dreaming of the Salvatore brothers again.

Opening my bedroom door slowly, wincing when I heard a small creak, my heart raced. If I got caught, I was in big trouble. Before I stepped out onto the large gallery landing, my eyes wandered around the hallway. My mum and dad's door was shut completely.

They were both heavy sleepers, but I was still nervous. Luckily, I was at the front of the house and they were at the back.

I edged out of my room quietly, closing the door behind me and instantly regretting it when the door creaked again. I tiptoed quickly towards the stairs, rushing down them and avoiding the second from last step that always made a noise.

I smirked.

Taking a deep breath, I unlocked the front door and left it ajar as I stepped outside.

There, standing at the bottom of the steps was Knight.

He looked even better close up.

I had to be mindful to stop my jaw hitting the floor, and instead I let my eyes wander up his body.

He completed his 'bad boy' look with skinny jeans tucked into black high-top converse.

"Like what you see?" He winked, stepping towards me up the stairs, his own dark eyes roaming up and down me.

"Not really." I turned my head quickly, trying to find anything to focus on and ignore the breath that was snatched from my lungs as he closed the gap between us.

"I can't stay away from you," he whispered, his minty breath on my face.

My head turned slowly, my arms crossing over my chest before I dropped my head.

His hand reached up, his thumb pressing under my chin and lifting my head so our eyes met.

"I don't know what it is about you, Cherry, but there is something that pulls me towards you. My soul maybe? It's like a magnetic attraction, I feel drawn to you by an unexplainable force. As much as I want to resist you, I can't." His thumb was still under my chin, his teeth sinking into his bottom lip.

My heart was jackhammering in my chest, my breathing fast.

"Like a moth to a flame." His breath hitched. "But like the silly moth, I can't stop myself from floating towards you, knowing full well I am going to get burned."

I closed my eyes, my lips parting as I tried shallow breaths to try and calm my erratic heart.

"But I don't care," he whispered, his breath fluttering across my lips.

Now it was my turn for my breath to catch.

My eyes burned through his, and I lost myself in them for a moment.

I stilled as his lips brushed against mine, a small smirk playing on his mouth.

"I won't kiss you unless you ask me to…" His whisper trailed off, his spare hand running around my waist, pulling me closer to him, holding me tight.

My subconscious was begging me to ask him. My heart screaming and lurching itself at my ribcage. But my brain was the one controlling this.

I needed to be smart and not give into temptation, no matter how good it looked at six-foot and wrapped in a leather jacket.

"I can't." The words slipped past my lips. "Not now."

I shook my head, breaking the connection between us.

He dropped his hand from my chin, his arm pulling away from my body slowly as they fell to his side. A stupid smirk still sat on his perfect bow lips.

"I won't give up on you, Cherry." He licked his lips, his hand reaching up and pushing his loose brown hair out his eyes. "Even if you have friend-zoned me." A beautiful chuckle came out of him.

I smiled back, blushing, my cheeks a crimson red.

"Friends?" I said sweetly, stepping towards him and holding my hand out for him to take.

"If that's all I can be at the moment, then of course." His voice was quiet, I could see the hurt and disappointment in his eyes, and I would be lying if I said

I didn't feel the sharp pang that shot through my heart as my stomach dropped.

"Friends," he muttered, taking my hand and pulling me to him, his lips brushing against my cheek.

"Goodnight, Peyton," he whispered in my ear, the hairs standing on the back of my neck, goosebumps spreading across my skin like wildfire.

I didn't have a chance to respond. He was already walking away.

But I didn't move. I stood and watched as he disappeared into the darkness.

And that's when it hit me.

The realisation that I had just turned down Knight Arlen Pierce.

I couldn't miss my opportunity with Casanova.

I knew people wouldn't understand, but I was a hopeless romantic and to think that my soul mate is my pen pal is something I can't explain.

I didn't want to risk ruining that with some boy that sung me a few lines from a cheesy love song––no doubt.

But I was grateful that he was still in my life.

Selfish. That's what you are. My subconscious snarled at me.

I ignored her.

Shaking my head from side to side before turning on my heel and walking back into the house, I headed to my bedroom.

I couldn't get the image of Knight out of my head, and of course, as soon as my eyes were closed, my dreams were filled with him.

My Knight.

Even if he was just my friend, I was grateful that he still wanted to be around.

Chapter Twelve

The week flew by pretty quickly. Knight had messaged me a couple of times, but mainly just for idle chit chat.

Poppy hardly came over this week as her and Stefan were living in each other's pockets. But to be honest, that suited me. We had a test next week, so I crammed as much studying in as I could.

Mrs Tides stood, grabbing the envelope tray off her desk as she started handing the letters out. I felt my throat tighten, my heart slamming against my chest.

What if he never wrote back again?

I would be so humiliated. It was bad enough last week when everyone's eyes were on me.

Tides stopped at my desk, smirking, then handed me two letters.

"Guess he missed cut off last week." She winked before continuing through the desks.

I wanted to tear them open right there and then, but I wouldn't. I never did.

I wanted to wait until I was at home and alone.

"Psst," I heard Poppy mutter.

My head turned to face her, a small smile breaking across her face.

"Can I come home with you tonight?" she asked, giving me her best puppy dog eyes.

"Course, you know you don't have to ask." Rolling my eyes, I turned my attention back to the letters in my hand.

I tried to stop the tremble.

I couldn't believe I got so affected by a handwritten letter that was created by a stranger.

The bell rang through the halls which echoed loudly. Everyone pushed from their chairs and grabbed their bags.

"Don't forget we have an English exam on Wednesday, a mock ready for the end of year exams," Mrs Tides' voice raised as she clapped her hands together.

"Brilliant," I heard Poppy mutter under her breath. She hated exams.

But then again, no one liked them. They just had to be done.

"Stop moaning, I'm sure you'll cope with not seeing Stefan for a couple of nights." I scoffed, a small laugh escaping me.

"It's got nothing to do with Stefan," she snapped.

I held my hands up in defence. "Sorry," I mocked, my

eyes widening as I stopped outside my locker and filled my bags with books.

She didn't say anything for a moment, just kicked the floor with the toe of her shoe.

"Sorry," she muttered.

"What you saying sorry for?" I asked.

"I'll tell you later, don't want nosey bitches listening, especially not Clarissa." She threw her head back slightly, indicating to the mean girl of Augustine Prep. To be fair, she was always polite to me and Poppy, but she has her enemies and loved nothing more than some juicy gossip to sink her teeth through. Then, her and her minions do what they do best. Smear it around the school like shit, making sure not one surface or person is left untouched.

I nodded; no words were needed. I locked my locker, threw my bag over my shoulder and walked down the corridor and out to my mother's waiting car.

We climbed in, "Hi mum," giving her a flat smile. I didn't utter another word to her after that, I would speak to her once we were home. She side eyed me; I gave her a small shrug as she pulled away. She could feel the tension in the car. I didn't know what was eating at Poppy, but I was desperate to find out.

Maybe her and Stefan had broken up? Or was it worse?

I shook the thoughts from my head. I inhaled sharply as my mum pulled onto the drive of our house.

My mum hadn't even put the car into park when Poppy dashed out the back, holding onto her bag tightly and busting through our front door.

"Oh, well…" my mum rushed out, flustered as she sat still, both hands still on the steering wheel.

"Mmm," I hummed, reaching for my own bag by my feet and opened the car door.

"If you need anything, let me know. I'll pop a pot of tea on… tea makes everything better." She smiled at me as she undid her seatbelt and climbed out the car. I followed silently. I couldn't still my heart. I really hoped Poppy and Stefan were okay.

She was so much happier and lighter with him.

Closing the front door behind me, I kicked my shoes off and left them in front of the shoe unit before running up the stairs, taking two at a time.

Pushing through my bedroom, I saw Poppy sitting on the edge of the bed, hunched over, silent tears rolling down her cheek.

"Poppy," I whispered, dropping my bag to my feet and running towards her, sitting next to her and wrapping my arm around her shoulders.

Her silent sobs became louder as she leaned into me. I wanted to ask her what was wrong, but I knew with Poppy that you had to wait until she was ready to tell you what was going on.

I felt like we sat this way for hours, my arm around

her shoulders as her body gently trembled through the tears.

It had to be Stefan.

Or her parents.

No, it couldn't be her parents. My mum would have been called.

My mum showed up, pushing the door open with her foot as she walked into the bedroom, holding a tray. Poppy lifted her head, her red, raw eyes seeking my mum.

"Oh, darling," my mum whispered as she placed the tray with the tea and plate of biscuits on down on the bedside unit and rushed over to Poppy's side, pulling her up from the bed and embracing her as Poppy sobbed loudly now.

I felt useless.

I shuffled back on the bed, reaching across and grabbing my tea. I sat, watching, crossing my legs underneath me as my mum continued to comfort Poppy. I was grateful my mum came in when she did.

I wasn't great in situations like this. Part of me wanted to get up and leave them to it, but the best friend in me couldn't do that to her.

"Darling, do you want to tell me what's happened?" My mum spoke softly, leading Poppy back to the bed. She took a seat, wiping her eyes with the sleeve of her school blazer. My mum stepped to the side, grabbing the hot cup of tea and handing it to Poppy with a sympathetic smile.

The silence fell over us all, and my mum's eyes darted from mine to Poppy's. This continued until Poppy's voice came out as more a squeak.

"I'm late," she sobbed.

I felt my blood run cold. Surely not?

It must just be stress, what with exams and everything else. She wouldn't be that stupid. I couldn't help but feel a little anger stir deep inside me.

My inner thoughts thrashed about. I closed my eyes for a moment. Of course, she wouldn't be that stupid. She was safe. Accidents happened.

My Poppy.

"Oh," my mum managed to breathe out after a––what felt like forever––silence filled the room.

My mum sat down on the bed next to her, placing her hand on Poppy's knee and giving it a gentle squeeze.

Poppy turned her head to face me, her red eyes brimming with tears, her bottom lip trembling.

I gave her a sympathetic look, but words failed me.

"It's okay, darling, it will all be okay," my mum reassured her as she pulled her to her side, wrapping her arm around her.

My phone beeped, and my heart jackhammered against my ribs.

I reached forward, fisting it from the duvet. My heart fluttered when I saw Knight's name.

LOVE ALWAYS, PEYTON

Pey,

I'm outside.

Come and see me.

Knight x

I tapped across the screen, telling him to go away.

"Who's that, darling?" my mum asked, hers and Poppy's heads turning to face me.

"Oh, no one important. Just Knight. He is outside, but I told him to go." I gave a weak smile.

"What? He is here?" Poppy rushed out, her voice panicked, her eyes wide.

"Yeah... well... not anymore, I don't think." I shrugged. Poppy flew from the bed and ran to the window, looking out to see Knight walking away.

She slid the window up quickly.

"Knight!" she called out, her voice hoarse from the crying.

"Poppy?" He sounded confused. I ran behind her, popping my head up over her shoulder as I watched him walk slowly towards the house.

"Yeah..." Her voice quivered before the tears rolled down her cheeks again.

"Oh, Pop," he called up, his head tipping back as he looked at her.

"Have you spoken to Stefan?" she sobbed.

"I have... he is okay." A small smile crept onto

Knight's lips.

"He isn't answering my messages." She shook her head from side to side, her arms still holding onto the open window above her head.

"His mum has taken his phone. I walked over to just chat to Peyton about it all..." He winced slightly; he didn't know whether I knew what the situation was.

I didn't.

He knew more than me by the sounds of it.

All I knew was that she was late.

I didn't know if she had taken a pregnancy test or if she was in fact just late.

But going on what Knight just said about Stefan having his phone taken off of him, it must mean only one thing. They already knew the answer.

She was pregnant.

"You're actually pregnant," I whispered. I couldn't quite believe the words that were coming out my mouth.

"Yeah," she mumbled, her face falling forward. I heard my mum gasp.

Poppy looked over her shoulder to see my mum standing behind us, her hands over her mouth.

"I am so sorry, Mrs Fallon." Poppy's voice broke again.

"Oh, sweet girl, don't apologise." She pulled Poppy away from the window and cuddled her. I took her place, holding the window up and fitted it into the catches to stop it from falling.

My eyes fell to Knight.

Why was he so handsome?

He mouthed 'sorry.' I just gave him a small smile. He had nothing to be sorry for. I felt awful for Poppy and Stefan to even be in this situation.

"Pey, darling, tell your friend to come to the front door, I will let him in." My mum smiled before her eyes went back to Poppy, and she kissed her on the forehead. She let her go and then made her way to the door.

"My mum is coming to let you in." I smiled down at him.

He didn't say anything, just disappeared as he stepped forward.

I shut the window and inhaled deeply. I turned on my heel and faced Poppy.

"I'm sorry, Pey."

"Sorry for what?" I couldn't help the little laugh that came out of me, my head tilting to the side.

"For not telling you."

"Well, you would have told me... Eventually." I stilled. "Wouldn't you?"

"Of course, I would!" She sounded shocked that I had even asked that, but I just didn't know. She threw herself at me, hugging me.

"Love you, Pey."

"I love you too." I hugged her back. We stood like this

for a moment, when I heard a gruff voice.

"Oi oi, am I interrupting something?" Knight's voice crashed through us. I heard Poppy snigger.

"Only in your dreams, Knight." She pulled away from me and flung herself into Knight's open arms.

I felt a pang of jealousy strike through me.

But I had no right to be jealous. I put him in the friend zone.

His arms wrapped tightly around my best friend's body, but his eyes were on me the whole time. I felt my whole body burn.

My stomach stirred and fluttered.

He pushed her away gently, his arms resting on the top of hers.

"It'll be okay. Stefan won't let his parents have a say." He smiled at her, pressing his lips on her forehead before he looked at me again.

"Am I allowed to cuddle you, seeing as we're *just friends?*"

I didn't say anything, just gave him a silly smile as he stepped towards me. His long arms wrapped around me, pulling me to him. His face nuzzled into my neck. My heart raced, my skin tingled.

I wanted to fight what I felt, but I couldn't.

He inhaled deeply, filling his nose with my scent.

I stilled.

"I won't give up on you," he whispered.

I felt my skin smother in goosebumps, and a small shiver crashed through me, causing me to shudder in his arms.

"Cold, Cherry?"

"A little," I lied, my voice weak and pathetic.

He let me go, his eyes looking down at me as he winked. He pulled his bottom lip in by his teeth, sucking in a breath as he did.

My skin felt like it was on fire, his glare burned into my soul.

His breath hitched as my eyes met his. The intense stare was too much. I couldn't keep my eye contact with him. I was defeated, and my eyes batted down.

"Sorry... Do you two need a room?" Poppy snapped as she stormed over to us and sat on the edge of my bed, her eyes volleying between both of us.

"No," I muttered, stepping out of his space and taking a seat next to her.

Knight kept his eyes on me, turning slowly to face both of us.

His hand pushed through his styled curly brown hair that sat on his forehead.

"So, what's next, brat?" His voice was laced with humour.

"I'm not a brat." Poppy's brows pinched, her nose turning up.

"No, no, of course not." He sniggered, winking at her

and giving her his best playful look. He rocked forward on the balls of his feet then fell back onto his heels.

"I don't know... I need to talk to Stefan and see how the land lies. I know what I want to do, and I am adamant I know what he wants to do..." Her voice trailed off as my mum approached.

"Stefan is here, Poppy. Shall I send him up?"

"I'll go down to him... I think we need a little privacy." Her eyes moved to me and Knight before they focused on my mum. She stood up, not another word mentioned as she followed my mum out of my bedroom and downstairs.

An awkward silence fell over us, and Knight's lips curled slightly in the corner.

"Did you get your pen pal letter this week?" he asked as he sat on the floor, bringing his knees up and resting his arms around the front of them, his hands overlapping.

"I did, well, two actually." I felt smitten for a moment, my heart fluttering at the thought of the letters sitting in my rucksack, untouched.

"Why two?" His interest piqued, his brows lifting and pinching before they smoothed back out on his perfectly beautiful face.

"He missed cut off last week––"

"What? So, you didn't get one last week? Were you embarrassed?"

"Mortified." My eyes batted to my nails as I picked

them.

"He is a fool." Knight breathed; I could feel him looking at me. I didn't look back at him.

I couldn't bear to see the pity in his eyes.

"Did you get your letter?" I quickly changed the subject.

"Yeah, just the one for me though." He laughed softly.

"Least your pen pal doesn't forget." I shrugged my shoulders, trying to make light of my embarrassing situation.

"You're right, she doesn't seem like the type to forget. She seems very regimented, very organised." His eyes moved from mine as they fell to his feet. "Unlike yours."

"Mmm, indeed," I agreed. I felt uneasy having this conversation with him, but I don't know why. This is what friends do. They talk about everything. Love lives included. But the thought of Knight being in love with someone makes me feel sick to my stomach.

I can't be greedy. He isn't mine. And I am not his.

We are just friends.

The room fell silent again for a while, and we both looked at the open door, trying to hear any noise that came from the hallway downstairs, but it was deadly quiet. You could hear a pin drop.

I pushed off the edge of the bed, pacing towards the window and overlooking the drive. It was empty.

My brows creased, I was expecting them to be out there unless my mum had taken them through to the lounge, so they had some privacy away from me and Knight.

I felt him behind me, his hand snaking around my waist as I stood looking out the window. My breath caught; my lips parted as his mouth sat next to my ear.

"I can't stay away from you," he whispered. "There have been so many times that I wanted to come over, just so I could see you."

My heart raced, my breathing fastened.

"Knight..." I managed on a shaky breath.

"Tell me you don't feel the same, Peyton."

"I don't..." *Lies. You spin a web of lies. My subconscious snarls.*

"I think you're lying, Cherry." His hand was still firmly splayed across my stomach, my skin burning. His hand wasn't even touching my skin, it was sitting on top of my shirt. His fingers started trailing across my stomach, skimming down my skirt as his fingertip brushed across my bare thigh, making my breath hitch. His hand moved back up, tapping gently on my hip before he gripped me and spun me around to face him.

Our bodies pressed against each other's.

His lips hovered over mine.

My heart sat at the base of my throat.

"Am I interrupting something?" Stefan's voice sliced

through us, making us both jump back. Knight pushed his hand through his hair, and I played with the tips of my fingers. Head down, I walked to my bed.

I flushed with embarrassment.

Stefan didn't say anymore, and Knight just nodded at the unspoken words between them, giving me one last look before disappearing out of my bedroom and into the hallway.

I inhaled deeply a few times, trying to calm my erratic heart.

Knight Pierce did things to me that I didn't understand.

I felt so consumed and whole when I was with him, but when he left, he took a piece of my heart with him.

It didn't make sense. If this soulmate myth was to be true, then why was I feeling something towards a friend? I wanted to be with Casanova. He was my soulmate.

Not Knight.

I unpacked my school bag and stripped down, throwing my uniform in the wash. I stepped under the scalding shower, trying to wash the effects of Knight off of me. I dried my hair and slipped into my pyjamas. I really needed to study but I felt exhausted. I also had to speak to Poppy and see how her conversation went with Stefan. The shock had worn off a little now. I still couldn't believe that she was pregnant with his baby at the age of seventeen.

I looked at my bed to see the two letters from Casanova sitting there. It took everything in me to walk away. I wanted to get my hair dried and have an hour down time and speak to Poppy before I did anything. It bothered me that she didn't say bye to me. She just got up and left.

Maybe I had annoyed her? But I hadn't done anything wrong. I was allowed to be shocked; this wasn't little news, was it? It was massive news.

She was going to be a mum and Stefan a dad.

She didn't come back. I sat and waited, but she never turned up. I assumed she had gone back home and I reached for my phone. I tapped Poppy's name as I sat, waiting for her to answer.

"Yes?" She sounded sad, quiet.

"Hey." I couldn't help but be a little cautious, I felt like I was walking on eggshells.

"What's up?"

"Just wanted to see if you were okay? And how it went with Stefan?" I nibbled on my bottom lip as the silence fell over the phone line.

I let out my breath when she finally started speaking.

"I'm doing okay, a little nauseous."

"I'm glad you're okay..." I stopped for a second. "And Stefan?"

"He has been amazing. His parents on the other hand..."

LOVE ALWAYS, PEYTON

"I'm sorry, Pop."

"It'll be okay though; my parents are back tomorrow... I know they're going to be mad, but what they going to do? Disown me?" She laughed at her own comment.

"Of course not." I shook my head from side to side as if we were having a face-to-face conversation.

"Stefan's parents have told them he is to have nothing more to do with me, or the baby." Her voice quivered.

"What?" I whispered, but you could hear the disbelief in my voice

"Mmm," was all she managed when I heard the choked sobs down the phone.

"Where are you?"

"Back at home, with Champ." Poppy sniffed.

"Come back over, bring Champ. You shouldn't be at home on your own."

"Are you sure?"

"Poppy, you never worry normally." A little laugh left me. "Just come over, I'll put the kettle on. See you in two." I smirked at the phone, cutting it off.

Throwing my phone back on the bed, I ran downstairs and into the kitchen. My mum and dad were sitting in the *good* lounge. No one was allowed in there. It was the adult's lounge.

I filled the kettle up with water and flicked it on. By

the time I had gotten the cups out, Poppy was outside the front door with Champ.

No words were exchanged as I let her through the door, Champ running straight down to the hallway and into where my mum and dad were.

"Champ!" my dad called out excitedly.

I smiled.

Poppy looked awful. Her eyes were red raw and swollen, her cheeks blotchy, and her makeup smeared down her face.

I thew myself at her, knocking her off her feet a little as I wrapped my arms around her.

We stood like this for a while when we heard footsteps approaching. I pulled away, looking over my shoulder and seeing my father walking towards us.

"Poppy, darling," he cooed as he pulled her in for a cuddle.

She wasn't just my best friend. She was family.

We were both ready for bed and snuggled under my duvet watching *The Vampire Diaries*.

"Why did you say you were late when you already knew you were pregnant?" I couldn't help but ask, it was playing on my mind. It bothered me.

I heard her sigh before she rolled on her side to face me.

"Because I was all over the place, and as horrible as

this sounds... I wanted to know what was happening with Stefan before I told anyone, as such." She winced slightly, knowing it would sting me, which it did. But I didn't say what I wanted to. I wanted to cuss her out and moan. But that wouldn't help. It would only tarnish our friendship slightly, and I didn't want to lose her, and I knew she didn't want to lose me either.

"I get it," I mumbled, turning away from her, my eyes focusing on the television.

The air grew thick.

"I wasn't being stupid and reckless Pey, we just got caught up in the moment. You know where you have to have someone as soon as your close..." her eyes widened slightly.

"Of course you don't" she smiled sadly, dropping her eyes to the floor.

My throat tightening, my lips pressing into a thin line.

My mum appeared at the door with her usual nightly cup of tea. I loved having a cup of tea before bed.

"All okay girls?" she asked as she perched herself on the end of the bed, her eyes volleying between the both of ours.

"Yup, dandy." I plastered on a fake smile across my face.

She raised her brows, handing me and Pop a cup each. "Hungry?" she asked.

"I am a bit peckish," I admitted, my stomach grumbling.

"Me too, but only if it's not going to put you out," Poppy said sweetly, batting her lashes.

"Of course not, you're my girls. I'll make you some sandwiches, won't be a minute," she muttered, standing from the bed and tottering out into the hallway.

"Don't be mad at me." Poppy leant up on her elbows, leaning closer to me.

"I'm not mad."

"Bullshit," she spat out through her laughs.

"Okay, maybe a little." I showed her my thumb and finger, making a small gap between them.

"You can't be mad, I'm pregnant." She lifted her shoulder up to her ear, shrugging it off slightly then fell back into the pillow.

I hummed.

"So, have you read the letters from lover boy yet?"

"No." I sighed. "I was going to do it tonight, but then you came over." I smiled.

"Only because you asked!" She raised her voice, interrupting me.

"And if you would have let me finish, you would have heard me say that you are more important," I snapped.

"Oh," was all she managed, side eyeing me. "Sorry!"

"I suppose I forgive you." I winked just as my mum walked in with sandwiches and a slice of Victoria sponge.

"You spoil us, Mrs F," Poppy chimed as she took her plate from my mum.

"Anything for my girls." Her voice was calm as she handed me and Poppy our plates.

"Thanks, Mum." I smiled at her, her eyes glistening.

"I will leave you be, get some sleep." Her voice hushed now as she closed my bedroom door behind her.

Once we had eaten, I reached for the letters that I had placed on the bedside unit before Poppy had come over.

"Do you mind?" I asked as I gripped them.

"Of course not, I'm going to message Stefan on the off chance that he has his phone back, then get some shut eye. I am exhausted, growing a human is exhausting," she said mid yawn while tapping away on her phone. She pulled the duvet up and rolled on her side.

"Night, Pop."

"Night, Pey." Her voice was barely audible, her soft snores filling the room within seconds.

I smiled while staring at her.

I was excited and anxious for her.

All my emotions rolled into one.

My fingers fiddled with the envelope of his missed letter, and I held my breath as I pulled it out and began to read.

Chapter Thirteen

Dimples,

Funny, I don't get the ick when I write your silly nickname.

Just teasing.

It's not a silly nickname, it's pretty cute actually.

No, not massively into sports, I do like my football and rugby, but I am not one of these that has to watch his team's games every week, and I am definitely not one of those lads that cries when his team loses.

That's part of life.

Winning and losing.

I'm sorry, but how can you ~~fuck~~ oops...
I mean, how can you mess up the recorder?
That made me really laugh.

Not musically gifted — noted.

Well, maybe if this all goes well and we get to meet and sparks fly, I can teach you a couple of easy notes on the guitar. But you don't touch my guitar without my permission, okay? That's the first rule of guitar learning. I learned that from my master, Phoebe Buffay.

Horse riding, aye? I would be useless at horse riding; they scare me if I am still being honest with you. I know what you mean by having to grow up, my father is not a very nice man, but he likes to still drum into me what he expects of me. Which is not what I want.

I have a question for you.

If Peter Pan appeared at your window and offered to take you to neverland, so you never had to grow up, would you go?

I think I would. In a heartbeat.

I would take his hand and not look back.

I don't have a lot here for me.

A couple of friends and you.

My mum left when I was a kid, I don't remember much and now my dad just gets drunk of an evening after being the big, rich CEO.

Sorry... I am self-wallowing, but it is so easy to sit and write everything down in a letter to someone I barely know.

I don't have a girlfriend, well... I have someone I like, I'm just not sure whether she likes me back. I have a date this weekend, but I'm not sure how I feel about it, to be honest.

And no, your dream sounds wonderful. Don't ever give up on it. Fight for it, Dimples.

P.S.— I want an epic love too.

My dreams are nothing compared to yours.

You are very brave, just don't let anyone take them from you.

Love, (I like that we are now putting this word in our letters...)

Casanova

I didn't waste time, I jumped straight into this week's letter, my heart thumping in my chest as I began to read.

Dimples!

I am so so sorry I missed the cut off.
Things happened, time ran away with me and before I knew it, I had missed the drop off.
Please forgive me.

I will miss reading yours this week, it's been far too long. Well, it feels like it's been a lot longer than a week.

I don't have much to report other than I went on my date, it was a little horrid.
I fudged up, and being honest again... I definitely do not think she is into me.

So, no, I do not have a girlfriend, nor does

it seem I will have one anytime soon.

Please write back,

I miss you.

Tell me everything,

Love,

Casanova

I sat for a moment, re-reading both of his letters. I could feel the blood thumping in my ears, my tummy swarming with a thousand butterflies. How could I feel something for someone I didn't even know? The feelings consumed me entirely.

My heartbeat was fast, a giddiness falling over me as I lost myself in his words, yet I found myself wanting to lose myself in his eyes.

I imagined what he looked like, opal eyes finding mine, his golden blonde hair complimenting his caramel skin.

His jaw was already chiselled and would only get more defined with age.

I burned, the apex between my legs aching. I gasped at the feeling. What was this?

I had never felt anything like it before.

I dropped the letters into my lap, reached over and grabbed a pen out of my bedside unit.

I wanted to write back while these feelings and emotions were still coursing through me.

Dear Casanova,

My heart is still racing after reading your letters. To say I felt lost and stung when my teacher stood at my desk with nothing to give two weeks ago, would be an understatement; it was humiliating. I thought I had pushed you away. I thought that you were fed up with me already.

Is it wrong of me to be happy that your date was horrid? If we are being honest, which it seems we are, I had a date too; it wasn't what I thought it was going to be. I would be lying if I said you weren't on my mind most of the time. What if we are soulmates and we move on? It's not a risk I am willing to take, are you?

I am sorry to hear that about your mum, and well, your dad too. Once we meet, my house is always a safe haven. You never have to be invited; my front door is always open for you.

I am glad that you found humour in my recorder story. I will show you one day. And I solemnly swear, that I will not touch your guitar. And yes, Phoebe Buffay is the master.

And in answer to your question...
I would fly to Neverland, but only if you

come with me. I couldn't bear to be alone over there. We can join the lost boys and never grow up.

Things have been a little weird around here, I don't have enough paper tonight to be able to tell all, but maybe I will in my next letter.

Casanova, I have no intentions of stopping my dreams. My father will be mad, but this is his dream, not mine. I will not be a kept woman or stuck behind a desk. I want so much more than that.

I am so glad you wrote back, the thought of going without hearing from you broke my heart a little.

It's mad to think that I have warmed to

LOVE ALWAYS, PEYTON

Someone I have never met.

And Casanova,

I will always write back.

Love, (I am so glad we are writing this too)

Dimples.

I read back through my letter a couple of times before sealing it into its envelope and slipping it––along with Casanova's letters––into my bedside unit, ready for Monday.

I laid my head on my pillow, my smile spreading across my lips and my heart fluttering in my chest.

I couldn't wait to dream of how my Casanova looked. He may be completely different, but that's how I imagined how he looked.

My heart sunk for a moment at the thought of Knight. My friend.

Every night he plagued my dreams. But only now, he doesn't plague them. He fills them, stirring feelings inside of me.

I felt torn between Knight and someone I didn't even know.

But for whatever reason, I was drawn more to Casanova than I was Knight.

And I don't know why, but my heart hurt.

Cracking and shattering a piece of it.

It was possible to fall for two different boys, right?

Chapter Fourteen

Three Months Later

A lot had changed around here, and Poppy was now living with us. Her parents kicked her out as soon as they found out she was pregnant. Both of my parents tried to talk to them, to tell them how Stefan was with Poppy and how they both felt for each other, but they didn't want to know. They didn't want to listen.

Stefan has been stopped from seeing Poppy, he is under lock and key and doesn't have a chance to sneak away.

Knight still pops in every now and again to see me, but even his visits have dwindled.

My mum has been fantastic with Poppy, she even went to her twelve-week scan with her and vowed to never let her go through this alone.

It was our last week at school before we broke up for six weeks, then I would be off to university. We found out our Uni placement next week. I was anxious, but more excited than nervous.

It was also my birthday month.

Poppy celebrated her eighteenth, and my mum and dad paid and booked for her driving lessons so she could have a little independence if she wanted it, but she is still waiting to book her test.

"You all ready for school, girls?" my mum chirped as we sat at the breakfast bar, inhaling our food. It was agreed with my parents and our head mistress that Poppy would finish out the term and sit her exams, then she was free to leave and would already have her letter and space at her chosen university.

I didn't know whether she would go back into education, but I hoped she did.

"Yeah, as ready as can be," I answered for both of us. Poppy was just stirring her cereal around the bowl with her spoon.

"You have two more exams and you're free for six weeks," my mum continued, her eyes bouncing from mine to Poppy's.

"I know, I can't wait. Looking forward to not stressing about studying." I couldn't help but laugh.

"I bet," my mum muttered, but she sounded distracted, her eyes now pinned to Poppy. "Are you okay?" she asked, and I could hear the worry in her voice.

"I will be." She sighed. "I just want to see Stefan; he is missing out on so much," she wailed.

"I know, darling, but me and Jason are working on

it." My mum looked defeated, but she kept a big smile on her face. I reached across next to me and grabbed Poppy's hand, rubbing my thumb across the back of her knuckles.

She pushed away from the breakfast bar, grabbing her bag off the floor and walking towards the front door.

I looked at my mum, and my eyes softened. My mum looked so sad.

"Any luck?" I asked, sliding off the breakfast bar stool and grabbing my own bag, pulling it over my shoulder. I knew my mum was trying everything to get Melinda and Tom to come around.

"Nothing." She shook her head from side to side, keeping her voice hushed. We were pretty certain Poppy had gone outside, but we didn't just want to assume.

"What are we gonna do?" I sounded helpless, but we were running out of ideas.

"Have you tried speaking to Knight again?" My mum leant her elbows on the breakfast bar, her eyes boring into mine.

I shrugged my shoulders. "I suppose I could try," I muttered. "I'll see when he is free." I walked around the side of the breakfast bar, kissing my mum on the cheek.

"Ready?" I asked.

"The question is, are you?" Her brows raised, a small smirk gracing her face.

I nodded.

"You've got this." She winked, stepping behind me

and following me out to the driveway where Poppy was standing. Her hand was sitting over her non-existent bump. She was miles away.

"Hey." My voice was soft as I approached her, wrapping my arm around her shoulders. "Let's get today over with." She didn't say anything, just slipped into the back of the car.

The pen pal programme had been halted while we did exams, then during the holidays, we were moving over to emails which I was excited about. Even though I liked keeping the letters in my box, now I would just print the emails off and put them in there instead. Mine and Casanova's relationship was going from strength to strength, and he seems to think that meet ups will be allowed soon, following a rumour he heard going around his school. But I can't see it happening, not yet anyway.

I shook the thoughts of Casanova aside for a moment as I pulled my phone out and tapped Knight's name.

Punk,

It's me.

When are you free? I miss you, feel like it's been forever… oh wait… it has.

P x

My lips curled into a smile as I watched the ticks

change colour to show he had read it, my heart thumping as the screen lit up with three dots.

> *Who you calling punk, punk?*
> *:P*
> *When are you free? You're the one that is always too busy for her best friend. Can you do tonight, Cherry?*
> *I can come over about five. That work for you? X*

I typed a quick response, telling him five was fine. I then text my mum, telling her Knight was coming over tonight and could she take Poppy out for a few hours so I could have some time to get some information out of him. My mum's phone lit up with my name, but luckily, Poppy was too busy staring out the window to notice. I saw my mum side eye the phone, but she quickly diverted her eyes back to the road.

I was excited to see Knight. Our friendship had started to blossom, but I felt like it had halted the last few weeks due to Poppy and Stefan.

I missed his scent, his beautiful hazel eyes and that smile.

He was so beautiful.

But totally not into me anymore, nor was I into him.

"Have a good day, girls, go smash your exams!" My

mum's voice pulled me from my inner thoughts.

"Thanks, Mum, I'll see you tonight." I leant through the middle of the two front seats of the car, kissing her on her cheek again.

"Bye, Mrs F," Poppy mumbled. "Come on, bitch tits, hurry and get out the car, I need to pee."

I rolled my eyes, shuffling towards the open car door, stepping down and holding the door for preggers. She slipped out, readjusting her skirt. She didn't look back at me, nor did she say thank you. I shook my head from side to side softly, shutting the door then turning to face my mum.

"Don't forget to check your phone," I mouthed, holding my thumb up then I turned on my heel to follow Poppy.

No one knew she was pregnant, only me, Mum, Stefan, Knight and the head mistress.

Luckily, she won't have a massive bump by the time we leave school, so easy to keep secret. Then we have a nine-month gap before we start at Uni.

She kept quiet; I know she normally feels nauseous around this sort of time, so I always found it better to leave her be.

I gave her a small nod as we walked towards the exam hall, I waited outside while Poppy ran to the loo. In a matter of minutes, she was back by my side as we strode into the exam room. Today was our maths exam, and we would be in this room most of the day, only stopping for a half hour lunch break and two fifteen-minute refreshment breaks.

Once sat at my desk, I gazed down over the exam paper. Nerves crept over me, but I sat tall, pushing them back down where they belonged.

I had this.

I was going to be just fine. The head mistress announced it was time to start, and all eyes were down and pencils scribbling on the paper. I tried to quiet my mind and lose myself for a couple of hours. I wanted it over now, I wanted to see Knight.

—

By the time the day was over, I was mentally exhausted. I always struggle with maths and today took it out of me. We had one last maths exam tomorrow which I was dreading, but at least it was the last day.

I waited outside for Poppy to appear. She looked tired. I looped my arm through hers as we walked out into the fresh air. The sun beat down on our skin, and it felt good.

My mum––like always––was sitting outside, waiting for us. I heard the car doors click as she unlocked them. I opened the door, letting Poppy in first then shuffled in next to her before I shut the door.

Putting my backpack on my lap, I reached for my

phone, turning it on.

It vibrated instantly. My stomach flipped when I saw a text from Knight.

Cherry. I'll be over in about an hour. Slight change of plans my end. I hope that's okay? Can't wait to see your beautiful smile. X

My skin tingled. But then my heart dropped. I hated the way I reacted to Knight. From the very first moment I laid eyes on him three months ago, he made me feel things that I have never experienced before. I feel bad for feeling the way I do towards Knight because of Casanova. I know it sounds silly, but I feel like I am cheating on him even though I'm not.

I hate feeling torn, and that's exactly how I am feeling now.

Torn and confused.

I pinged a message over to Knight, telling him that was fine. I couldn't ignore the excited butterflies that were fluttering around in my stomach.

Pulling up on the drive, Poppy darted out the car, letting herself in through the front door and then disappearing.

"Mum, I am worried about her," I mumbled.

"I know, sweetie. I managed to get her mum to

answer my phone calls. I think they'll come around, just need to keep reminding them of how much they're going to miss out on their daughter and grandchild's life. I know it's not what you want for your children, a teen pregnancy, but it's life. These things happen for a reason. This baby is a blessing for Poppy. The baby has been sent to her, so she always has someone who needs her." My mum sighed. "I'll go make sure she is okay. I'll take her out to the shops, see if she wants some maternity clothes and update her wardrobe. That way, it'll give you and Knight a couple of hours to try and plan something to get Stefan over..." My mum's voice trailed off as she tapped her fingers on the steering wheel. "I want to go over to that boy's house and shake his fucking mother for doing this to our Poppy."

I gasped. My mum hardly swears, and it felt wrong coming out of her mouth.

"Mum!" A nervous laugh bubbled out of me.

"Sorry, darling." Her eyes flicked up to look at me in the rear-view mirror. "I am just so bloody annoyed." She tsked.

"I know, Mum, me too." I grabbed my bag and left the car, my mum getting out the same time as me.

"Good luck," I said with a grimace.

"Good luck to you too, let's hope we can get this sorted for her."

After a little pleading from my mum, Poppy finally agreed to get changed and leave the house with her. I am pretty sure she only did it because she didn't want to keep listening to my mum begging her.

As soon as she was gone, I ran into my wardrobe to get changed. I slipped on a pair of high-waisted, light blue jeans and an off-the-shoulder white bardot top. I accessorized with a thin gold chained necklace with my initial and a pair of gold, small studs earrings.

I brushed through my long brown hair, pulling it into a ponytail then stared at myself in the mirror, my head tipping to the side.

I was fussing.

I felt fidgety.

I looked at my phone. Knight would be here any minute.

Running my ring finger under my eyes and smoothing some lip balm over my lips, I decided on keeping my hair down. It made me feel safe and a lot more comfortable.

My phone pinged; it was him, letting me know he was here.

I inhaled deeply, closing my eyes to try and slow my erratic heart.

My eyes flicked open to see myself in my mirror, smiling.

I left the bedroom, running down the stairs and opened the front door.

I felt the air leave my lungs when I saw Knight turn

around slowly to face me. My eyes trailed up and down his body as I took every inch of him in. He was sporting skinny black jeans that were ripped at the knee, a white long tee that sat just above his thighs and gripped over his changing body. And of course, he had his leather jacket on. His curly hair sat perfectly, flopping onto his forehead like it always does. I loved it.

I didn't have a moment more to think about it when he threw himself at me, his arms around my waist, mine around his neck. I laughed as he squeezed me tight, lifting me off my feet and swirling me around. He settled me back down, letting my feet touch the floor as he inhaled deeply, and I did the same, drinking him in.

He smelt delicious. Musky tones drifted through my nose, followed by a fresh scent that I was familiar with but couldn't quite work out. I could smell the smoke on his breath, and as much as I hated smoking, I liked the smell on him.

"Missed you," he muttered into my hair.

"Missed you more," I teased as I stepped back.

"Not possible, Cherry."

"Come inside." I smiled, taking his hand and leading him into my home.

I don't know why, but I felt nervous. A current was swarming through me, a tingle even.

"Drink?" I asked as I closed the door behind him. He dipped his head down, looking at his shoes before looking up through his hair, silently asking me if he should take his shoes off.

I nodded. "Please."

He kicked them off, placing them in front of the cupboard in the hallway.

"Ready?" Pushing my hands into my back pockets, I rocked on the balls of my feet.

"Ready." His tongue darted out and swept across his bottom lip.

I smiled, turning and walking down the hallway. My skin smothered in goosebumps. I could feel his eyes on me, burning into the back of me.

I looked over my shoulder, his eyes were trailing up and down my body before they focused on mine. I quickly turned my head, a little relieved when we were in the kitchen. He stood round the side of the breakfast bar, and I continued walking, stopping in front of the sink. I pushed onto my tiptoes and reached for two glasses. Once again, I felt his stare penetrate me.

"Stop staring," I muttered.

"I can't help it," he admitted.

I blushed, turning quickly and stepping away from the sink.

"What do you want?" my voice quivered.

"What I want is unavailable, so I'll just have a water please." He winked as he walked closer to the sink. I was grateful that the kitchen counter was separating us.

Turning the tap on, I ran my finger under the water and waited for a minute until it went cold, then pushed the glass into the stream, filling both our cups.

I held his out over the counter for him to take, and our fingers brushed slightly, a zap burning my skin.

I took a large mouthful; my mouth and throat were so dry. Padding over to the seat in the large window overlooking the drive, I fell into it, Knight following and sitting opposite me.

"What did you summon me for?" He wiggled his eyebrows at me, his shoulders moving a little as he chuckled.

"I didn't summon you."

"Well, you technically did."

I rolled my eyes.

"Have you heard from Stefan?" I didn't want to beat around the bush, just wanted to get straight to the point.

"A bit, why?"

"Just a little worried, Poppy is getting herself in a state... as you can imagine. She has had her scan and she went without Stefan." I stopped myself, my eyes meeting Knight's––that have been on me the whole time. "She needs him... is there anything you can do?" My voice was a plea.

I heard Knight sigh, his hand pushing through his beautiful curly hair.

"I can't even get to him. Yes, I see him in school, and

he looks like shit. But as soon as the bell rings at the end of the day, he is chaperoned out and bundled into the back of his dad's car. It doesn't help because his dad is the chancellor of Tyron Prep." Knight's eyes went wide as that bit of information slipped past his lips.

I almost choked on my mouthful of water.

"What?!"

"Fuck, Pey, you can't say anything." Knight shook his head; I could see the worry creeping onto his face.

"I won't," I whispered.

"You promise me, pinkie swear it." He smirks.

"I'm not pinkie swearing, what are we, five?!" I laughed.

"Nothing is more sacred and trusting than a pinkie swear," he continued, pushing off of his chair, stalking over to me.

My breathing quickened; my lips parted.

He kneeled in front of me.

"Repeat after me." His tongue darted out as he swept it across his bottom lip, wetting it. His little finger was sticking out, hovering in front of me.

"I, Peyton."

I rolled my eyes, swatting him away.

"Go away," I said through a laugh.

"No." He shook his head. "Now, repeat… I, Peyton," he said, loud and clear, a smirk on his lips.

I felt like such a fool, my cheeks flushing crimson.

LOVE ALWAYS, PEYTON

"I, Peyton."

"Solemnly swear." He grinned like an idiot.

"Solemnly swear." I mumbled.

"I will not tell anyone about Stefan's dad being Chancellor Tyron."

"Wait, Chancellor Tyron!?" I shrieked. "The bloody school is named after Stefan's family!?"

"Fuck it," he groaned, falling back onto his heels. "Just stick ya damn pinkie out."

I stifled my laugh, shuffling forward so I was sitting on the edge of the seat. I did as he asked and held my little finger out.

"I'm trusting you, Pey," he whispered as he sat back on his knees, moving closer to me and closing the gap.

My breath hitched. He did things to me I couldn't explain, but I would never let him know. We were just friends.

"I know," I whispered back, breathing out.

His little finger linked around mine as he shook his hand.

"There, you can't say anything." His hazel eyes twinkled, his lips pressed into the most beautiful smile I had ever seen. He broke contact then wrapped his arms around my body as he nestled his head on my chest.

I stilled. Frozen almost.

"Don't panic, I am just having a *friendly* cuddle," he muttered softly.

I felt myself sag a little, my arms finding their way around his neck.

"I know," I mumbled again.

The room fell silent as we sat like that for what felt like an eternity.

And I didn't want it to end.

Ever.

Chapter Fifteen

We were sitting in the lounge, the music channels playing in the background, just for some background noise.

"How's things going on the pen pal front?" Knight asked, pulling my eyes from the television.

"Yeah okay, things are speeding up. It's coming up to four months already, and I think the meet up is being arranged before we go back to school." I tried to hide the excitement in my voice, I knew Knight held a torch for me––well, that's what my mum said.

"How about you?"

I felt a sting shoot through me at asking him about his pen pal. I had no right to feel that way.

"Eh." He shrugged his shoulders, as if he wasn't fussed at all. "It's going okay, things are a little stagnant at the moment. I think she likes someone else, but that could just be me. You know, because I like someone else…" I blushed, my eyes falling to my lap. "So maybe I am giving off the same vibe. I dunno, don't get me wrong, she seems lovely, and things might be different when we meet in the next few weeks, but I'm not getting my hopes up." He winked, his fingers twirling in one of his styled curls. "I don't think she's my soulmate though."

"No? Why?" The words left before my brain could stop them.

"Because I already know who my soulmate is." He looked up at me, he looked so vulnerable.

"Oh," was all I managed. I felt the air being knocked from my lungs.

"But she doesn't feel the same." His eyes fell to his lap, his smile fading.

"Knight... I..."

"Cherry, you haven't got to say anything. It's cool. It's life, it happens." He still didn't look at me, his eyes stayed pinned down.

"I'm hoping it's just a silly crush, and it'll soon go, and I will move on." His voice changed, it was upbeat... happy maybe?

"I like you Knight, more than a friend... but I can't help but wonder what will happen with Casanova."

His eyes widened, his jaw laxed.

"You told me his nickname?" He couldn't hide the shock, he fidgeted on the large sofa he was lazing on, now sitting up.

"Oops." I couldn't help the laugh that bubbled out of

me. "Now it's my turn to let something slip." I shrugged my shoulders.

"Casanova, aye? What a lad."

"Of course you would think that." I stood, walking towards him and swatting him as I walked past.

"Where you going?" he asked, standing up and following me like a lost puppy.

"I am going to get us a drink, punk," I teased, looking over my shoulder at him and winking.

"Oh, punk, aye?" His voice was low, gruff as he walked quicker to close the gap between us. I picked up the pace then ran towards the kitchen as he chased me. I couldn't stop the loud squeal that came from me as I ran behind the breakfast bar, my hands flat on the worktop, Knight the other side. His eyes darkened, hooded even. His head dipped slightly but he didn't take his eyes off of me.

"I can see your heart thumping through your chest... Nervous, Cherry?"

I had lost the ability to speak. I shook my head fiercely from side to side––when in reality, I was nervous. I was also excited.

"Oh, *really?*" he muttered, stepping to the side and walking towards me. I dragged my hands to the edge of the worktop, curling my fingers around the edge, tightening my grip.

"Knight..." I said breathlessly.

"Yes, petal?" He continued his slow torturous steps towards me.

I stepped back, the worktop hitting my lower back.

"If my memory serves me right, it's your birthday Saturday, isn't it?"

My eyes trailed up and down his body. He was only in his T-shirt now, the sleeves hugging his muscular arms. His signature black ripped skinny jeans clinging to his thighs.

"Yes," I whispered.

"Sweet eighteenth," he teased. "Not too much of an age gap now, seeing as I am already eighteen." He winked. "Seventeen, eighteen... whereas any younger... well, it seems a little..."

"Wrong." My voice was a squeak.

"So wrong." His breath was on my face, his eyes burning into mine as he craned his neck. He had grown taller, broader. He wasn't the skinny boy I met a few months ago. I steadied myself by holding onto the worktop behind me, his body pressing against mine.

I felt the current swarm me, the heat flushing to my cheeks.

"Why won't you just admit you feel something for me?"

"I have nothing to admit..." I lied.

"You're lying." His lips hovered over mine. "Stop holding out for this Casanova."

LOVE ALWAYS, PEYTON

My eyes darted back and forth to his hazels.

"Let me kiss you, I don't want to steal another kiss..." His voice was shaky, as if he was trying to restrain himself.

"Knight..." I breathed; he was so close now. My eyes moved to his perfect bow lips.

"Think of it as an early birthday present." His lips brushed across mine, ever so slightly. "Please, Cherry... can I kiss you?"

My heart was in my throat, it was racing in my chest.

"Yes..." The word was just off my tongue as he pushed his lips over mine. I heard a groan in his throat, and a low rumble vibrated through him.

My eyes closed; my heart sped up as his tongue swept against mine. I had never kissed anyone like this before, but my heart and body knew exactly what to do. My tongue danced with his, my heart thumping and swelling in my chest.

His large hand came to my face, his finger and thumb holding my chin as his kiss deepened, his tongue slowing down before he pulled away.

A small whimper left me as he broke the connection. I didn't want him to. I wanted his lips back on mine. My fingers moved to my burning, swollen lips.

"Happy birthday, Cherry," he whispered, his eyes closed. He sounded defeated. His fingers fell from my chin and he stepped back away from me.

"I've got to go... I'll call you later, okay? And I'll see

what I can do about Stefan, leave it with me." His voice was strained as he continued stepping away from me, turning on his heel and walking out of the kitchen. I jumped when I heard the front door shut, the noise rattling through me.

I just stood, confused, alone, and wanting so much more from him.

I wasn't alone for long when I heard the front door go. I turned the television off in the lounge and walked down the hallway to see Poppy carrying a handful of shopping bags.

"Hey, beaut, you okay?" I asked her, smiling warmly.

"Shattered, but we got some baby bits. Want to see?" She smiled back at me, a sparkle in her eyes. It was good to see her happy.

"Errrr... YES!" I exclaimed, clapping my hands together excitedly.

"Down here? Or upstairs?" she asked as she hovered by the stairs. My mum stood behind her, pointing upstairs behind her back.

"Go up, I'll make us a tea." My voice was soft as I stood next to her.

"Perfect, see you in five. I need to pee anyway." She laughed, carrying her bags and wandering up the stairs before disappearing. My mum's eyes watched as Poppy disappeared, then she nodded her head towards the kitchen, pressing her finger to her lips.

Did she think she was on a secret mission or something?

I couldn't contain the laughter that bubbled out of me as I wandered behind her into the kitchen.

I had literally stepped across the threshold when my mum grabbed my arm, dragging me in front of the oven and clicking the extractor fan on the cooker hood to make some background noise. I couldn't help the roll of my eyes.

"I think you're being a little over the top," I scoffed.

Her eyes widened as she swatted my arm.

"Not at all, I don't want her to know we have been meddling. She is in such a wonderful mood after our shopping trip."

"I get that, but this is a little extreme..." I smirked, lifting the kettle off its base and feeling how full it was. There was more than enough water in there for two cups of tea. I placed it back on the stand, flicking the bottom of the kettle where the switch was and letting it boil.

"So, what did Knight say?"

My mum was back next to me. The sound of his name made my stomach drop but my heart race.

"He is going to try and get to Stefan; he hasn't seen much of him," I muttered, turning away from her and grabbing a couple of mugs down from the high kitchen unit. My mum was stuck to me like glue, following me as I moved around the kitchen. Leaning to get the tea bags and sugar, I threw them in the cup, followed by a heaped teaspoon of sugar for Poppy.

I knocked into my mum, tutting as I put the pots back and grabbed the milk from the fridge.

"Seriously, Mum," I snapped, shaking my head.

"How has he not seen much of him? Are they not best friends? And the fact that they go to the same school––"

"He just hasn't, okay?" My voice was harsh, but I didn't want to break my trust with Knight.

"What's he going to do about..." She looked past me and towards the stairs. "Stefan," she whispered his name.

"He just said he will deal with it." I shrugged my shoulders as I poured the boiling water into the cup.

"Right... so we aren't actually any closer to getting Stefan here." She huffed, shaking her head as she snatched the milk bottle out of my hand and strutted to the fridge.

"Mum, can we just give him a couple of days? Don't see it as a failure just yet." My voice cracked. I hated the thought of my mum being pissed off with me, but I hated the fact of Poppy doing this alone so much more. "Trust me... please?"

"Of course, I am just worried... that's all," my mum muttered as she walked towards me, taking my face in her hands and kissing me on the forehead.

"I know... I am worried too. But I have faith. Knight will sort it." I nodded confidently as I grabbed the mugs

LOVE ALWAYS, PEYTON

by the handles and walked towards the doorway of the kitchen.

"Keep me posted," my mum called out as I headed for the stairs. I didn't respond, but she knew I would. I told her everything... well, everything until Knight Pierce came crashing into my life.

I shut the thoughts down that were swirling around my head. I felt so confused, but I also felt like I had cheated on Casanova. I was such an idiot. I wanted to tell Poppy, but I felt selfish, she had all of this going on and all I wanted to do was tell her about my kiss with Knight.

I didn't have a chance to think about it any more as I walked through the bedroom. Poppy was curled up on the bed asleep.

I let out a little sigh. Stepping towards her, I placed her tea on the bedside table and covered her with my bed throw. I felt a little lost as I looked around the room. I could do with another few hours of studying, but I just wasn't in the mood. I padded over to my bedroom window, sitting on the chaise lounge overlooking the drive, my knees bent as I sat looking out the window, drinking my tea and enjoying the silence.

As always, as soon as it was quiet, my mind drifted to him. I can't remember what it was like not having him on my mind twenty-four seven. It was ridiculous.

I jumped, my phone beeping underneath me. I

fumbled, pulling it out and smiling, my heart racing when I saw a message from Knight.

Cherry,

I can't stop thinking about your lips.

Fuck it, I can't stop thinking about you non-stop.

Sorry for being a bit of a douchebag best friend… but anyway…

I am camping outside Stefan's house. As soon as I see my move, I am making it.

Your Knight in shining armour is coming to save the day.

LOL.

Like what I did there?

I miss you.

Knight x

I giggled as I read his message, my cup resting in-between my thighs as my thumbs happily danced across the screen.

Punk,

Stop thinking about me.

But truth be told, I can't stop thinking about you either which makes me feel like a horrible person because of Casanova.

LOVE ALWAYS, PEYTON

You're the best, best friend, FYI.

Also, are you really camping outside his house? Have you got a little tent? ;)

Ha, you're so original. If there was an eye rolling emoji, I would insert it now.

Twat.

Love, Pey x

P.S. I miss you too. A little bit. Okay, a little bit more than a little bit.

I couldn't wipe the smile off my face. But then, in an instant, my smile fell from my lips, my eyes focusing on the wall as I thought of Casanova. I was such a horrible person.

I needed to write to him. Rushing off the chaise lounge and running into the walk-in wardrobe, I reached up for my box of letters, flicking through them until I found a spare piece of paper and grabbed my pen.

Moving back into the bedroom, I sat on the floor, crossing my legs underneath me and resting my paper on the lid of the box.

It took me a minute to compose my thoughts. I had so much going on in my mind that I couldn't decipher where I wanted to start.

Dear Casanova,

I actually cannot believe this is the last handwritten letter that I have to write. Going forward, we will be moving onto emails. I'm not sure how I feel about it to be honest, I like the letters. But I am a sucker for small romantic gestures like love letters.

How have your exams been? I feel like this week has dragged, but it's the last day tomorrow, then it's my birthday! Finally, eighteen. I am one of the youngest in my class which sucks at times, but at least I will always be a little younger than my friends. Every cloud and all that.

How have things been at home? How has your father been? Have you got many plans over the summer holidays? Like I have said numerous times in our letters, you are always welcome to my house.

I can't wait until we finally get to meet. Do you wonder what I look like? Have you built an image up of me in your head? I have with you. Wow, I felt silly writing that.

But seeing as I am already blushing and feel like an idiot... I will tell you what I _think_ you look like.

I can imagine you sporting a side parting in your golden blonde hair. Short round the sides, long on top. Your skin would glisten under the sun, a beautiful sun kissed glow radiating off of you. Your eyes are the perfect opal, just like the ocean.

What about me? You don't have to tell me

if you don't want to, but I felt comfortable spilling that to you.

My friend is doing okay, no update on her boyfriend, but we are working on it.

I have an almighty ache in my heart and a pain in my stomach that feels like I am being gutted. I kissed someone. My best boy-friend. He feels more for me than I do him... I think. I don't know.

I don't even know why I am telling you this, but I suppose it's because I feel guilty.

Guilty that I did that to you.

I know we are only pen pals, but I feel some sort of connection with you.

Do you feel the same?

Please don't hate me.

I had to tell you.

I'm sorry.

Love, Dimples xx

I sighed, folding the letter neatly and slipping it into an envelope before writing his name on the front. I didn't want to look at the letter again as my guilty conscious was already working overtime, so I shoved it into my rucksack and tried to forget about it.

I looked over at Poppy, she was still sound-o. I didn't know whether to wake her up or leave her be.

She had scattered the bags over the bed, ready to show me, and I didn't make it in time. I kicked myself, I felt like I had been the worst friend to her at the moment, but that was only because I was so out of my depth. I didn't know what to do for right or wrong.

My phone beeped again, my heart jumping. Poppy stirred.

I moved slowly, grabbing my phone and seeing Knight's name again.

Good. I am glad I am on your mind, now you can join the torture.

Update. I have seen movement. His dad has just gone out, his mum has yoga at seven, so I am hoping I can sneak in like a ninja and get him out.

Keep your phone close.

And, Pey, don't give up on me just yet.

Please.

Forever always, Knight x

I swallowed down the large lump that was wedged in my throat, or was it my heart?

"Everything okay?" Poppy distracted me as she sat up, looking around the room and frowning. "How long have I been asleep for?"

"Not long, hun, only about half an hour." I smiled. "I thought you could do with the rest. Teas on the side, I'll go make you a fresh one."

I walked over, grabbing her cold cup of tea and walked out the room.

I needed to clear my head. Walking into the kitchen, my mum was sitting at the breakfast bar, reading a magazine.

"Just making Poppy a fresh tea, she was asleep when I went up there."

"Okay, love, any update?" She lowered her voice as she stared at me.

"Knight is outside his house; his dad has just gone out and apparently his mum has yoga at seven... I dread to think how Knight knows that..." I shuddered at the thought.

"Maybe he thinks she is one of those MILFs or

whatever they're called." She waved her hand around in the air.

"Oh my God," I said slowly, covering my ears while the kettle boiled.

"What?! It's a thing, isn't it? You know, MILFs and cougars."

I dropped my head back, waiting for the ground to swallow me whole.

"Mum, please stop saying MILF and cougar."

She shook her head as if it was me that was in the wrong. I turned my back towards her and made Poppy her fresh cup of tea.

"I'll keep you posted," I muttered as I walked out of the room and back upstairs to Poppy.

"Here we go." I stood in front of her, handing her the cup.

"Thanks, sweet," she muttered, bringing the hot tea to her lips and taking a sip.

"How you feeling?" I asked as I sat next to her.

"Better, I think." She nodded, her eyes looking at the tea in her cup. "I don't want to do this alone, and I know I'm not alone because I have you, and your mum and dad. But I want Stefan here with me so bad."

"I know you do, and we will get him to you, just got to work out *how* to get him to you." I laughed softly, leaning into her.

"Is he still being kept as a prisoner?" she asked,

sadness lacing her voice.

"Yeah, but Knight's gonna fix it, okay?" I reassured her, scooping her hand into mine and squeezing it. "I promise." I nodded.

Her eyes found mine, they were filling with unshed tears. She didn't have to say anything. I dropped her hand, took her cup and placed it on the floor before hugging her. I held her tight. I didn't want to let her go.

"I don't want my baby to grow up without their dad," she choked.

"They won't," I muttered into her golden blonde hair. "Stefan will be here; he will always be here."

The truth was, I didn't know that he would be here. I could only hope that Knight could get Stefan here. Then, once he was here, I was never letting him leave again.

Chapter Sixteen

The night drew in quickly. I felt exhausted. I needed sleep.

Poppy was folding her new baby bits, a smile plastered on her face. She looked so relaxed, sitting on the end of my bed, one knee tucked under her, the other hanging off the bed.

Her face was clean from smudged tear-stained makeup, her golden blonde hair pulled into a messy bun on the top of her head. She wasn't showing yet, but she would be one of these that would have a neat bump and that's it.

"Just gonna get ready for bed, you okay?" I asked, my hand resting on her shoulder as I stood next to her.

"Yeah, I am." Her eyes glistened, her smile growing.

"Good," I mumbled and disappeared into the bathroom. I turned the shower on, letting the steam fill the room before peeling my clothes off. The summer was in full swing, and I felt sticky. Stepping under the shower, I let the water cascade over me. I needed to wash my hair, but the thought of washing and drying it at ten p.m. was too much of an effort.

Once washed, I turned the shower off and wrapped myself in my towel. I stopped in front of the large bathroom mirror, cleansing my face and brushing my teeth.

I looked tired; bags formed under my eyes. I felt like I was carrying the stress Poppy was feeling as well as my own, and my stress was minimal compared to hers. Tugging my hair out of its bun, I ran the brush through it and let it fall down my back. My mind drifted back to Knight, his lips on mine and how I wanted his lips to move down my jaw, my neck, my collar bone... I had to stop. I hadn't done anything sexual, and the thought scared me. Whereas Knight, he no doubt had many sexual experiences. Another notch on the bed post and all that. But not with me.

He wouldn't do that to me. But would Casanova? Would I be a game? I couldn't help the groan that left me, frustrated that I let my mind wander.

I stormed into the dressing area, grabbing some frilly hemmed shorts and a vest top. Dropping the towel, I pulled the white vest over my head, then pulled the cerise pink shorts up over my hips and tucked my vest into them. I padded back through to the bathroom, hanging my towel up. I didn't want to feel the wrath of my mum. She had a thing about towels being left on the floor.

LOVE ALWAYS, PEYTON

As I walked back into the bedroom, Poppy was in my bed, the duvet kicked down the bottom of the bed.

"Sleeping with me again?" I smirked.

"Do you mind? I don't like sleeping on my own." She gave me the best puppy dog eyes, her green eyes widening.

"Of course not," I smiled, opening the sash window halfway and letting the small summer breeze fill the room. Plugging my phone in and checking the time, I saw a message from Knight.

I looked over my shoulder. Poppy was already dozing off. I quickly opened his message.

Pey,
We've got movement.
I'll be in touch.
K x

Frowning, I looked at the time he sent that message––nearly two hours ago. My heart lurched from my chest, my palms sweaty.

Had something happened?

Punk,
I've only just seen this. Sorry.
Everything okay?
That was two hours ago.
I am worried.

225

Pey x

As soon as the message sent, it beeped.

Fine.
Go to sleep x

I felt a little annoyed at his blunt message, but I didn't know what was going on over at Stefan's house.

I let out a sigh, putting my phone down and laying on my back.

All of a sudden, I was awake, my eyes pinned to the ceiling.

I didn't realise I had fallen asleep when I was woken by someone calling my name.

"Peyton..." My name was clear before being filled with muffled conversations. "Peyton, baby," I heard again. I sat up, looking over at Poppy who was snoring softly. I tapped my phone, it was one a.m. I groaned.

Laying back down and rolling on my side, my eyes fell heavy again before my name woke me again. It took me a moment to realise it was coming from the window.

I knew who would be out there.

I moved from the bed quickly, running to the sash window to see Knight and Stefan.

"Cherry, let us in!" Knight's voice was loud but rushed. I didn't respond, just ran for the bedroom door and out onto the gallery landing when I heard my mum's bedroom door open. I stilled.

"What's going on?" she asked hastily, rubbing her eyes as sleep filled them.

"Knight is outside, with Stefan." I was panicking. "He has asked me to let him in." I was worried in case Stefan's father was following them.

"Fine, go. Your dad will be livid knowing that they're both in the house. You know what he is like." Her head shook from side to side, softly. "Just be quiet," she warned, her voice hushed before shooing me away and closing the door.

I ran across the hallway and down the stairs. Unlocking the locks on the door, I swung it open quickly. Knight rushed through the door, pulling Stefan with him.

My eyes glanced at Stefan, he looked awful. Then my attention moved to Knight. His cheek was cut slightly, his eye bruising.

"What happened?" My voice was quiet, my heart hurt.

"It's nothing for you to worry about." He smiled. "Where shall we go?"

I nodded towards the kitchen, my eyes wandering up the stairs before I followed them both.

"Drink?" I asked, automatically filling up the kettle.

"Tea, please," Stefan said, his eyes looked sad as they pinned to mine.

"Knight?" I faced him, but he looked like his mind was elsewhere.

"Huh?" His brow furrowed on his handsome face as he turned his head, looking over his shoulder at me.

"Tea?" I repeated again as I clicked the switch on, the kettle humming as it started to boil.

"Yeah, if that's okay?" he muttered as he stepped towards me, his hands in his back pockets of his jeans.

Stefan sat, staring out the window.

"How did you get him out?" I lowered my voice as I spoke to Knight but kept my eyes on Stefan the whole time.

"I'll explain later..." His voice trailed off before he stood next to me, his hands flat on the worktop.

"Are you okay?" I was worried, his face looked sore, and his eye was blackening more and more by the minute.

"I'm fine, honestly."

"Was it Stefan's dad?"

"Pey, don't worry about it." His head flicked up, his eyes narrowing on mine. His tone was low and gruff, as if he was warning me.

I kept silent, rubbing my lips into a thin line as I threw two tea bags into the bottom of the cups.

Once the tea was made, I slid one across to Knight and walked over to Stefan, handing him his.

"Thank you so much for this, Pey, honestly..." His voice trailed off, the crack in it apparent.

LOVE ALWAYS, PEYTON

"It's fine." I smiled warmly at him, my head tilting to the side slightly. "I'll go get Poppy," I muttered, turning on my heel and walking out the kitchen. I didn't say anything to Knight as I walked past him. Of course, I was worried about him, I only wanted to know if he was okay, and he snapped at me like that. I sighed as I climbed the stairs, my heart aching.

I tiptoed into the bedroom, standing next to Poppy. I felt bad for waking her up, but she would be so annoyed with me if I left her asleep while Stefan was sitting downstairs.

My hand rested on the top of her arm as I gently shook her. "Pop, wake up," I whispered; her eyes fluttered before falling back shut again. I shook her a little harder this time "Poppy, hun, wake up." My voice was a little louder now as I continued to shake her.

"Yeah?" Her voice was muffled, her arms stretching up as she yawned, her eyes falling heavy again.

"Stefan is downstairs."

Her eyes pinged open, widening.

"What?!" She sat up quickly, standing from the bed.

"He is here." A smile crept onto my face as her eyes glassed over. "Come, let's go... but be quiet. Dad will go mad," I whispered as we approached the landing.

She nodded, not saying another word. I walked her downstairs, cautious that she was walking down the stairs in the dark after being in a heavy sleep. I gripped onto her arm, I didn't want her losing her footing and slipping.

She walked slowly towards the kitchen, her eyes seeking Stefan's as soon as she saw him. The sobs that left her were heart breaking. Stefan stood up, his lips curling at one side as his own eyes welled.

Poppy ran towards him, leaping into his open arms and wrapping her legs round his slender frame.

"I've missed you so much," she choked in-between planting soft kisses over his lips.

"I've missed you more," he said quietly, but enough for us to hear. The words echoed around the room. I felt a burning lump in my throat, my own eyes filling with unshed tears.

I cleared my throat, my eyes looking at Knight. His deep hazel eyes were pinned to me, but I looked away quickly. They were intimidating, burning through me.

"Stay the night, it's late." I sighed, looking at the time. "Just take the couch or something." I waved my hand around in the air before letting it fall back to my side. I had to be up in a couple of hours for school. Poppy ignored me, and Stefan gave me a small nod before I turned around and walked out the room.

I trawled up the steps, feeling sluggish instantly. I was exhausted. Padding into my bedroom, I fell onto my bed, face down into the pillow. A relieved, relaxed sigh left me, my eyes falling heavy. I kept my eye on the door, waiting for Poppy to join me. I kept blinking, trying to

LOVE ALWAYS, PEYTON

fight the sleep that was crashing over me like a wave when I saw a dark figure standing by the door.

"Cherry." His voice hummed through the room. "You asleep?" He stepped in the room, walking cautiously over to the bed.

"No." I huffed; exhaustion clear in my voice.

"Can I sit here? Poppy and Stefan have gone to her room..."

"Yeah," I bit; I couldn't help the tone in my voice. "But you'll need to stay out of Dad's sight... go shut the door."

He stilled, looking behind him then back to me.

"Won't that piss your dad off more?" he asked.

"Not as much as walking past in the morning and seeing you in here."

His head fell forward, then he turned and closed the door quietly.

I shuffled along the bed, so I was closer to the edge. I had a double bed, but I didn't want to be close to him. I was annoyed with him. It didn't help because I was so tired, so the little things were irritating me more.

I felt the bed dip as he climbed on. I forced my eyes closed, but annoyingly, I didn't feel tired anymore. All I could focus on was the electricity that was coursing through me. The tension between me and Knight was too much. It was like a forcefield. We were being pulled closer to each other whether we wanted it to happen or not. It was as if the universe wanted us to be together. It was the raw magnetism that I felt, it was overwhelming.

I stilled as I felt Knight roll onto his side, his breath on the back of my neck.

"Pey, don't be mad at me..." His voice was barely audible. "I'm sorry. I didn't mean to snap at you."

Rolling on my back, I turned my head slowly to face him. "But you did."

"I know, it's just been a rough night. I had some issues with my father, then shit went down at Stefan's." He pulled his bottom lip in-between his teeth, his eyes on my lips.

"What happened?" I whispered; the breath being sucked from my lungs. His stare was burning through me, setting something inside of me on fire. That's how I felt. The apex of my thighs ached, my stomach flipping.

"My dad likes to rough me around from time to time..." His eyes were now on mine.

"Knight..." I was shocked, the words escaping me.

"It's fine, I'm used to it." He shuffled closer to me, his hand cupping the side of my face. My lips parted, ready to speak when Knight shook his head gently from side to side. "I don't want to talk about it anymore tonight... please?"

I pulled my eyes from his, the pain and sadness in his eyes broke my heart. I could feel the tension that was growing. It was too much. My eyes fluttered shut as I rubbed my lips together.

I could feel his stare penetrating through me, my eyes opening and focusing on his.

"Kiss me," I whispered.

"Pey?" He pinched his brow together, his hand still cupping the side of my face as I rolled on my side, so we were both facing each other.

"Kiss me," I asked again, and this time, he didn't question it.

He moved his lips towards me, slowly, too slowly. His breath was steady before he pressed his lips against mine, his tongue sweeping across mine as my lips moved with his. The burn only grew, a whimper leaving me when he pulled his lips off mine.

"What's wrong?" I could hear the panic in his voice.

"I didn't want you to stop." I blushed; I felt the heat on my cheeks.

"Oh, baby..." He groaned. "I never want to stop, but if I didn't stop... then I don't think I would have been able to control myself." He winked, his tongue darting out and sweeping across his bottom lip before pulling his full bottom lip in-between his teeth.

"Then don't," I whispered, shocked at the words that I just muttered out aloud.

"Pey..." His tone was warning.

His hand trailed down my side, past my ribs and across my hips. His fingertips brushed against my hot skin. He stopped on the skin exposed before my shorts, his fingers circling slowly, teasing.

I pressed my thighs together, biting my own lip.

"Talk to me," he whispered, his fingers stopping for a moment as his eyes burned into mine.

"I can't explain this feeling... I feel a dull ache... a burn..." I blushed again; I was so embarrassed.

"You're turned on."

"What?! No!" I threw my arm across my face. I was mortified.

He reached up, grabbing my arm and pulling it away from my face.

"I'm not asking you; I'm telling you... that feeling... it's normal." He smirked, his fingers back circling over my sensitive skin. "And I fucking love it." He groaned before covering his lips back over mine. It was like I had fireworks ready to explode in my stomach, the butterflies uncontrollably swarming.

I heard him suck in his breath, his eyes closing.

"Are you sure you want to do this?" I could see the worry in his hazel eyes as they volleyed between mine.

I nodded; I didn't want to speak. I felt too embarrassed.

"I'm not going all the way with you, Pey, I'm just going to relieve you a little..." His lips played into a smirk, his breathing harsh. I knew if I thought about this, I would fight with my subconscious and stop this from happening.

But not because I didn't want it to happen, I did, but he was my friend, my best friend.

His fingers worked their way into my shorts, his fingertips gliding across the top of my thigh slowly. His breath hitched. "Fuck," he whispered when he realised I was naked under my shorts. His voice was so low, it was almost inaudible.

I felt the goosebumps smother over me, my skin even more sensitive than usual. I was really letting this happen. And I was so glad it was with Knight.

The thought of anyone else scared me.

I was distracted when he hovered his lips over mine. He propped himself up on his elbow, so he was over me. He didn't move his eyes away from me as I slowly rolled on my back. My heart was racing in my chest, but I didn't want him to stop.

Skimming his fingers across and closer to where I so desperately wanted him to touch, he then dragged them back across to my hip. My brows furrowed.

"Patience, baby," he cooed, his fingers sweeping back over, this time even closer.

"It's not too late..." he whispered against my lips, his breath intoxicating me in that instant.

"No," I breathed out, not taking my eyes off of him.

And before I could think anymore, his finger glided down my core, dragging it back up and rubbing my sensitive clit slowly. I had no control over the gasp that escaped me, his eyes stayed on mine, his lips still teasingly close. My lips parted as the pleasure ripped through me.

"Does that feel good, Cherry?" he whispered against my skin, his lips moving slightly and pressing to my jaw.

His finger moved from my clit, his finger teasing at my opening.

"So wet," he muttered, his lips moving to mine, covering my mouth as he gently pushed his finger inside of me. I tightened, stiffened as I adjusted to the unfamiliar sting that coursed through me.

"You okay?" he breathed, his finger slipping out of me, circling at my opening once more before pushing it back into me, the burn spreading through my body. An unfamiliar tingle swarmed over me. I felt hot, and a moan rolled off of my tongue.

"That's it, baby." His voice was slow and low, his lips by my ear as he nipped. His finger pulled out of me, spreading my wetness across my clit. The bubbling in my lower stomach was overwhelming.

I felt myself tighten around him, my breathing faster now, my skin smothered in goosebumps and a shiver vibrating over my body.

"Knight," I moaned, my hand moving to his shirt, my fingers wrapping around the thick white material of his T-shirt as I clung onto him tightly.

"Let it go." His eyes didn't leave mine for a single moment, his lips back hovering over mine, his breath on my face. He darted his tongue out, swiping it across my bottom lip before slipping it into my mouth, kissing me as our tongues danced with each other. His finger grazed across me, slipping back into my opening as his thumb circled over my clit slowly. My legs trembled as I felt an almighty wave crash over me, tightening around his finger and moaning into his mouth as I came. His mouth devoured me, his tongue caressing every part of me as he rode me through my orgasm. I felt a shudder sweep over me as he pulled his finger out, shifting his weight and laying in-between my legs, his hands around my face as his thumbs pushed a couple of loose strands of hair away. His eyes moved from my lips to my eyes, from my eyes to my lips.

I couldn't hide the smile that was plastered over my face. His lips pressed into a smile when he saw mine.

"You okay?" he asked quietly.

"I am." I sighed, blissfully happy.

"I can't believe we did that." Knight let out a soft chuckle. "Does this make us friends with benefits now?" He wiggled his eyebrows which caused me to burst into laughter.

"Stop it." I smacked at his arm.

He winked at me, hovering close to my lips, waiting for my acceptance. I smirked, putting my hands on the side of his face and pulling him closer to me. Our lips connected, and a fire raged inside of me.

Is it wrong I want so much more from him? He was like a drug; I have had one taste and now I want more. I felt addicted from that one sweet hit.

"Okay if I go freshen up?" he mumbled against my lips.

"Of course," I whispered, watching him push away from me and climb off my bed and into the bathroom, closing the door behind him.

My heart thumped, my insides alight.

I laid for a moment, just replaying the most intimate moment of my life over and over. It was so much more than I could have imagined.

I nibbled on my bottom lip; my mind filled with what Knight had just done to me. I could feel the heat spreading over me once more.

I couldn't lay here anymore. I needed to cool myself down, and a splash of water on my face would do the trick. I swung my legs round, pushing off the bed and padding towards the bathroom door, a smile creeping on my face as I opened the door to see Knight, standing completely naked under the shower, pleasuring himself.

I stood frozen. Knight's head turned and he looked at me over his shoulder, his eyes wide.

I couldn't take my eyes away from him, they trailed up and down his back. His muscles rippled under his skin. I never noticed just how toned he was.

"Pey... I..." he stammered, turning to face me.

LOVE ALWAYS, PEYTON

I didn't say anything, just walked towards him slowly, not taking my eyes off of him as I closed the gap between us.

The room was thick with tension.

Sliding the shower door open, my eyes moved from his down to his hand. My lips parted, eyes widening when I saw his cock in his hand. It took me a minute for me to bring them back up to his face.

"I'm sorry, I didn't even think to knock," I muttered, feeling like a complete idiot. I wanted to move, to run out the room, but I couldn't. My feet felt like they were cemented to the floor. Knight let out a deep sigh, turning slowly. The water hit the shower tray, drops hitting my bare feet.

My eyes moved to his as I watched his hand turn the dial on the shower, the water stopping. A few water droplets ran from his soaked hair and down his face.

The burning desire grew deep inside me. I squeezed my thighs together to stop the dull ache that consumed me.

Stepping out the shower, he was in front of me, our bodies millimetres from touching. He was so wet, the water running over his body.

My mouth dried. My lips parted.

He pressed against me; I could feel just how hard he was. My breath hitched.

He didn't take his eyes from me, the water running

off of his hair, dripping between us.

"See what you make me feel, Cherry?" His breath was on my face as he exhaled through his pursed lips and inhaled deeply through his nose. His breaths sounded ragged.

I didn't say anything, just watched as his eyes darted back and forth to mine.

"Does it hurt?" I blurted out after a moments silence.

"What? This?" He smirked, taking my hand and putting it over him.

Blushing, I nodded, all of a sudden feeling shy.

"No, sweet. No pain, just a little uncomfortable." His voice was lowered, shaky even.

I quickly retracted my hand; my eyes eyeing his hard length. His hand replaced mine, wrapping his fingers around himself as he slowly moved his hand up and down his cock. His breathing fastened, his eyes still on mine. It was killing me, fighting the urge to not look in-between his legs. The burning grew deeper inside of me, the ache overwhelming.

"Can I touch you?" I whispered.

He licked his lip, his breathing shallow.

My eyes darted down, watching his hand move up and down himself, nibbling on my bottom lip. He nodded, placing my hand over his. I was trembling, but not from nerves.

I was intoxicated by him.

"Cherry, do you know how long I have waited for this..." he stammered, his breathing harsher as he continued moving his hand up and down his cock slowly, my fingers wrapping around his hand.

I couldn't help but watch his face. His eyes were hazy, looking down between us, his curly hair sitting on his forehead, water still dripping occasionally down his skin from his soaked hair. His jaw clenched; his lips parted as his breath shakily left his lungs.

He wrapped his spare hand behind my head, pulling me to him as our lips crashed together. The groans leaving his throat were delicious. His tongue caressed mine so slowly, teasing me.

I needed more of him.

I stopped his hand, replacing his with mine. Wrapping my fingers around him, my eyes fluttered open and widened at the feel of him on my skin. He was like silk, softer than I imagined but thick. So thick.

He winced. Instantly letting go, I stepped back, a small gasp leaving me as my eyes searched his.

"No baby, no..." he whispered, wrapping his fingers around my wrist and pulling me towards him, and back into the shower cubicle. He twisted the dial, the water cascading over his body first until it ran hot. He tugged my wrist, pulling me close to him. Our bodies touched for a small moment.

"Touch me again," he begged. "Just don't squeeze as

tightly this time." I heard the humour in his voice.

I pressed my hand flat against his chest, his heart was racing underneath my touch. I glided my fingers down slowly, making my way to where he wanted me. Where I wanted to be. Wrapping my fingers around his thickness, I slowly moved my hand up and down. Knight's forehead pressed against mine, and his head dipped as his eyes watched me. His moans hummed through me.

"Pey, fuuuuuuck." He dragged his words, his head falling back then snapping forward. His eyes were hooded as he gazed into mine. His hand came over mine, pulling it away quickly then he span and finished himself off. I watched his muscles tense in his back, one of his hands pressed against the tiled wall as a shudder ripped through him, deep groans escaping his lips.

My breathing was fast, harsh. The water was falling over me, but I didn't care. I was soaked, and not just from the shower.

Knight turned the dial off, turning slowly to look at me.

"Oh dear, you're *wet*," he purred, wrapping his hand around my back and pulling me closer to him.

"And your top is see-through..." He licked his lips, his eyes falling down to my top.

I blushed, pushing against him slightly and covering myself.

He let out a throaty laugh. "Cherry, don't become shy

now. I've already seen it." He winked as he planted a kiss on my forehead then moved round me and grabbed a towel, wrapping it around his waist.

"I'm gonna go change..." I muttered, still stood in the shower. It took me a moment to get my brain to engage and move my legs. I walked straight past Knight; my clothes soaked as I looked around my wardrobe. I peeled the wet clothes off of me, letting them sit by my feet as I stepped out of my shorts, my tee falling to the floor.

Rummaging through my drawers, I grabbed a pair of shorts and an oversized tee. Pulling them on, I furrowed my brows, looking at the soaked clothes beside me. My mum would question them.

I couldn't worry about that now. I had to be up in three hours for school. I picked them up, throwing them in the washing basket when I heard the bathroom door go.

"Damn it, I missed you getting changed." Knight groaned as he wrapped his arm around my waist and kissed me on the cheek.

I smirked, my hand resting over the top of his before he pulled it away from me.

"I need to sleep," I whispered, walking away from him and climbing into bed.

I didn't look back, just pulled the duvet of my bed back and fell into it. My eyes were so heavy, but within moments, I felt the bed dip.

"Have I pissed you off?" Knight asked, laying close to

me as his arm laid over my back, and my eyes searched his.

"No..." I muttered, my arms moving under my pillow, my eyes threatening to close. "I am just exhausted."

"Okay, Cherry, sleep," he mumbled, kissing my cheek and resting his head on the pillow next to me. I fought with my eyes as I wanted to watch him fall asleep, but I couldn't fight it anymore.

The truth was that I was confused. I didn't know what I was feeling. I felt torn. Torn between Casanova and Knight.

Chapter Seventeen

My head felt heavy, my eyes hurting as I heard a muffled ringing. I moaned out, swatting my hand down on the bed next to me, looking for the source of the noise when I heard a groan.

My eyes pinged open, my heart jackhammering in my chest when I saw Knight peeking through one eye, his hair all messed up, his lip lifted on one side before it broke into a smile.

"Morning." His voice was husky and low. He was laying on his front, only wearing his boxers. The sun peeped through the chiffon material curtains, and his skin glistened. I couldn't stop my hungry eyes from taking every inch of him in.

"Morning," I squeaked, bringing the duvet up as I tried to cover myself.

"Stop covering yourself up," he moaned, rolling on his back, his hand grabbing the front of his boxers. My eyes followed his hands, widening when I saw the bulge.

"Morning glory." He winked, sweeping his tongue

across his bottom lip, our eyes locking. I needed to move away from him, I couldn't stand the tension that was brewing between us. The pull was too much, like a forcefield. I couldn't breathe, he literally took my breath away. The air was being pulled from my lungs from just his stare. Throwing the covers back and darting into the bathroom, I slammed and locked the door behind me.

I couldn't give into the temptation again. Wrapping my fingers around the edge of the wide, square sink in the bathroom, my head dropped as my eyes focused on the water dripping from the tap, hitting the porcelain sink before dissolving. I internally groaned, rolling my head back before lifting it slowly and looking back at my reflection.

I looked wrecked.

But not in a bad way.

Knight had claimed me, and part of me wanted him to claim every single part of me. My fingers tightened around the sink, my teeth sinking into my bottom lip as images of him flitted through my brain.

I forced my eyes closed, squeezing them tight.

Casanova.

Casanova.

Casanova.

My heart filled with dread. The thought that I had done that with Knight and things were going so well with Casanova... I know we weren't a couple, but still, I wanted us to be when we finally got to meet.

Had I fucked it up?

No, no. Peyton. Stop.

You and Casanova are just friends. As are you and Knight. Friends. Knight knows that. He has always known that.

My trembling fingers lifted the tap, and the water spurted out. Both my hands cupped under the stream, letting the water fill before splashing my face.

It instantly woke me, slapping me with a pinch of reality. I shook my hands out then reached and shut the tap off. Grabbing the towel and dabbing my face, the scent of Knight intoxicated me once more as it drifted through my nose. My stomach clenched before whirling in a three-sixty.

Reaching for my toothbrush and smothering it in toothpaste, I brushed the taste of him out of my mouth. Even though we hadn't kissed since last night, I could taste him on the tip of my tongue. It only made my craving worse. Once done, I stripped down to nothing and stepped under the shower. The warm water slipped across my skin, instantly relaxing me. I kept my eyes closed, I didn't want to open them as the memories of last night would crash through me, making this torture even worse.

My shower was short and sweet. Walking out, I wrapped myself in the towel that Knight was covered in last night. I ignored the fire that ignited in the pit of my stomach, the delicious ache that I had become familiar with over the last few hours. Shaking my thoughts away, I opened the door to see Knight standing in the dressing area of my room.

We both stood staring, neither of us pulling our eyes from each other. Knight stepped towards me cautiously. He was still only in his boxers, his eyes hazing and moving up and down my wet towel-covered body.

"What a sight..." he mumbled, his hand moving closer to me, when I heard a knock on the door. My heart dropped out of my chest, my eyes widening as I shoved Knight into one of my wardrobes, slamming the door shut on him and leaving him in darkness.

"Darling, it's me," my dad called out.

"One second, Daddy! I've just got out the shower!" Panic rose through me as my eyes scanned the dressing room for Knight's clothes. I couldn't see them. I darted into my bedroom, trying to tidy my bed a little, my eyes still looking. I was out of time. He must've put them somewhere.

Another knock on the door.

"I'm coming," I shouted out, running towards the door and opening it, plastering my best smile across my face.

"Daddy!" I beamed, my fingers gripping onto the door tightly. "You okay?" My voice was so high. I was trying to play it cool, but I couldn't.

"Where is the boy?" He pushed past me, his eyes scanning the room as he paced a few steps back and forth.

"What boy?" I played dumb, following closely behind him.

"Don't make me out to be a fool, Poppy is downstairs with Stefan, so where is the other one?" His voice was calm, but that scared me more.

"Oh, Knight?" A giggle bubbled out of me, my hand tightening on my towel around my body. I was sweating. Nerves were bolting through me. "He left last night, once Stefan and Poppy were reunited, he left." God, I hated lying, but I would hate it more if my dad found Knight standing in his boxers, hidden in my wardrobes.

"He did?" My dad's voice was shocked, laced with a little disbelief.

"Yeah." I smiled. "No reason for him to stay here. His job was to find Stefan, which he did."

"Fine..." My dad's lips broke into a small smile, but the stern look was still plastered across his aging face. "How are you feeling about today?" my dad asked as he perched himself on the edge of my bed. I was so nervous, but I managed to keep my eyes on his and not once look in the direction of where Knight was hiding.

"Yeah okay, confident. I am looking forward to this being over now." My hand tucked a loose strand of hair behind my ear, my eyes batting to the floor.

"Good, that's my girl," he muttered, standing from

the bed and placing a kiss on the top of my head. "Go get them, champ!" His voice was louder now, booming around the room. His hands fisted in his suit trouser pockets as he strolled towards the door before stopping and turning to face me. My eyes darted behind the door. Knight's white tee sat––screwed up––behind the door, just inches away from my dad.

Shit.

"Tell your friend, thank you for bringing Stefan here." My dad smiled again and gave a quick wink before he walked out the bedroom door.

My heart was racing, I felt sick.

I rushed to push the door shut, my back against the cool wood, my head tipping back and resting on the hard surface. I closed my eyes, taking deep breaths through my nose and exhaling through my lips.

I needed to still my erratic heart.

I jumped when I heard a noise come from the dressing area. Knight's hands locked together, rubbing over each other, his tongue in his cheek as he walked towards me.

"Naughty girl, tsk." His voice rumbled through me as he closed the gap between us.

"Don't," I warned, my eyes narrowing on him. "I can't." I shook my head, my voice trembling. "You are misting my judgement, my conscious. You're like a drug. I can't stop craving you, but you're bad for me. Not now, I can't," I muttered. I saw Knight's face drop slightly, his eyes following me as I stormed around the room, flapping and huffing out loud.

"I'm *bad* for you?" He repeated my words. Of course, he would hone in on that.

I threw my hand down, one gripping the top of my towel that was threatening to fall. "I didn't mean it like that." I rolled my eyes before connecting them with his.

"Then how did you mean it?" His voice was still, quiet.

"I meant it in a way that I can't get enough of you. I want you, every second of every minute, of every hour!" I couldn't help the rise in my voice. "You have completely consumed me. I am fixated on you, but the thought of that scares me..." My throat burned, my eyes welling. "But this shouldn't be happening. I have Casanova... we're friends. *Best friends,* and here we are... well, here you are, making me feel like this. I am addicted to you, obsessed even. You plague my mind, haunt my dreams, and you have done from the first moment I laid eyes on you months ago..." I was deflated, I felt so disheartened. My voice was hoarse from the burn in my throat, as if an iron rod was pushed down into my windpipe.

"I'm sorry..." Knight's voice was barely audible. Instantly I felt the loss, the loss of the connection that we held. His eyes focused on his feet, shuffling awkwardly from one foot to the other. "I'm sorry I *consumed* you.

Have you any idea of how I *actually* feel for you?" he asked, the tone of his voice not altering at all. He shook his head, his curly hair pushed away from his face with his large hand. "Forget it," he grunted, turning and grabbing his tee from behind the door then disappearing into the dressing room.

I felt my heart crack, a pain searing through me.

But maybe this was good?

Maybe we needed this? I *needed* this.

I couldn't afford to be distracted today, especially not by Knight Pierce.

—

Once dressed––and a whole tube of concealer to try and cover my bags and my sins––I wandered downstairs.

Poppy's head turned to face me as I walked into the kitchen, Stefan cosied up next to her. Their fingers linked and entwined through each other's as they ate their breakfast.

"You look like shit," Poppy muttered through a mouthful of cereal.

"Gee, thanks." I tutted, plodding over to the fridge.

"Poppy..." Stefan snapped. I watched as Stefan kept his eyes on hers, until she eventually shook her head in a playful manner then rolled her eyes. "Sorry, you look beautiful." She snapped her head towards Stefan, plastering a fake, sarcastic smile over her lips. "As always."

"Think I preferred the truth to be honest." I scoffed, pouring myself a large glass of orange juice.

"How did you sleep?" I asked, my eyes volleying between them as I stood opposite them, but over the other side of the breakfast bar.

"Like a baby. You?" she asked, her eyes lifting from her cereal.

"Not bad." I nodded, reaching for a banana and peeling it. I needed to eat, but I had lost my appetite.

A shiver swarmed over me, the hairs standing on the back of my neck when I felt his presence crash into the room. I was just grateful my dad had left.

"Morning!" Poppy chirped, her eyes on Knight.

He didn't say anything, just held his hand up before walking past me and flopping down in the large chair that sat in the window.

Huffing, I placed my glass in the sink and walked out of the kitchen, my eyes meeting with my mum's as she came down the stairs.

"Morning, darling, you okay?" Her perfectly shaped brows furrowed, pinching in the middle. Her hands came to my face to hold my head then one of her hands moved to her forehead. "Oh, sweetie, you feel a little warm, are you feeling okay?" she asked. She was clearly concerned. I couldn't tell her the flush was because of Knight.

"I'm fine, Mum, promise. The house is just warm," I

muttered.

"Okay, princess, one day to get through." She smiled, kissing me on the cheek and walking into the kitchen.

"Oh, Knight... you're still here..." I heard my mum's muffled voice.

I didn't want to stick around and listen to what he had to say, even his voice was torture. I stepped into the entrance hall, opening the cupboard and grabbing my backpack. I had a quick peek through to make sure I had the correct textbooks. Throwing it over my shoulder, I opened the front door as quietly as I could. I was grateful Champ was in the garden otherwise he would've barked, causing an unnecessary commotion. Slipping out the front door, the summer air filled my lungs. I sat myself on the front steps of my house, watching the clouds drift through the sky from the light summer breeze.

I internally groaned when I heard the front door go. I didn't even have to look behind me to know it was him.

He slumped down next to me, laying back on his elbows, his knees bent as he looked ahead.

Nothing was said, we just sat next to each other in silence.

There was so much I wanted to say, but I couldn't. I just didn't have the right words to say. The urge to reach across and slip my hand within in his––to entwine my fingers through his––was so strong, but I stopped myself. How could I do that after what I said to him upstairs?

"Pey..." I could hear the agonizing pain in his voice, his head turning to look at me. I didn't look back, I couldn't. I was ashamed of my behaviour.

"Please talk to me, I can't stand it. It's only been half an hour and it's killing me." He sounded strained; I could feel his eyes burning into the side of my head. The pull inside was overwhelming as I slowly turned to face him.

"Don't hate me," I whispered, because if I spoke, he would hear the crack in my voice and just how much this was hurting me.

"Cherry, I could never hate you. *Ever.*" A small laugh left him. He sat up slowly, rubbing his elbows then scooted closer to me, his arm stretching out and wrapping around my shoulder, pulling me to him. His scent crashed over me like a wave, drowning me in an instant. I felt his lips on the side of my head, his lips hesitant before they pressed against my hair.

"You're confused, I get it. I brought raw, new emotions to the surface last night..." He stopped for a moment, leaning forward and looking at me. "Don't get me wrong, I fucking loved it, but I get that it's a little overwhelming."

I nodded, my fingers knotting together.

"I want so much more with you, you know that. But it's not me I have to talk to, to convince. It's you. You are so hell-bent on Casanova and this whole soulmate bullshit that you can't see what's right in front of you." He sighed, dropping his arm from my shoulders. "If you would just open your eyes a little more, forget the pen pal shit, and just look... you would see your soulmate has been in front of you all along." I watched as he pushed himself up off the steps and took a couple of strides forward, his hands pushing deep into the front of his jean pockets. "But you won't. You won't give us a chance until you have explored things with that douche Casanova..." He shook his head, one of his hands pushing through his beautiful hair. "But soon, my Cherry, soon you will see just how perfect I am for you," he muttered, turning on his heel and walking away from me.

I don't know why, but that felt like goodbye.

And it obliterated my heart.

Chapter Eighteen

The bell chimed and I placed my pen down for the last time on my maths exam paper. I couldn't believe it was over. We had done it. Now for the fun bit, waiting for the results to see if we got accepted into our choice of university.

I was anxious, Knight's words played over and over in my head throughout the exam which annoyed me and broke me at the same time.

He was right. I had gotten so consumed and wrapped up with Casanova that I ignored everything else around me.

The teacher's voices echoed round the hallway as we were dismissed. I reached down, grabbing my bag and heading out into the crowded corridors.

We were told this morning that we had to meet in our English room for the last letters from our pen pals, then we were moving onto emails.

I walked slowly through into Mrs Tides' room, dropping my backpack to my feet as I reached for my letter. My heart dropped; my palms sweaty as I fumbled in my bag. Dropping to my knees and opening the bag more, my eyes searched every pocket looking for it. I knew it was in there, I put it in there.

But it wasn't.

It was gone.

"Everything okay, Peyton?" Mrs Tides asked as she stepped towards me, the rest of the room filling with the chatter of the girls.

"My letter is not here." My voice was hushed.

"Oh…"

"He is gonna think I have ignored him." My lip trembled.

"No he won't, you are moving onto emails in a few weeks but this is actually why I called everyone here." She smiled, handing me my letter from Casanova.

I stood slowly, watching Mrs Tides walk away from me and back to the front of the class.

"Okay girls, settle down!" she called out, clapping her hands and trying to silence the room. "As you know, this is your last handwritten letter to your pen pals, but moving on… in two weeks time, we will be moving to email addresses, *if* you wish to continue…" She smirked, her eyes finding me. "And the reason I say that is because next Saturday, we are holding a school fete where you will finally meet your pen pal." I could hear the excitement in her voice, the girls nattering next to me, some squealing.

"All I would like you to do is write your pen pal nickname then your real name underneath. Then we will get them made into pinned name badges which will be laid out at the fete on Saturday next week." Reaching in her drawer, she pulled out a tub of white name stickers and black sharpie pens.

Everyone swarmed her, grabbing their stickers and pens. I stood and waited until everyone had scarpered. I wanted Poppy here, but she didn't have to be here because she had Stefan, and Stefan was her pen pal. And that's just it, if she could meet her soul mate through the pen pal programme, what is to say I won't?

I wandered aimlessly towards Tides' desk, grabbing a sharpie and jotting my name down on the sticker.

Dimples.

Peyton Fallon

"You excited?" Tides asked as she took the sharpie off of me and placed my name sticker in the pot.

"I am." I smiled. And that was the truth, I was. At least this way, I could finally see if I had anything with Casanova, or if he merely was just a pen pal friend.

I started worrying. What if I wasn't attracted to him? What if he wasn't my type? I felt a cold sweat smother me, my palms sticky.

Tides' mouth was moving but I couldn't decipher what she was saying. I was too lost in my thoughts.

"Bye, Miss," I muttered, turning and grabbing my bag off the floor and walking out of the classroom to see Poppy standing by the locker, waiting for me.

"Hey, hun... you okay? You look like you have seen a ghost," she muttered as she held onto my shoulders. "Yeah, fine... just... we are meeting our pen pals Saturday, next week––at a fete thing," I stammered; arms waving in the air, my eyes fixed on her.

"That's a good thing, it's so exciting! I can't wait to see what he looks like... I bet he is a God." She swooned, pulling me towards her so my legs were forced to move. "Come on, let's get out of here and say goodbye to Augustine Prep once and for all." She cheered, walking towards the door.

It hadn't even sunk in that we wouldn't be coming through these doors again for lessons. Our time at Augustine's was done.

I had put the conjoined university for Augustine as my first choice, whereas Poppy put URC which was two hours away, even though I wasn't even sure if she was going to go now. I put URC as my second choice. My father didn't want me too far away, so when I have study days, I could work with him.

I needed to work out when I would sit down with him and tell him that I didn't want to work for his company.

LOVE ALWAYS, PEYTON

The thought didn't even bear thinking about. It was going to be hell.

"How did Knight get a black eye? I have been meaning to ask you, but you know, I was preoccupied last night." She winked, nibbling on her bottom lip.

I turned my nose up slightly, not wanting to think about how her and Stefan spent their night. I was so desperate to talk to her about what happened with me and Knight, but it just wasn't the right time. "He didn't actually say as such, just his dad roughs him around a bit." I winced. I––all of a sudden––felt guilty, I didn't even ask how he was feeling this morning. The cut on his cheek had scabbed over and didn't look as angry, but his eye was a full-on shiner.

"Ah shit, I was worried you were going to say that..." she muttered as she pushed through the double doors at the end of the corridor.

"What do you mean?" I asked, my eyes moving to her as she focused on my mum's car.

"His dad is horrible to him, like beats him for stupid shit... Stefan said he is meant to be moving into his nan's or something this week." She shrugged.

"Well, I hope he does, so he can get away from that monster." My voice felt strained. How could anyone hurt their children?

And just like that, my heart broke all over again for Knight.

My poor, beautiful Knight.

My mum and Poppy chatted the whole way home, but I wasn't really listening. I felt absent from the conversation. All I could think about was Knight and how much I wanted him safe and away from his father. It wasn't right, and yet last night, all he cared about was getting Stefan to Poppy.

I was relieved to see my house approaching, I needed to sleep. I was exhausted. Dragging myself from the car, I followed behind Poppy and my mum. Stefan was here, he didn't go to his last exam. He was worried that if he left the house, he wouldn't get back to Poppy and he vowed that he wouldn't be leaving her side again. Dropping my bag to the floor, I dragged my tired legs up the stairs and straight into my bedroom. I had a mix of emotions overwhelming me. Falling onto the bed, face down, I promised myself that I would lay here for a moment, just to rest my eyes.

"Hey, darling, wake up." My mum's voice was hushed, and there was a gentle nudge on my arm.

"Mum?" I muttered, lifting my head up from the pillow. My eyes were like slits, and heavy. I just wanted to go back to sleep. The lack of sleep last night was catching up with me.

"Dinner is on the table, then you can come back up and rest." She smiled, her hand running up and down my arm over my blazer.

LOVE ALWAYS, PEYTON

"Okay," I muttered, pushing myself up and crawling off the bed. I was grateful it was just my mum here, because how I just climbed off the bed wasn't very lady like, especially not in a skirt.

My mum's hand rested on the lower part of my back, ushering me out of the room and down the stairs.

I gasped when I reached the bottom. The long hallway was surrounded by balloons, and a massive flower arch was across the kitchen double doorway.

"Wow," I whispered, a little overwhelmed as my eyes scanned the room. "What's all this for?" I asked, stopping in front of the kitchen and asking my mum.

"Well, one, for doing amazingly in your exams, and two, you are eighteen tomorrow so why not start the celebrations early."

"Thanks, Mum," I mumbled, leaning into her as her arm wrapped and cocooned around my shoulder.

"You're most welcome. Come on." She smiled, kissing the side of my head and leading me into the kitchen where I saw Poppy, Stefan, Knight and my dad. My heart swelled.

All my favourite people in one room.

Well, apart from Casanova.

I felt the tears prick my eyes, my cheeks flushing as I stepped into the room. The balloons and flowers continued through the kitchen and into the lounge, then finished off with another large flower arch leading to the garden.

My eyes were pulled straight to Knight, the fire burning deep inside of me as he lifted his lip one side, smirking at me. My dad broke our connection as he embraced me tightly, kissing me on the cheek.

"I am so proud of you; I can't wait for you to join the team." He sounded so happy, his eyes crinkling in the corners slightly.

I really needed to tell him, but I just couldn't do it. Not now. I didn't want to break his heart.

He turned slightly, grabbing a champagne flute off the breakfast bar and handing it to me. My eyes fell to the glass that my fingers happily wrapped around before they blazed back up to his.

"Just the one, we're celebrating," he mumbled, grabbing his own glass before stepping back and standing next to me.

"Please, raise your glasses in a toast to my beautiful daughter. Peyton. You make us so proud; you are so caring and kind. You will put anyone else's needs above your own and I can't wait to have you working with me." He looked down at me again, a massive smile spreading across his face before he turned his head and faced forward, re-raising his glass and holding it in the air.

"To Peyton. Happy birthday, my sweet girl."

"Happy Birthday." The voices were loud as they echoed around the room.

LOVE ALWAYS, PEYTON

Poppy bounced up to me, wrapping her arms around me as she hugged me, her lips by my ear.

"I've got to say, Knight is devouring you with his eyes... I can't stand it, it's so hot." She drawled out the last word, fanning herself with her hand.

"Stop it." I giggled, pushing her off of me. My eyes batted to Knight's as they trailed up and down my body. "I need to get changed, you coming?" I asked her, eyeing up her uniform.

"Yeah, I'll be up in five..." she muttered, her voice trailing off, her eyes on Stefan. She was obviously distracted by him.

I laughed, shaking my head and bringing my glass to my lips, taking my first mouthful. The light bubbles of the champagne melted on my tongue, the unfamiliar golden liquid slipping down my throat like silk. It was delicious.

I rushed to place the glass on the side, excusing myself and disappearing upstairs. I was hot and stuffy, I needed to strip off.

Pushing my bedroom door open, I shrugged my blazer off as soon as I was over the door threshold. My fingers fumbled with my tie, pulling it off for the last time and throwing it on the bed. I smirked. This moment felt so bittersweet. The end of an era. I stared into the room, my fingers and thumbs pushing the buttons out of their holes slowly. I heard the floor creak, footsteps following. My eyes were down, watching as I undid the buttons, my fingers stopping when I reached a few from the bottom.

"Finally managed to pull yourself away from Stefan for a moment?" I burst into laughter, spinning round to see Knight standing in the doorway. His eyes slowly moved from my feet, dragging up my body. One look from him, and I can hardly catch my breath. I heard the woosh from my lungs.

He stepped into the room, looking over his shoulder before his hooded eyes pinned to mine. Pushing the door with his foot, he closed it behind him. His hand pushed through his curly hair as he stalked towards me, his thumb running across his bottom lip as he closed the gap between us.

I was so hypnotized by him, my eyes not moving from him at all.

"Do you need help getting that shirt off?" His voice was low, slow. It took me a moment to register that my shirt was half un-done, my bra on show.

I pulled it over my chest, trying to cover myself the best I could.

"Oh, Cherry, don't cover yourself up for my benefit. I am quite enjoying the view." He winked; his face so close to mine before his lips pressed to my cheek. A cold shiver spread across my body, followed by goosebumps.

I stood frozen as Knight continued behind me, jumping onto my bed and lying on his back, his eyes on the ceiling.

I turned, a small smile on my face. "I'll be two minutes," I muttered, disappearing into the dressing area and throwing a lounge suit on. Pulling my long, chocolate-coloured hair into a high ponytail, I walked back into my room.

Knight propped himself up on his elbows, so he was looking at me, his long legs dangling off the side of my bed.

"I got to say, as much as you look beautiful, you looked a lot better in the open shirt and the little chequered skirt." He chuckled loudly.

"Stop it, dirt bag." I nibbled on the inside of my lip, the corner of my mouth turning up as I tried to stop the smile that was threatening.

"So, how was the last day of school? Fun?" he teased, patting the spot next to him for me to come and join him.

"We can't be up here long..." I mumbled, padding over to him and diving onto my bed, laying on my front, my head turning to the right slightly, so I was looking at him. He pushed his elbows away, so he was lying flat on my bed again, his hazel eyes burning into mine.

"I know, we aren't going to be here long. Just thought we could have a moment together." He smiled at me.

"School was okay, long. Glad it's over with... I think," I muttered. "You?" I couldn't help but stare at him, he really was a work of art. So handsome.

"Yeah, glad the shit-show is over with. Looking

forward to the next stage of life." He smirked. "University... we should get our letters soon. You excited?"

"I am, yeah, not that I am going very far. I am going back into Augustine's, aren't I."

"Oh, course yeah, no different for you then. Whereas me, I am going three hours away. Going to Oxford hopefully." His little smile faded momentarily. My brows pinched, my eyes saddening.

"What's wrong?" I whispered.

"I am just looking forward to getting away from my father." He closed his eyes for a moment, his palms pressing onto his forehead. My eyes moved to his cheek, his cut still prominent on his face, his skin around his eye yellowing slightly at the corners, the rest still purple and black.

"I bet," I muttered. I shuffled up the bed slightly, my head resting on his chest. His heart was jackhammering in his chest, the beat comforting. His arms moved from his head and wrapped around my body.

I felt safe, and I hoped he did too.

"You do know that my house can be your safe place, right?" I said quietly. I felt a little awkward, but I wanted to just remind him.

"I know, thank you, angel," he muttered, squeezing his arms tighter.

"I'll be out of there soon anyway; I am moving in with

LOVE ALWAYS, PEYTON

my nan tomorrow." His voice was hushed, his arms still tightly wrapped around me.

"I heard... Where does she live? Is it far?" I couldn't help the crack in my voice, the thought of him not being able to walk to mine broke me. I was so used to him being near all the time, the thought of him leaving me so soon terrified me. I didn't even want him to leave for Uni, but I would never be able to stop him. Never be able to make him stay with me instead of escaping the hands of the monster that is known as his father.

"No, Cherry. Not far at all... I'll be even closer," he whispered. My head lifted from his chest, my eyes gazing into his.

"You will?" I stammered slightly, my heart thumping. I am sure he could feel it.

"Yeah..." His voice trailed off, his hazel eyes glistening, his lips pressing into a smile, his beautiful teeth showing. My heart skipped; my breath caught.

"Where?" I managed to breathe out. It scared me. It scared me just how much he affected me.

"I wasn't gonna tell you yet..." A light laugh bubbled out of him, and my body moved up and down with his. My arm was still over his chest, my chest pressing against him.

"Tell me..." I narrowed my eyes on him, my lips twitching.

"I'm moving next door."

"Next door?" I repeated, my eyes widening.

"Your nan is Mrs Edwards?"

"Yup."

"She your dad's mum?" I rushed out.

"No, my mum's..." His voice dropped off, his jaw clenching.

"Oh," was all I could muster. My mind was being filled with a little lost boy, his hazel eyes searching for his mum.

My heart broke.

He leant up, his arms pulling me closer to him as he placed a kiss on my forehead, inhaling through his nose deeply.

"Come on, we better get downstairs. The birthday girl can't be gone for too long," he teased, rolling me off of him and standing from the bed. He held his hand out for me, which I took gladly. A spark coursed through me like a zap. I quickly retracted my hand, as if his skin was fire, burning me.

"What's wrong?" He threw me a puzzled look, his hand still out for me to take.

"Nothing," I lied, taking his hand again and ignoring the spark that burned through me again. As soon as I was on my feet, his spare hand pushed my chest, so I fell back on the bed.

"See you downstairs, Cherry." His head fell back as he let out a loud throaty laugh before running out of the room.

Dick.

I pushed from the bed, giggling to myself and following him out the room.

My heart thumped; my stomach stirred with butterflies.

Knight had consumed me.

And I was petrified.

Chapter Nineteen

I was awoken by Poppy shouting and shaking me. "Happy Birthday!! Woohoo, you're legally allowed to get hammered!"

I groaned, I felt exhausted.

"Come on, get up. Your mum has gone all out!" she squealed with excitement.

"Okay," I groaned, throwing the covers off of me and sitting on the edge of the bed. I just needed a moment to wake up. I felt like I had been hit by a train.

Poppy was flitting from foot to foot, she was like a child.

I stood from the bed, slipping my feet into my slippers and moving towards the door.

"My God, you are acting like an eighty-year-old, not an eighteen-year-old." She rolled her eyes, laughing at me.

"I am knackered, this week at school has done me," I moaned as we walked to the hallway together.

"Try growing a human and then tell me you're tired," she snapped.

"I know, I'm sorry." I sighed.

"I'm sorry too, a little hormonal," she muttered.

I took her hand in mine as we reached the bottom of the stairs, walking towards the kitchen. My mum was standing there, her arms open wide and tears streaming down her face. I ran into her arms, hugging her tightly.

"Why are you crying?" My voice was light, playful even.

"I can't believe you're eighteen," she choked out as she squeezed me tighter and planted kisses on the top of my head.

"Oh, Mum." I felt myself get a little teary.

"I'm fine, I'm fine," she muttered when I felt another body hug me.

"It's okay, guys," Poppy chimed as she tried her best to wrap her tiny arms around me and my mum.

I snorted out a laugh, a few stray tears running down my cheeks.

"Poppy." My mum laughed, kissing my head then turned her head and kissed Poppy's forehead.

"Love you both, very much." She sniffled, her voice cracking.

"Love you too."

"And me!" Poppy said as she hugged my mum again.

"My young women!" my dad called out as he stepped into the kitchen.

"Cassie? What's wrong?" He moved quickly to be by

my mum's side, Poppy stepping aside.

"I can't believe the girls are so grown up." She sobbed into my dad's shirt.

"Oh, Cassie." He shushed her, wrapping his arms around her tiny frame. "What are you like, aye?" He let go of her, his hands cocooning around her face as he gazed into her teary blue eyes.

"I know, I know." Her light laughter filled the room.

"We've got two beautiful young women in our life, and don't forget that we have a little grandbaby on the way." He beamed, Poppy smiling at my father.

"Exactly, I am sure I can find some time for you to babysit." She laughed, her hand rubbing over her belly.

"See, we get to do it all again, darling. No tears, it's a happy day." He pulled my mum's lips towards his as he kissed her.

Most teens would get sickened and embarrassed by their parents kissing, but I didn't. It showed me just how much they still loved each other after all of these years. And I couldn't wait until I found an epic love like theirs.

"Right, let's do presents! Before your old man has to pop to the office. I'll only be gone an hour. Not too long, and I can retire," he chimed, winking at me. A pang of guilt bolted through me.

"Yes! Presents!" My mum ran both ring fingers under her eyes and then clapped her hands together.

I looked around the room, there was so much food.

Cakes, sweets, pastries, pancakes, eggs, bacon, muffins. All of my favourite food all laid out over the large dining table.

I was feeling very overwhelmed.

Stefan appeared in the doorway.

"Morning, birthday girl." He smiled as he wrapped his arms around me.

"Thank you," I muttered before he let me go and stood by Poppy's side, kissing her on the lips.

"Morning, son," my dad called out, his eyes softening when he looked at Poppy and Stefan together.

I honestly had the best parents in the world.

I pulled my phone out of my pyjama short's pocket, hoping I would have had a message from Knight. But there was nothing. I felt the ache in my heart, the disappointment shining out of me. Stefan moved closer to me, his arm reaching around my shoulders, his voice low as he leaned towards my ear.

"He won't have forgotten, I promise."

I inhaled deeply, plastering a smile over my face as I stepped towards my parents and the pile of presents that sat in the centre of the table. They were all wrapped in turquoise-blue with white ribbons.

"Mum, Dad, thank you…" I could hardly speak; I was so overcome with emotion.

"Always." My dad nodded, giving me a soft wink as his arm found its way round my mum's waist.

"Eighteen presents, they're all numbered." Mum smiled at me, her head leaning to the side as she rested it on my father.

"Wow." I laughed a little, I felt very grateful.

I had one present left to open, it was a small box with a plastic silver door key on it. White ribbon was threaded through the top. I furrowed my brow, opening the ribbon gently and lifting the lid off. Inside the box was a car key. My jaw dropped, my mouth wide, my eyes filled with excitement as I looked up at my mum and dad.

"Is this for real?" I squealed, holding the key tightly in one hand, the present box in the other.

"Take a look for yourself." My dad beamed, his head nodding towards the driveway.

I spun, running quickly to the front door and seeing a grey convertible Mercedes sitting on the drive.

I stood on the steps of the house in complete shock. I heard light nattering behind me, my mum and dad standing beside me.

"Do you like it?" my mum asked, taking my hand in hers.

"Like it? Oh my God, Mum, Dad... I love it," I choked, the tears streaming down my face.

"You deserve it." My dad's voice was smooth as he kissed me on the top of my head. "Happy birthday, darling." His arm wrapped around my shoulders. "Want to take it for a spin?"

"Really?"

"Yes, really. Go get changed, I'll meet you in the car."

I ran upstairs quickly, taking two steps at a time and grabbing the lounge suit I had on last night. I didn't care. I didn't want to make my father wait.

Running back down the stairs and straight out the door, I smiled when I saw my dad sitting in the car. He had put learning plates on the front. I slipped in the front seat, adjusting my chair, and my fingers wrapped around the leather steering wheel.

"Dad, I am so happy." My eyes were glistening again.

"I know, angel, I know. And you deserve to be. You deserve every ounce of happiness in this world."

"Dad," I whispered. I couldn't stop the tears from falling. I palmed them away as quickly as they were coming.

"Come on, don't cry. Let's go for a spin."

I left the key in the middle of the car--between me and my dad--and pushed the button to start it. It purred smoothly.

"Ready?" he asked.

"Ready." I nodded, pulling away as I pushed gently on the accelerator and drove out the driveway.

The roof was down, the sun was shining, but I didn't feel one hundred percent complete.

And it was because Knight wasn't here.

Knight

The same day

I looked around my old room. It was empty, but it didn't feel any different to when my stuff was in here.

My nan had sorted a removal company to turn up today and take my bigger furniture over from my dad's to her home. I had a rucksack of clothes; I didn't have much. My father was a wealthy man, yet I felt like the poorest kid in the world.

But this was a step in the right direction, the first step to me finally climbing out of his grasp.

I just wanted to get to Peyton. If I had my way, I would have been there for when she woke up. But I couldn't. I had to get this all done. At least I had sent her a message, so when she woke, she would see it. She was the first thought of the day, and my last of a night.

I took one last look at my room, letting out a deep sigh and closing the door behind me.

Walking down the stairs, I stilled. My father was barricading the front door.

"Where are you going, son?" he slurred, stepping towards me slightly.

"You know where I am going," I said through gritted teeth, my jaw clenching, my fist balling, the other tightening its grip around my strap.

"I don't think so. You. Are. My. Son." He growled as he steadied himself by holding onto the newel post.

"I am leaving." I shook my head, pushing past him. He reached out, grabbing the back of my leather jacket and pulling me towards him. His head pressed against mine. The smell of bourbon was on his breath.

"You aren't fucking leaving." His teeth were gritted, his eyes bulging.

I didn't answer back. I had nothing to say to him.

"Do you understand me, boy?" he spat in my face.

Again. Not a word left my lips.

He shoved me to the floor, the back of my head hitting the bottom step. I pushed the pain down, the throbbing unbearable.

"Answer me!" He leant down so he was over me.

"You can't stop me, Dad." My voice was steady, even though I was terrified. I never knew when he was going to lose it completely.

"Can't I?" He laughed through his words as he stood up. "Shall we see about that?" His voice was threatening.

"Go on then," I goaded. He took a step back, a little shocked at my response. "You always do anyway, so what's so different about today?" My voice was getting louder as I pushed up off the stairs, standing in front of him.

"Hit me, go on. One more for the road." I felt the

pent-up anger bubbling inside of me.

"Watch your mouth, *boy,*" my dad's vicious tone swiped.

"Or what?"

With that, my father stepped towards me, towering over me like he always did as he grabbed my head and smashed it off the wall. The pain splintered through me, a high-pitched ring in my ears before I felt a warm trickle run down the side of my face.

"Knight!" I heard his voice... my vision was blurry. I was dazed. "Knight!" he called again before the room went black.

—

"Hey, bud, you okay?" I heard Stefan's voice. I winced, my eyes opening slowly as I looked around. The pain in my head was searing through me.

"Yeah, fine, fine," I mumbled.

"Oh, my darling boy." My nan's voice hummed through me. "Are you okay?" She shoved Stefan out the way and perched herself on the edge of the sofa.

"I'm fine, Nan." I gave her a small smile.

"My handsome boy, that father of yours. I called the police when Mr Pretty here said you didn't show at your girlfriend's house." Her face lit up.

"She's not my girlfriend, Nan, just a friend."

"Who is a girl, so that makes her what, Mr Pretty?"

She turned, looking at Stefan.

"A girlfriend." Stefan shrugged his shoulders, waiting for my nan to turn back to face me before he burst into laughter.

"I think we should get you to the hospital." My nan went to stand and I wrapped my fingers around her wrist and shook her head.

"I promise, I'm okay." I nodded slowly. "Some painkillers will help though."

"Stefan!" she shouted.

"I'm right here, Beryl!" He raised his voice.

"Who do you think you're talking to? Where are you fucking manners?" She eyed him, and Stefan shrank back and apologised. Now it was my turn to laugh.

"Go and get the pain killers out the bathroom, please. The one opposite my bedroom, then pour my poor grandson a glass of iced water. Not from the tap, no, that shit is horrible. Fresh, filtered water from the fridge." She nodded at Stefan.

Stefan nodded back before stepping out of the large lounge to go upstairs.

"Are you sure you're okay?" she asked. I could see the worry over her face. She didn't need my fucked-up shit at her age. She was seventy, but you wouldn't think it when you saw her. Her hair was still coloured brown, only a few wrinkles setting on her face.

"I am, Nan, I promise."

"Okay, my darling, let me put a pot of tea on. Then I'm going to check your head."

I just gave her a weak smile; I didn't say anything else. Stefan reappeared with the paracetamol packet, his eyes searching for my nan.

"She's making tea," I said quietly, my eyes looking at my phone.

"What's wrong?" Stefan asked as he sat on the end of the sofa, turning his body to face me.

"I haven't heard from Peyton; I messaged her this morning but she never replied... she is probably busy with Pop and her birthday celebrations." I sighed, locking my phone and placing the screen down so I didn't keep checking it.

"Are we still going to the bar tonight in Silvertown?" I muttered, my nan appearing with a tray. On it was a pot of tea under a tea cosy, china cups and biscuits.

Stefan nodded.

"Here we go, boys, take a biscuit." My nan smiled, placing the tray down on the coffee table.

I grabbed a digestive, holding it before my nan popped two tablets out and handed them to me and pushed the glass of water into my hand.

I swallowed the tablets down then took a bite of my biscuit.

My nan fussed about, pulling me forward so she could look at my head.

"Your father is a monster." She tutted, moving my hair so she could get a proper look at the gouge on my head.

"I really think you could do with a couple of stitches..." she muttered before sitting on the chair and taking the tea cosy off of the teapot and pouring us all a cup of tea before adding a dash of milk and a sugar cube.

"Fine." I rolled my eyes before taking the cup off of her and bringing it to my lips. She always made the best cups of tea, and I honestly think it was because it was made in a teapot and drank out of a china cup. "Can I at least finish my tea in peace?" I mumbled, taking another mouthful.

"Of course." She nodded, sitting there proud as punch that I had listened to her.

I shook my head, annoyed, but she was right. I should really get it checked.

—

After four hours sitting in the emergency room, I was all good to go. My head was glued, and my nan was given some stronger painkillers for me to take. Stefan offered to come but I told him to go home with Poppy and I would catch up with him later. While we waited for the taxi, I pulled my phone out my pocket and furrowed my brow at the empty screen. Why hadn't she replied? Stefan wanted to tell her that I was at the hospital, but I asked him not to. I didn't want her worrying about me on her birthday. I couldn't help the sigh that left my lips, my arm dropping down by my side, my phone still within my clutch.

"You are sighing as if you have the world on your shoulders, my boy." My nan turned slowly to look up at me.

"I'm okay, Nan." I gave her my best smile before fisting my phone in my back pocket. I didn't want to drone on about how I was so in love with a girl who I didn't actually know felt the same back.

The taxi pulled up, stopping my thoughts in an instant as we climbed into the back. I was grateful for the short car ride. My head was throbbing.

Walking up the driveway, my eyes wandered over to where Peyton's house was. I needed to know what the plans were for tonight. Seeing my nan in and then kissing her on the cheek, I slipped back out the front door. I couldn't stop the nerves that crashed through me every time, at the thought of being near her. She did things to me. My heart thumped in my chest as soon as her eyes locked on mine, my stomach swarming with what felt like a thousand butterflies. I needed to feel close to her, whether she liked me the same as I did her, I didn't care. I would rather have her in my life as a friend than not at all.

Stepping up to the big oak gates of the house, I punched the code in. I watched as they opened slowly, too slowly for my liking.

I hadn't even had a chance to wrap her present up, I felt like such a douche. But she would understand.

I ran my hand through my curly hair, mindful of the side that had just been glued. It burned, my head throbbing in pain every time my fingers brushed near it.

I took a deep breath, trying to still my erratic heart when I pushed the doorbell. I could just let myself in, I normally do…but today, it just felt right to knock. I waited, standing on the wrap-around porch.

The door swung open, and my breath caught at the back of my throat as I laid eyes on her. I could never get over just how beautiful she was. Her ice-blue eyes penetrated through me, her dewy skin glowing in the summer sunshine. Her hair blew softly in the gentle breeze that danced around us. She was wearing a light blue summer dress, and small sleeves kissed her shoulders, the neckline sweeping across her visible collar bone. It took every ounce of strength I had to stop myself from placing my lips over it, kissing tentatively.

"Knight," she breathed.

"Hey," I muttered, my head dipping down as I focused on my shoes for a moment, my hand running around the back of my head.

"Where were you?" Her voice was so small as my eyes met hers again. She looked sad.

"I just had some bits to deal with this morning…" My

voice trailed off as I looked over at my nan's house, the cherry blossom tree that sat in the front garden creating confetti. I rubbed my lips together, my eyes cast over her beautiful face once more.

"I thought you would have been here this morning, but I haven't even heard from you." Her voice stopped; I heard the sharp intake of breath that she took. My brows furrowed, my lips parting as I went to speak.

"No, Knight. I don't want to hear it," she snapped, stepping back, her fingers wrapping around the door as if she was getting ready to close it on me.

I don't think so.

I stepped towards her, pushing my foot in the door to stop her from closing me out.

"I did text you!" My voice was loud as it bounced off the walls and down the long hallway of her house.

"What?" She shook her head as if in disbelief. I pushed my hand into my back pocket and pulled out my phone, opening the messages.

"Here." I shoved the phone into her hand a little forceful. Her fingers wrapped around, her brows pinching together as she looked at the message.

"But I didn't get it..." she mumbled as her eyes flicked up to look at me, her head cocking to the side.

"I text you," I whispered. "Pey, the fact that you even thought I wouldn't text you on your birthday..." I couldn't even finish my sentence, choking on the words. "I would always text you…"

"I'm sorry, Knight…" She pressed her lips into a thin line and opened the door for me to come in.

I didn't say anything, just pushed past her and dropped my leather coat on the pretentious footstool that sat by the door.

I don't know why I was letting it bother me so much, but it did. I stormed down the hallway and into the garden where I saw Stefan and Poppy. I made my way over to them, grabbing a glass of champagne as I did.

"How did it go?" Stefan asked, his arm wrapped tightly around Poppy's waist as he held her close.

"How did what go?" Poppy asked, her head turning to look at Stefan before they came to mine. I didn't look at her, just focused on the distance ahead of me.

"Fine," I bit, my jaw clenching. It wasn't just Pey that had put me in this mood, it was a mix of everything.

"Did you need stiches in the end?" Stefan's questions continued. Why couldn't he just shut his fucking mouth?

"Stitches?" Her voice crashed over me, my eyes widening as I glared at Stefan.

I spun quickly, her eyes searching mine.

"There was a little accident this morning," I muttered, keeping my voice low.

"With who?"

"My father." I rushed the words out as if they were poison on my tongue.

I heard a small whimper come from her, her eyes widening before they were filled with guilt and sadness.

"Sorry, Knight," Stefan mumbled behind me.

"You knew!?" Poppy screeched.

"Yes, I knew."

"And you didn't think to tell us?" Poppy continued before she walked away from Stefan and linked her arm through Peyton's. *Great.*

"Knight didn't want to tell anyone…"

My God, this guy just didn't know when to shut his mouth.

I rolled my eyes, tipping my head back for a moment and closing my eyes. The silence was welcoming. I just needed a moment.

I lifted my head slowly, blurring everything else out around me apart from her. The only one I cared about.

"Can we talk?" I stepped towards her, holding my hand out for hers. "Please?"

She didn't say anything, just stared at me for a moment before turning from Poppy and walking down towards the pool house.

I dropped my head, my feet moving towards her whether I wanted to go or not. My heart was leading the way.

Following through the door that Peyton had just walked into, the heat from the pool house knocked the air from my lungs.

LOVE ALWAYS, PEYTON

Peyton stood there, her arms down the side of her, her lips pursed into a pout.

"Why didn't you tell me?" Her voice was low, and I could see the sadness in her eyes, a veil of anguish covering her face.

"I didn't want you worrying about me, especially not today of all days," I admitted, both my hands pushed into my front pockets as I rocked onto the balls of my feet.

"Knight…" Her sweet voice hummed through me, my skin covering in goosebumps. She sauntered towards me, and I stilled. She intoxicated me. I wanted her, all of her. But I couldn't. Because I don't think she wants me.

"You should have told me," she whispered as she closed the gap between us, her arms linking around my neck, her lips hovering over mine as my neck craned down. "I always want you to tell me, okay?"

Every fibre in my body was vibrating, the current swarming through my blood from her touch.

"Okay," I breathed out, my breath on her face.

I pressed my forehead to hers, my breathing shaky. The way she affected me was indescribable.

"What did he do to you?" she asked, her body not moving from my grip, her arms still linked around my neck.

"Hit my head off of a wall," I whispered. Saying the words out loud sent a shiver through me.

The gasp that left her lips broke me, and her bottom

lip trembled.

"Hey, angel." My hand broke away from her waist as I brushed my thumb across her cheek, wiping a tear away. "Don't cry, I'm not worth your tears, and he definitely isn't." A smirk played onto my lips before I pressed them to her forehead and inhaled her scent.

"I am okay, a bit of glue and I'm good as new." I winked at her. "Plus, I am away from him now and even closer to you... I bet if I planned it right, I could see right into your room, so no more walking around naked, okay?" I just about finished my sentence before I burst into laughter, her laughing with me.

"Shut up," she mumbled, smiling before planting a kiss on my cheek.

"Oh, I have something for you..." she breathed out, her head dropping. She pulled this black, thin, rubber-looking bracelet off her wrist and held it between her thumb and finger.

"What is it?" My brows pinched as I looked at this tiny band.

"A friendship bracelet, or a shag band..." Her nose scrunched up. "Well, that's what Poppy says. You give it to someone you want to shag..." She couldn't even finish her sentence before laughing.

"Stop..." I trailed off, shaking my head as I took the band from her.

"So, you want to shag me then?" Wrapping my arm

around her back, I pulled her to me, breathing in her scent.

"It's a friendship bracelet," she muttered, her voice low, raspy.

"Gotcha." I winked, taking it from her and slipping it onto my wrist.

"Do I give you one?" I asked, looking at the grey one on her wrist. She pulled the band off and gave it to me.

"There, give it to me." She smirked, holding her wrist out.

I laughed.

"I, Knight, give you, Peyton, this *shag* band." I wiggled my brows, slipping it onto her tiny wrist.

"There, shag buddies." I nodded, stepping back and fisting my hands in my back pockets. "So, what do we do if we shag?" I asked, causing Peyton to choke on her breath, her eyes wide.

"Well, if we *do* shag, we snap them." She nibbled on her bottom lip.

"Oh, well..." I smirked. "That's fitting, I suppose." I shrugged my shoulders and winked at her.

"Come on, let's get back outside. I am so hot in here." She laughed.

I wanted nothing more than to stay in the pool house with her, to expose her skin and see the sheen of sweat glistening over her from my touch, my mouth... I wanted to taste her. To have her.

To claim her as my own.

Mine. Always.

Chapter Twenty

Knight

The evening was soon upon us, the sun setting behind the trees as we all sat in Peyton's garden. The drinks were flowing, and her mother and father were also with us.

"Are we still heading out?" Poppy asked, yawning.

"I would like to, but only if you're not too tired." Peyton smiled sweetly at Poppy who was cuddled into Stefan.

"I'll be okay, even if I come for a couple of hours."

"Sounds good." Peyton looked at her phone for the time, her eyes widening a little. "We better go get dressed so we can get out and get back." Pey smiled, holding her hand out for Poppy as she pulled her from the sofa we were all sitting on.

They disappeared into the kitchen, when I felt Pey's father's eyes on me.

"Make sure you both look after them, don't let her

get too drunk."

"Oh, no, I won't." I shook my head. "I wasn't going to drink anyway so I could keep an eye on her." I nibbled my lip, picking the skin around my thumb.

"That's a good idea, what about you Stefan?" Mr Fallon crossed one of his legs over the other one as his gaze burned into Stefan. Mrs Fallon was trying to hold her laughter in, her lips twisting.

"I was going to have a couple," Stefan muttered, his eyes moving to mine before focussing back on Mr Fallon.

"Were you? Do you think that's a good idea, you know, what with Poppy pregnant and carrying your child?"

I tried to stifle my laugh. Even I could see Peyton's father was trying to get a rise out of Stefan. If I were him, I would have burst out laughing while talking to Stefan, but he didn't. His face remained unchanged. Unaltered. Emotionless. He had a good poker face.

"No, sir." Stefan dropped his eyes to his lap, breaking the connection with Peyton's father. Mr Fallon turned his head to me, his lips turning up at one side and smirking as he winked at me before he plastered his stern face back on as Stefan looked back up at him.

"Just going to grab a drink..." I trailed off, excusing myself from the outside seating area and disappearing inside. Once out of sight, I couldn't help the laugh that escaped me. I made my way to the fridge, opening it and

LOVE ALWAYS, PEYTON

grabbing a glass bottle of water as I unscrewed the cap and took a mouthful.

"All okay, Knight?" Mr Fallon asked as he walked into the large kitchen area and stopped at the wine chiller.

"Yes, sir." I nodded, placing the water down on the worktop for a moment.

"I heard you have moved in with your nan, is that right?" His eyes were on mine as he held the wine bottle in his hand by his side.

"It is."

"I am glad." He smiled, but it was small, weak even. My eyes were pinned to his, and I couldn't read his expression.

"You are always welcome here, son, never feel like you have to be invited. This is a safe place. It always will be, never forget that," Mr Fallon said as his smile grew. "I am just happy you are away from your father, and don't worry, I have someone who works with me who will make sure he doesn't walk free anytime soon." He nodded then gave me a wink before he turned on his heel and walked back towards his wife as he whistled a tune. My heart finally started calming down after it was slamming against my ribcage.

Grabbing my bottle of water again and placing it at my lips, I heard her voice. A small smile graced my face as I turned towards where her voice was echoing.

My arm fell slightly, the bottle dropping from my lips

when I saw her walking towards me, looking like pure perfection.

My eyes roamed up and down her perfect fucking body. My pulse raced, and my cock throbbed against my jeans. She was trying to kill me. I was sure of it.

My brain was showing her in slow motion as her hips swayed, and her hand flicked her long brown wavy hair over her shoulder before her icy blues found mine. Her lips curled into a beautiful smile.

I couldn't pull my eyes from her, even if I wanted to.

She was wearing a figure-hugging little black dress. It sat mid-thigh, her glorious tanned skin on show. It made her already long legs look even longer. I was grateful that her chest was covered, I didn't want any man looking or glaring at her. The thick straps sat over her shoulders before running into a high tank neckline. She finished the look off with black chunky-soled Dr Martens.

She looked fucking incredible.

"You like?" she asked, giving me the full three-sixty spin. My eyes pinned to her tight, peachy arse before my brain brought me back to real time.

"You look phenomenal," I whispered, pushing the bottle to my lips and gulping down a few mouthfuls of water to wet my dry mouth.

Her smile was still clear on her face, her eyes looking down at her dress before they flicked back up to mine.

"Ready?" she asked, her tone excited.

"I am." I nodded, putting the bottle of water down and walking towards her. And now, I was even more grateful that I wasn't drinking, because I could watch her every fucking move and every other fucker's that may think it was a good idea to go near her.

No chance.

No one was getting remotely close to her, only me.

Mr Fallon offered to drive and pick us up as he didn't want the girls getting in a taxi. Even though we would be with them, he would rather pick us up than have a stranger drop us home.

After a short ride into Silvertown, we were dropped outside the heaving bar. Peyton and Poppy were excited.

"Got everything, girls?" Her father turned in the chair of his Aston Martin, eyeing the girls.

"Yup, ID, keys..." I mumbled.

"Looks, charm and personality." Poppy piped up before bursting into laughter.

"Smooth." Stefan snorted.

Poppy leant forward and swatted Stefan in the arm, still smiling as she did. He turned from the front seat, giving her a wink.

I opened the passenger door, climbing out and then held my hand out for Peyton to take, which she did––gladly. She kept her legs pressed together as she swung round, getting out of the car as dignified as she could. Pulling her close to me, I laced my fingers through hers. I was being possessive; I know I was. But no one was getting near her tonight but me.

I pulled her to the door, pushing into the queue, Stefan and Poppy behind us.

"What you doing?" Stefan muttered behind me.

"Getting into the bar, what do you think I'm doing?" I snapped back.

"But why push in?" He laughed.

"I didn't push in, they haven't noticed. Too busy filling their lungs with that shit in their death sticks."

Stefan rolled his eyes as we stepped forward towards the entrance. "Pot kettle black..." He coughed.

"I've quit," I muttered through gritted teeth.

"ID?" The large bouncer asked as he eyed the four of us.

The girls scrambled in their bags for their cards, me and Stefan pulled ours from our pockets as we showed him. He didn't say anything, just stepped aside and smiled at Peyton. "Happy birthday, princess." His voice sliced through me.

I raged through my nostrils, hot air breathing out of them.

"Cool it." Stefan squeezed my shoulder. "Don't get kicked out before we even get in."

He was right. I took a deep breath as I walked them over to the tables in the VIP area that her father had booked.

LOVE ALWAYS, PEYTON

"Why are we in here?" Peyton asked, still holding my hand as the other one removed the red rope that separated us.

"Because it's your birthday?" I said, a little sarcastically over the loud music. "And your father thought it would be better if you and Pop's had an area to sit." I smiled sweetly at her.

I finally let her go, even though I was reluctant. I knew she was safe sitting behind the rope and at the table.

I watched her like a hawk. Her arm reached for the champagne that was in the middle of the table. Popping the cork and filling the glasses on the table, Poppy denied her glass, patting her little belly and reached for the bottles of water that sat in a chiller––also on the table.

She eyed me and Stefan. Stefan stared at me, his brows raising slightly, his eyes batting down to his lap.

"Oh, come on, please? Someone have a drink with me! It's my birthday." Peyton pouted, giving me her puppy dog eyes.

"Fine," I growled, reaching for the flimsy champagne flutes, as did Stefan.

"To me!" Peyton called out, pushing her glass into the middle of the table so our glasses all touched before she threw it back in one go, wincing then cheering while holding her empty glass in the air.

"Another?" she called out.

I just shook my head; I knew the way this night was

going to go.

I was uncomfortable as I sat on the chair by the table, my eyes pinned to her. I watched her like a hawk, I didn't want to take my eyes off of her for a moment.

She was dancing with Poppy, her hips shaking to the beat, her eyes closed as she let the music consume her.

Once the song stopped, Poppy dragged her to the bar and lined up four shots for her to knock back.

I pushed from my chair, barging past the bodies on the dance floor. Wrapping my fingers around her wrist, I pulled her towards me. My stomach flipped, and my heart lurched from my chest from that small bit of contact with her.

"Don't drink all of them," I warned.

"Oh, pipe down." Poppy rolled her eyes.

"No, don't just shove shots down her fucking throat," I growled at Poppy, stepping towards her and glaring down into her eyes.

"You're such a kill joy." She huffed, shaking her head and re-ordering another round of shots. I could feel the anger rising in me.

"I'm not a kill joy, far from it, but she is already smashed and you're ordering her more drinks!" I was fucking livid.

"Stop it!" Peyton slurred, finishing the last of the shots before grabbing onto the bar as she tried to steady herself.

LOVE ALWAYS, PEYTON

I moved closer to Pey, wrapping my arm around her and holding her up.

"Enough," I snapped at Poppy. She sighed, flicking her long blonde hair over her shoulder and storming away into the crowds.

The bar tender stood, looking at me, four shots lined up and ready. I fisted in my pocket with my spare hand and threw him some notes before knocking the four shots of sambuca back. The burn intensified with each one.

Fucking disgusting.

I swooped Peyton up and walked her over to the seating area. Poppy and Stefan were nowhere to be seen.

Perfect.

Pulling my phone out of my pocket, I clicked Pey's dad's number.

"Knight?" His voice was gruff.

"Yeah, sir. It's me. Any chance you can come and get us?" My voice was more a plea than an ask.

"Noooo! I don't want to go homeeeee, I want to dance and drink and party!" Peyton screamed in my ear, wriggling out of my grasp and disappearing into the sea of the crowd.

"How drunk?" Fallon's voice turned, he sounded angry, and rightly so.

"Pretty wasted," I mumbled, my eyes searching for her.

"I told you––" He didn't get a chance to finish his

sentence.

"I know you did, and I didn't get her drunk. This was all Poppy's doing and now her and Stefan have fucked off and Peyton is back on the dance floor. Sir, I've gotta go. I'll see you outside." I cut the phone off and shoved it into my back pocket.

My heart raced as I stormed towards the crowded dance floor. I stopped, my heart falling from my chest. Some fucking creep had his hands all over her, dancing behind her while grinding his hips against her arse.

My fists balled, a low rumble ripping through me as I headed towards her. Wrapping my hands around her wrist, I pulled her towards me.

"Hey!" she called out while laughing.

"You her boyfriend?" Said the creep as he squared up to me, his bushy brown brows furrowing. The sweat was dripping down his face. His rancid, yellow teeth gritted as he grabbed Pey and pulled her back towards him.

"Don't you fucking touch her." I glared at him. Sure, he was bigger than me and older, but there was no way he was getting to her again. Grabbing Pey and pushing her behind me, I stepped towards the stranger.

"You're just a little boy," he antagonised me.

"I might be *just a little boy,* but step near her again, even breathe in the same air as her and I'll kill you." A smirk played on my lips, and my eyes volleyed back and forth to his bright green eyes. The anger bubbled away, a red mist hazing me as I headbutted him hard on the bridge of his nose. Blood trickled down his face. I didn't stop, the adrenaline was pumping through my veins. Not letting go of Peyton for one moment, I walked towards the front of the bar when I saw Poppy and Stefan.

I didn't want to speak to them.

I was too angry.

The fresh summer air hit me, filling my lungs and I closed my eyes for a moment, keeping Peyton close to me the whole time.

"Knight, stop being stroppy, let me go dance," she whined, trying to pull her hand out of mine.

"Not a chance, Cherry." I smirked at her, which caused a roll of the eyes. She tugged quick and hard, releasing her from my grasp. Dropping my coat, I darted towards her, wrapping my arms around her waist and throwing her over my shoulder.

"Don't be a brat," I growled, placing my leather jacket––that was on the floor next to me––over her arse and legs.

I was relieved when I saw Fallon pull up, his eyes on Peyton before slowly moving to Poppy. And they didn't move from hers. I couldn't give a shit if she was in the bad books with Pey's dad, she should have never let her get that drunk. What if they were out on their own? A cold shiver crept over me, I couldn't even bare thinking about it.

I shook the vile thoughts that were haunting me as I dumped Peyton on the front seat.

"Hey, Daddy! I had so much fun! And loooooaaaaads to drink, oh and, and Knight broke a man's nose." I heard the childish giggle escape her.

Fuck's sake.

I let Poppy and Stefan slip into the back, both sitting there with a guilt-ridden, sheepish look on their faces. Couldn't give a shit. I wasn't covering for them.

"Is that true?" Mr Fallon asked as I shut the door behind me.

"Yes, sir," I muttered, my voice quiet.

"Why?" His brows raised as he looked at me in the rear-view mirror, and I could see the smile that was threatening on his lips.

"A bloke was dancing with Pey..." My eyes widened. "Grabbed her and that..."

Fallon's eyes darkened as he looked over at his drunk daughter who was curled up on the front seat, asleep, covered under my coat. They trailed back towards me, his eyes softening.

"Thank you for looking out for her, Knight." His voice was sincere. "You are a good friend to her, and I am very grateful to you right now." He nodded, clearing his throat before pulling away. "As for you two, sitting in the back like naughty school children, I have nothing to say to you tonight." He shook his head as if disappointed with them. I didn't move my eyes from where Peyton was sitting, even though I could feel the burning glare from Poppy and Stefan.

You are such a good friend. The words that her father just said to me played on a loop.

I wanted to be so much more than that.

Chapter Twenty One

Knight

The rest of the car ride was silent. I could feel the tension brewing. But I was going to take myself out of the situation, because if I stayed, me and Stefan would come to blows.

His pride was wounded, and I got that. He didn't like the fact that I had thrown him and Poppy under the bus. But I didn't give a shit, Peyton was my priority. She was always going to be my priority.

He would have done the same if it was Poppy.

Mr Fallon pulled into the drive, waking Peyton up, who seemed to have gained a second wind.

"After drinks!" she shouted as she stumbled up the drive. "Shots, shots, shots," she chanted.

Stefan and Poppy followed her with their tails between their legs. I just stood, watching Peyton walk into the house.

It stung.

LOVE ALWAYS, PEYTON

I didn't want to leave her.

"You okay?" Mr Fallon asked as he stepped beside me, letting out a deep, heavy sigh.

"I am." I nodded; my eyes pinned to the door.

She'll turn back and say goodnight to me, she just hasn't realised.

"Good." He squeezed my shoulder before walking towards the front door, when he stopped suddenly. "And Knight..."

"Sir?"

"Thank you again for tonight, I owe you." He smirked before climbing the steps to the house and walking in, the door still open.

"You're welcome," I muttered, stepping back slowly, not taking my eyes off the door.

Come on, Cherry, don't blow me out. But she didn't turn back.

I shook my head, kicking my converse on the driveway before throwing my coat over my shoulder and turning to walk away.

"Knight!" Her voice vibrated through me, the hairs on the back of my neck standing. I turned quickly, licking my top lip before rubbing them together when I cast my eyes over her.

She was just stunning.

"Don't go." She pouted, her eyes trailing up and down my body.

"Why?" I teased as I stepped towards her.

"Cos it's my birthday and you have to do what the birthday girl says." She shrugged her shoulders as she closed the gap between us. Her little hand splayed out over my chest, the burn smothering over me from her touch.

"Please?" she whispered, begging.

I tipped my head back, groaning.

"Okay... just because it's your birthday." I winked.

"Yay!" She reached up on her tiptoes, kissing me quickly on the cheek before spinning and taking my hand as she dragged me towards the house.

"I've lined the shots up." Her head turned as she looked at me, a small smirk appearing at the corner of her mouth.

"Great," I muttered before walking into the house and closing the door behind me.

I finally gave in, letting her hand me shot after shot.

"Pey, enough. You're going to be so rough tomorrow." I winced, the sambuca was vile.

"Ohhhh, Knighty poo, don't be like that." She pouted, pushing her brows down, creating a deep V on her forehead.

"I'm not being like anything, Cherry, but it's already gone three a.m. I am shattered, my head hurts, and I don't fancy having a raging hangover in the morning," I groaned.

She crossed her arms over her chest, her brows still deeply furrowed as she pouted.

"Fiiiiiine." She stomped her foot like a spoiled child as she stormed out of the kitchen and walked towards the stairs.

I stood, smirking as I watched her walk away.

"Knighty poo..." Her angelic voice sang down the long hallway.

I rolled my eyes. What the fuck was this new nick name?

"I want you to stay the night..." Her voice was getting closer as I walked slowly down the hallway.

"Please?" she whispered; her blue eyes looked glassy. Her perfect fucking lips parted as her breathing fastened, her hand wrapping around the top of the newel post of the stairs.

How the fuck could I say no?

I didn't want to leave her, I never wanted to leave her, but this was dangerous territory.

She rubbed her lips together, running her tongue over her bottom one quickly before walking up the stairs. And like a damn fucking puppy dog, I followed.

Peyton stumbled up the stairs, banging into the wall, then giggled. I grabbed her wrist, tugging her towards me gently before swooping her up, so one arm was under her legs, the other under her arms.

"You're a nightmare," I whispered as I climbed the

last step, my breath on her face, my eyes boring into hers.

"And..." She smiled sweetly, batting her lashes.

"And nothing." I laughed. Oh, sweet Pey, there is so much more I want to say to you. But tonight was not the night for that.

I stepped over the threshold of her bedroom door, walking towards her bed and dropping her on it.

"Knight!" She laughed, her hair fanning out behind her.

I stayed stood, looking down at her. Could I ever tire of her beauty?

She pushed up onto her elbows, her legs dangling over the edge of the bed before slowly pulling herself up. Her hand found my tee, and she ran her fingers over my chest and body before wrapping them around the material of my top and pulling me down towards her. Her eyes were on my lips, her breathing ragged.

"Knight." Suddenly the giggles had gone, her voice was low, a whisper as she said my name. Sometimes I wish it didn't affect me the way it did. I am completely bound to her. Helpless even.

"Peyton," I whispered back, smiling at her, even though my heart was thrashing in my chest.

"I want you to take my virginity," she muttered, her cheeks flushing but her eyes staying on mine.

My eyes widened.

The fuck?

LOVE ALWAYS, PEYTON

"Pey..." One of my brows dropped, the other high.

"No, listen." Her voice was stern now, her fingers still clasped around the material of my tee. "I, er, well..." she stammered, her fingers on her other hand grabbing the hem of my tee. She was nervous.

"Just with meeting Casanova next weekend, well, I'm worried... you know... about being inexperienced. And I don't want to be inexperienced. I want you to take my firsts, all of them." Her hands dropped from my tee, her fingers knotting together.

Just hearing Casanova's name infuriated me.

But selfishly, I wanted all of her firsts.

"Please, Knight," she whimpered, her eyes widening, her hands finding their way back to my chest. The heat that rose from my skin from her touch was just too much.

I inhaled deeply, my eyes closing as my large hand reached up, my fingers wrapping around her tiny wrists and pulling them away from my chest.

Leaning closer and pressing my lips to her forehead, I lingered a little longer as I inhaled deeply, my eyes closing. It took everything in me to pull away and restrain myself from going any further.

"Let's not talk about this tonight, Cherry, we need to sleep," I muttered, letting go of her and pushing her back onto the bed.

I inhaled sharply, turning and walking into the bathroom.

I needed to get away from her, just for a moment.

Wrapping my long fingers around the edge of the basin, my head dropped before I slowly lifted and looked at myself in the mirror.

What the fuck was I going to do?

Part of me wanted to do it, of course. God, I wanted nothing more than to be her first in everything. But then rage infuriated me that she wanted to use me to seem more experienced.

I felt the anger shake through me, but I pushed it down.

I was going to make sure she never wanted to be with another boy again.

Turning the tap on, I waited for the water to run cold before splashing my face. I had to shake it off.

Patting my face dry with the towel and folding it back up, I gave myself a last look in the mirror.

Walking back into the room, Peyton was asleep, laying on her front. She had an oversized T-shirt on and just little knickers.

She was trying to entice me. She was playing a game. She wanted me to give into the sweet temptation.

The smirk played on my lips, my cock hard just looking at her. I needed to just climb into bed and roll over. And lay as far as fucking possible from her.

Climbing in beside her, I lay as slowly and gently as I could. My eyes trailed up and down her body before covering her up with the quilt.

I lay on the edge of the bed, my heart hammering against my chest, my eyes pinned to the ceiling with thoughts swirling around my head.

I felt restless. I stilled when Peyton moved slightly, a sweet as fuck moan leaving her before she fell silent again.

Her moan made my cock twitch, and groaning, I palmed myself through my boxers. I couldn't do this.

Folding the covers back, I stepped out, pulling my side of the bed back over again and walking over to her work bag and rummaging through. I saw the letter from Casanova. Picking it up, I then dropped it quickly, as if the envelope burned my skin. I found a scrap piece of paper and a pen and quickly wrote a note.

Pey,

Just left to freshen up and get some sleep, because sleeping next to you is impossible.

(Your snoring is too much)

I'll be back before you wake. I promise.

Forever always, Knight x

Smirking, I dropped the pen back into her bag and padded over to her bed, placing the note on the pillow next to her. She looked so beautiful when she slept. Grabbing my clothes off the floor, I pulled them on and left her bedroom.

I didn't want to leave but I had to.

I couldn't be that close to her, especially after what she asked me tonight. I was hoping she would forget all about it in the morning, once the alcohol was out of her system.

Walking down the long driveway, the sun was peeping up over the light dusting of clouds in the pink sky. Climbing the gate and jumping down the other side, I jogged towards my nan's, picking the key up from under the gnome and letting myself in before falling face down into my bed.

I didn't have to wait long before I was in a deep slumber, my dreams being filled with her.

Always her.

—

I woke, startled, my eyes taking a minute to adjust to the room. I reached for my phone; it was nine a.m.

I darted out of bed and straight into the shower. Rough drying my body, I pulled a black tee over my head and grabbed my black ripped skinny jeans. Running my hands through my hair quickly——avoiding the glued area——I ignored the wild curls that were forming and brushed my teeth. Once back in my bedroom, I grabbed my phone then opened the bedside cabinet drawer, hesitating for a moment as I picked one of the condoms up and shoved it in my back pocket. I felt wrong for even thinking about it, but if she still felt the same this morning, then I needed to be prepared. I walked downstairs to see my nan sitting at the kitchen table.

"Good morning, sunshine." She smirked, drinking her tea, her rollers sitting in her hair.

"Morning, Nan." I smiled, grabbing an apple off the centre island.

"How's your head?"

"A little sore," I admitted, rubbing the apple on my T-shirt before taking a big bite.

"And your night?"

"It wasn't bad," I muttered as I walked past her. "Nan, I've just got to go and see Peyton, I'll be back soon though, okay? Then we can talk."

"Okay, my darling boy." She lifted her cheek towards me. I playfully rolled my eyes at her before stepping closer to her and kissing her on her cheek.

"Bye, Nan," I called out as I walked towards the front door. I couldn't help but feel a little panicked. I promised I would be there before she woke, and I didn't want to break it.

Running down my nan's path and up to her gates, I hesitated for a moment. Her conversation replayed over and over in my head on a loop.

Punching the code to the gate in, there was a loud clunking noise before they started opening. I squeezed through the small gap and up the stairs to her house, trying my luck at the front door.

It was open.

Walking through, I saw Mr and Mrs Fallon sitting at the breakfast bar with a coffee.

"Morning, Knight," Mr Fallon called out.

"Morning, sir." I stopped at the double door opening that lead from the large hallway to their kitchen.

"Is Peyton awake?" I asked, my eyes wandering up the stairs.

"I'm not sure," Mrs Fallon said, her lips pursing before she took a mouthful of her coffee. "She had a lot to drink, so I doubt it." She let out a little laugh. "But go up there, and if she isn't awake then wake her."

"Cassie." Mr Fallon looked at his wife, a little shocked.

"Well, she's already got the hangover, she needs to see that this drinking malarkey isn't all it's cracked up to be."

"Oh yeah, I forgot you were never eighteen and never got so drunk you couldn't speak." Mr Fallon's hand moved to her thigh, giving it a squeeze.

"Exactly! I've been there, done that and I've got a T-shirt or two." She cackled loudly, all the time looking at her husband with such admiration.

"You're fine to go up there, Knight. Poppy and Stefan are awake if Peyton isn't." Mr Fallon smiled at me before kissing his wife on the cheek. I just nodded, stepping back then running up the stairs two at a time. I stilled outside her bedroom door, my hand hovering over the door handle. Inhaling deeply, I pushed the door handle down slowly and smiled when I saw her still asleep.

I stepped over to her bed quietly, looking down at her. I was so drunk off of her, I always felt high around her, the crippling fear crashed over me when I was away from her. I didn't want the withdrawal to kick in from not being near her.

I needed to be near to her continuously. I was addicted to her. I kneeled on the bed before slowly sinking back towards the headboard, my head resting there but my eyes staying on her.

Soft mummers vibrated through her lips, and her eyes fluttered open before she screwed them shut.

"My head!" she whined, pulling the quilt over her.

I stifled the laugh that was threatening to escape me.

"Welcome to the hangover club, baby," I teased, the laugh bubbling out of me as I pulled the quilt off of her.

"Here," I muttered, turning and grabbing the two tablets that her mum gave me and a glass of water. "It'll help."

She snatched them out my hand, throwing them back and knocking the water back down in one, then handed it back to me.

I placed it on the bedside table, and her eyes were on mine. Her cheeks blushed slightly, her fingers picking at the skin around her nail bed. She was nervous, cautious.

"What's wrong?" I asked, my hands resting on my stomach, my fingers linked.

"Nothing," she mumbled, her eyes falling to the bedsheets, her brown hair falling around her face.

"Do you want to talk about last night?" I asked, breaking the awkward silence. I wanted to know whether she remembered or not.

"What about last night? How much I drank or how you got a little overprotective?" She smirked. I loved her smile. She sat on her bent knees, her large tee covering her but sitting on the top of her thighs. I can't even begin to tell you the restraint it is taking to not touch her, kiss her, taste her.

"Er, both?" I muttered.

"Are you sure it's that?" Her answer caught me a little off guard, but I was also grateful that she didn't mention Casanova's name.

"Or..." Her voice trailed off, her chin lowering, her eyes fluttering to mine. "Did you want to talk about what I asked last night?" she muttered, moving forward, crawling across the bed and climbing onto my lap, her bare legs either side of me.

"Pey." My voice was low, warning her.

"Knighty poo," she mumbled, her arms linking around my neck as she rocked her hips over me to move closer.

Fuck. That was like pure ecstasy. My cock hardened beneath her in my jeans.

"You don't want that, Cherry... you were drunk," I whispered, my eyes volleying back and forth to hers.

"I wasn't that drunk." She slid back slightly, dropping her arms from my neck.

"Baby..." I whispered, one of my arms wrapping around the back of her as I pulled her closer to me, my other hand cupping her face as my thumb ran across her bottom lip which caused her breath to hitch.

"I want nothing more than to be your first, but once it's gone... It's gone." I saw her bottom lip drop, her eyes closing as her head fell forward. "I don't want to ruin it for you," I admitted, my voice quiet.

The air was thick with tension, the room full of silence.

"Pey..." I whispered, my thumb resting under her chin as I lifted her face up, her lips parting as I did.

"I want you to be my first, Knight." Her voice was so quiet it was hardly audible.

"Pey," I replied, this time a little sterner, my eyes burning into hers.

"I'm sure, please... don't make me ask again." Her eyes met mine, holding my gaze. My heart raced in my chest, and my palms were sweaty.

I ran my hand around the back of her head, entwining my fingers through her hair and pulling her towards me so our lips crashed together. My tongue found hers as I slowly stroked it with mine.

A small whimper left her as I broke away. My hand was still on the back of her head, the other around her waist as I slowly pushed her off of me and laid her down.

She looked incredible, laying there with her eyes glistening, her oversized T-shirt bunched at her hips and her fucking black laced thong that didn't leave much to the imagination.

My cock twinged, pressing against my jeans.

Fuck, I was so hard for her.

I kneeled in front of her, my hands gripping onto her knees before they moved slowly down to the top of her thighs.

"Are you sure about this?" I muttered, and I couldn't stop my hungry eyes from wandering up and down her body.

"Yes." Her bottom lip was being pulled behind her teeth.

"Okay," I breathed. I took my hands from her skin, unbuttoned the top of my jeans and climbed off the bed. Pushing them down and kicking them off, I knelt back onto the bed, my eyes moving to the door quickly.

"What about your mum and dad?" I asked... that's all

we needed.

"They go for a two-hour tennis lesson at ten," she muttered, breaking her eye contact to look at her phone before she smiled. "They would have already left."

I nodded, kneeling back in-between her legs.

"Do you trust me?" I whispered as I leant over her, my body in-between her thighs.

"Yes," she whispered, her breathing fast.

"And if you want me to stop at any time then tell me, okay? Or if I hurt you... fuck, Pey, if I hurt you, you tell me stop, okay?" My eyes widened, my voice louder now. I needed her to agree, I needed her to tell me she would ask me to stop.

"I will." She nodded a little too eagerly.

"I'm going to touch you, okay? I'm not going straight into having sex with you..." I couldn't help the little laugh that was behind my voice. "Just trust me, okay?" I winked at her, my tongue sweeping across my bottom lip.

"I trust you," she whispered.

Chapter Twenty Two

Knight

I brushed my thumb across her cheek, my lips hovering over hers. I wanted to make this moment special for her, I always wanted her to remember it. Her chest was heaving up and down. I could tell she was nervous, but she didn't want me to know it. I tried my best to push it away.

Her hand moved around the back of my head, pulling me to her, so our lips locked. I couldn't help the groan that left my throat from just having her lips on mine. I placed a few soft kisses on her lips before trailing my lips down her jaw, past her neck and to her collarbone. My finger hooked under the neck of her tee as I pulled it away, exposing more of her skin. Her breathing was ragged, and I could hear the sharp intakes as my mouth continued its delicious trail across her skin. Kneeling up, my hands ran down her thighs slowly, until I reached the apex of her thighs, my fingers brushing across the front of her pussy. My breath was shaky and shallow. It was so hard to keep my fingers moving. They ran back up and under her T-shirt and trailed up her body, taking the bottom part of her T-shirt with them. I reached up, my lips pressing at the bare skin in-between her breasts. I could feel her innocent eyes burning into me. My fingers slowly ran down the side of her body as my lips continued their butterfly kisses. My mouth began to move to the right, planting soft kisses along until I got to where I wanted to be. My lips pressed against her skin, my eyes looking up through my lashes at her, waiting for the silent go ahead. A little moan left her as my hands tightened around her waist, my mouth over her puckered nipple. My tongue flicked across it gently before my hot mouth consumed her, sucking and licking. All the time she was watching me. My lips trailed back down to the centre of her breasts before I covered her other nipple, doing exactly the same.

After sucking and watching her nipple pucker, I blew gently across both of them. Peyton's lips parted as she watched my every move.

Pressing my lips to her skin, I trailed my mouth down to her belly, kissing over her navel and continuing my kisses until I got to her knicker line.

I shuffled down, my mouth in line with exactly where it wanted to be. Over her perfect pussy.

Hooking my finger in the side of her thong, I peeled them away from her, slowly moving them down her legs and discarding them.

What a fucking sight. I moaned appreciatively.

My left hand travelled up her body, grabbing her T-shirt and bunching it round her throat. I loved seeing her like this. So wanting and ready for me.

"Remember what I said, okay?" I muttered, my eyes falling from hers as they locked on her pussy.

"Mmhmm," she hummed.

"Sit against the headboard, baby," I whispered. I wanted her to watch what I was doing to her.

She obeyed, shuffling back slightly so her back was against the headboard and her legs were bent but dropped open.

"Perfect," I purred, shuffling up slightly. My hand moved back to her tee, holding it up round her throat. I wanted to see her tits. I wanted to see all of her.

I ran two fingers up her pussy lips, teasing her. Warming her up. Then I ran them back down and brushed them over her opening.

I did it again, angelic moans escaping her and I hadn't even touched her properly yet.

"Knight," she moaned out as I glided my fingers back up before my finger gently rubbed across her clit, a gasp leaving her.

I circled the tip of my finger over her clit, gently, slowly circling. I kept my eyes on hers, her chest rising faster now, her lips parted.

"Does that feel good, baby?" I asked, my lips pressing

on the inside of her thigh.

"Yeah," she whined, my finger rubbing quicker then gliding in-between her folds and circling at her opening before dragging back up and circling her clit again.

"Oh," I heard her moan. I did it again, gliding down her folds, this time pressing the tip of my finger into her pussy before pulling it out, my finger rubbing on her clit once more.

I tightened my grip on her tee as I pressed another finger over her clit, rubbing her harder now.

I wanted to show her how it felt, I wanted her to experience it all.

Gliding one finger through her folds, my finger stopped at her soaked opening, pressing the tip in slightly, stilling for a moment before pushing my finger deeper into her, her walls clamping around me almost instantly.

"Feel okay?" I asked, my finger still.

She nodded, her breath held.

Slipping it out slowly and massaging her clit with my finger again, I then slipped it into her, a little deeper this time. I continued this, easing her in, stretching her and getting her used to the feeling.

Her pelvis rocked up every time my finger pulsed inside of her, her walls clamping tightly.

She was getting close.

"Baby, let me taste you," I begged, my eyes watching my finger slowly pump in and out of her now.

"Knight," she whined, her legs trembling as I pulled my finger out to the tip then pushed it into her.

"Oh, Cherry, you're fucking soaked." I groaned, her hands in my hair, her hips circling over my finger as my mouth covered her, my tongue sucking and flicking over her clit. My finger pumped in and out of her slowly as I ran my tongue in-between her folds then circled over her clit. Her tight pussy clamped around my finger as I drew it out and pushed it straight back into her, my tongue slowing before gliding it in-between her folds again.

"I'm... Knight..." she moaned as she tried to talk.

Slipping my finger out of her and kneeling up, I reached over the edge of the bed, grabbing my jeans and pulling the foil wrapper out. Fisting myself out of my boxers, her eyes watched the whole time as I rolled the condom down my cock.

"You sure, angel?" I asked again as I knelt in-between her legs once more, my finger slipping straight into her.

"Fuck," she cried. "Yes." She panted as my thumb brushed over her clit. Leaning down, I couldn't stop myself from tasting her again, my tongue pressing flat against her. Moving my head from side to side, I buried my tongue inside of her, my finger slowly pumping in and out.

"I'm... Oh..." she moaned, her eyes closing. Pulling out of her quickly, I hovered over her, lining my thick cock at her opening.

"This is going to sting, but trust me, it'll get better each time," I whispered, my hands either side of her head. I wanted her to come over my cock, she was so close. Pushing into her slowly--just the tip at first--her eyes widened, her breath escaping her as I edged in a little more.

"You okay?" I asked through gritted teeth. I was close before, but now with her tight pussy around me, I was even closer.

She nodded, her teeth sinking into her bottom lip as my hips thrust into her a little more now. I stilled for a moment, wanting her to get used to me. She pinched her eyes shut, her hands tightening around the bed sheets. I didn't move until she told me to. It was killing me. Her eyes opened, and she nodded softly.

I pushed my hips slowly forward, filling her completely, and I watched as she winced.

"Trust me, baby, okay?" I cooed, my thumb brushing across her cheek.

Her lips curled into a smile as I started to move, so slowly, not wanting to hurt her any more than I already was. Pulling out to my tip, I stilled then pushed back into her. She felt amazing.

I did it again, slowly pulling out to the tip, stilling for a second then pushing deeper into her. My thumb rubbed over her clit as I continued this rhythm.

"Baby, I am so close," I muttered, pulling myself out of her and moving back onto my knees so my mouth was over her again. My tongue glided up and down her soaked pussy, my finger edging its way into her as my tongue danced over her clit. Her legs began to tremble, her moans filling the room as I sped my finger up now, pumping in and out of her quickly as my tongue flicked over her clit, keeping up with the tempo of my finger.

"Knight, I am going to come." She moaned, her hands grabbing the bedsheet as I grabbed her hips and pulled her towards me, my cock slipping into her, my thumb rubbing over her clit as I looked down in-between us, watching as my cock filled her and brought her to orgasm. Her fingers wrapped around the sheets, and her legs trembled as she came over my cock. The moans that escaped her were enough to bring me to my own orgasm, stilling as I filled her.

I rolled onto my side, panting as I studied her. Her cheeks were slightly pink, her chest dipping low and rising fast.

"Did I hurt you?" I asked, my hand cupping her face as I held her.

"No," she muttered.

"You promise me?" I needed her to tell me the truth. I felt like I went a little rough with her, I just got so carried away and caught up in the moment.

"I promise." She smiled, her face leaning into my

LOVE ALWAYS, PEYTON

hand. "I feel amazing, a little sore... but amazing."

"Let me go run you a bath," I whispered, dropping my hand from her face and placing my lips on her forehead, lingering for a moment longer before getting off the bed. Tying the end of the condom up, I then slipped my boxers back up my thighs and padded off to the bathroom.

Once the bath was done, I grabbed my jeans from the floor and shoved the condom in my back pocket before dropping them back on the floor. I didn't want her mum to find it, and I thought it was best that I discard it. When I was back in the room, Peyton was sitting crossed legged on the bed, her T-shirt riding up when I noticed in-between her legs. *I felt awful.*

"Baby, come, your bath is ready." Holding my hand out for her to take, which she did, I couldn't explain the guilt that washed over me.

I loved her with everything I had, but now I felt like an arsehole.

I felt used, but I also felt like I had used her.

My anxiety was ripping through me, but I had to push it down.

For her.

I was brought back round when I felt her lips on mine. "Thank you, Knight." She smiled, her eyes focused on the bathmat as she twiddled her fingers, her cheeks crimson.

"For?" I smirked.

"You know... doing that for me."

"Ah, yes. Well..." I stammered. Now it was my turn for my eyes to hit the floor. "What are friend's for?" I shrugged my shoulders. *What are friends for!? What the fuck?*

She giggled, I loved shy Peyton.

My fingers brushed across the exposed skin on the top of her thighs, grabbing the hem of her T-shirt and pulling it over her head. I took a minute to just marvel at her, I couldn't wait for the day that she was mine.

All mine.

Chapter Twenty Three

Peyton

I felt like my mind was a million miles away. I could see Knight's mouth moving, but I couldn't hear what he was saying. I was too busy letting my mind show me the flashbacks of my favourite moments from this morning. The way his delicate lips traced across my skin, his fingers dancing across my body. The thought of his mouth in my most sensitive area made me blush just thinking about it. I have been dreaming of that day for so long, for the day that Knight finally gave in and gave me something. I felt awful using Knight, but I knew he wouldn't say no. But the truth is, now I have had all of Knight, I don't think I want Casanova anymore.

"Peyton, did you hear me?" Knight's voice crashed through me, breaking me from my delicious thoughts.

"Huh?" I muttered.

"Prom? Have you got a date?" He was still sitting in just his T-shirt and boxers. I wanted to pull his top off and run my hands all over his body.

"Erm, nope. To be honest, I haven't really thought about it," I muttered, playing with the hem of my T-shirt.

"Wanna go with me?" A devilishly handsome look crossed his face, his eyes pinning to mine and holding my stare.

My heart raced, and I nibbled on the inside of my lip.

"I would love to." I smiled as I shuffled over to him, climbing in his lap, my arms locking around his neck.

I wanted him to take me again; even though I was sore, I wanted more of him.

"Looking forward to seeing Casanova next weekend?" His question filled me with so much guilt.

"I don't know," I admitted, and it was the truth.

"Well, that makes me happy." He scoffed, his lips curling into a smile as he moved his face closer to me, his lips hovering over mine before he pressed them softly to mine.

My hands moved from his neck, moving down his body and over his T-shirt as I ran them across his boxer shorts. His large hand wrapped around my wrists, stopping them in their tracks and shaking his head, his curly brown hair moving.

"Not yet," he whispered against my lips, tugging his jeans up. His finger ran under the grey band that sat on my wrist.

"What you going to do with this now?"

"Break it, I suppose." I shrugged my shoulders, my voice small.

My own fingers wrapped around the band and I slipped it off my wrist, snapping it easily.

"There, done." I smiled, my fingers running over his. "Shall I?"

"No, Cherry. I'll do it later." He smiled back at me, his hands wrapping around my waist and lifting me off of him.

I pouted, crossing my arms as I sat on the bed.

"Stop being a brat." He licked his bottom lip.

He moved closer to me, his hand cupping my face as he lifted my lips to meet his.

"I'll be back tonight, you can have me all to yourself." He winked, pushing his lips to mine, his tongue sweeping across mine, slowly. Torturing me.

I ignited inside, the apex of my thighs burning. I had to push my thighs together to try and relieve some of the tension.

I didn't want to wait.

I needed him.

I craved him. Always.

I was addicted. He was a dangerous fucking drug that I just couldn't get enough of.

Knight Pierce was my addiction.

Everything about him I craved.

His lips woke me from my thoughts as they pressed

softly over mine.

"I'll see you in a bit, okay?" he muttered against my forehead, his plump lips now pressed there.

I nodded.

I couldn't speak.

Because if I spoke, I would beg him not to leave.

He pushed off the mattress, standing and pulling his T-shirt down before walking towards the door, but not before turning and winking at me. Then just like that, he was gone.

It was like a punch in the gut. How could I already miss him?

I didn't move, I didn't want to get changed out of my top. I could smell him on me, even though he washed me last night, his scent was all over my skin. I wanted to savour every second of it.

Reaching for my phone, I sighed. My fingers hovered over the screen on an open message to Knight. Sighing, I dropped it.

Climbing off the bed, I felt agitated. I had to do something. It was driving me insane that he had consumed me this way.

Whilst getting changed, his smell still seeped through my pours as I dressed. Pulling my oversized vest and gym leggings on, I inhaled deeply.

I needed to keep busy, and exercise would do that. Pulling my hair into a high ponytail and slipping my trainers on, I walked onto the landing, pushing my phone into the waistband of my leggings.

"Hey, darling," my mum called out as I approached the kitchen.

"Hey." I gave her a small wave. "I'm going into the gym for an hour, try and sweat this hangover out." I laughed, rolling my eyes as I smoothed my hair down with my hand. If only it was an alcohol induced hangover that I needed rid of.

"No worries, darling, I'll be getting a roast ready soon. Poppy and Stefan were looking for you, think they're in the basement." She smiled, pursing her lips before taking a sip of her coffee.

"Okay, I'll go see them." I smiled, blowing her a kiss and walked towards the basement. The gym was on the same floor.

Walking down the stairs, I saw both of them laying on the sofa watching *Dirty Dancing*.

"Hey, all okay?" I asked, pressing my earphone into my ear.

"Yeah, fine, just wanted to apologise for last night," Poppy said, her lips pressing into a thin line.

"Oh, it's fine. Don't worry about it." I smiled. "Honestly, I had a blast." Laughing, I started walking towards the gym door.

"Where is Knight?" Stefan asked.

"Gone home, had to speak to his nan." I shrugged my

shoulders.

"Ah, yeah. Sunday ritual. Cup of tea and chat with his nan. Even before he moved in, he used to spend a few hours there." Stefan smiled at me, his arm wrapping around Poppy and moving closer to her.

"Yeah..." I muttered. "I'm going into the gym. Need to burn some pent-up frustration." I laughed, shaking my head from side to side.

Poppy's head popped up like a meerkat from the sofa, her eyes narrowing on mine, her skinny finger pointing at me.

"Did you?" she said, her voice blunt and to the point.

"Did I what?" I lifted my top lip, my brows furrowing as my nose scrunched.

"You know what." Her brows lifted, her head turning slowly before her eyes narrowed again.

"I have no clue what you're talking about." I waved my hand at her, as if dismissing her.

"Peyton--"

"I've got to go..." my voice trailed off, my finger pointing to the gym door as I started running across the room, opening the door and locking it behind me.

I knew exactly what she was going on about, and I wasn't about to go there with her.

Sitting on the floor, my knees were bent and up round my chest, my arms wrapped around them. I was panting. That work out killed me. The sweat was glistening over my skin. What a waste of a bath. I scoffed, slowly falling back and landing on the padded gym floor. My eyes focused on the brightly lit ceiling.

I still hadn't read my last letter from Casanova, but part of me didn't want to know. But I at least owed him that. Then, once I met him on Saturday, I would call it a day. I couldn't do it.

I was pulled from my thoughts when I heard banging on the gym door.

"Pey! Open up!" Poppy shouted, her voice urgent.

I groaned, my legs already aching as I stood.

The banging continued.

"I'm coming!" I shouted out. Aggravated, I unlocked the door and swung it open.

Poppy's eyes were brimming with tears.

"Pop, what's wrong?" My voice was full of worry now.

"It's Stefan's parents. They're here." She sobbed.

"It's okay. Let me call Knight," I mumbled, pulling my phone out of my waist band.

"He is already here." Her voice was breaking.

My heart fluttered; my stomach churned with these new feelings.

"Oh, okay," I whispered.

I followed Poppy as she walked quickly down the hallway. My heart thumped, the blood pumping through my ears as I heard the noise of raised voices. One being my father's.

I pushed past Poppy, walking out the door. "Stay in there," I ordered, jabbing my finger at her, looking over my shoulder as I stormed down the steps and onto the large driveway––and for once, she listened.

Knight's eyes widened as I approached, and I felt a rage burning through me. My dad was stood in front of Stefan, Knight was next to him, and my mum was stood back a little with worry all over her face. She hated confrontation.

"Mum," I said softly, and she jumped as my hand touched her shoulder. "Go inside with Poppy, she needs you." I had a small smile on my lips. She nodded, staying mute as she walked away from me and into the house.

I walked over and stood next to my dad, my eyes moving to Knight before they were on Stefan's parents.

"He isn't staying here," Stefan's father shouted, his face red from the anger.

"He is welcome to stay here for as long as he likes. You made him choose between you or his baby. Of course, he would choose Poppy." My dad's voice was calm as he played mediator. "I would be honoured to call him my son, he didn't get up and run when the first sign of trouble appeared."

"How do we even know it's Stefan's?" the mum piped up, stepping around her husband's large frame.

"Why wouldn't it be Stefan's?" I couldn't help myself, my fists balling by my side.

"Pey," I heard Knight growl.

"Because she is obviously a slut who sleeps around and who gets pregnant at seventeen." The mum threw her hand in the air, scoffing and shaking her head.

"Excuse me?" I snapped, taking a step closer.

"I said, she is obviously a slut," the mother repeated, a smarmy look all over her botoxed-as-fuck face.

"How fucking dare you." My voice was low but stern, and I felt the blood rushing around me.

"Mum," Stefan muttered as he stepped around my father, his hand resting on my shoulder, silently nodding at me.

"I know you're worried, Dad, we are too." His voice was calm, hesitant even as he continued closing the gap between them. "But I love Poppy with all of my heart. She isn't that type of girl you are referring to, and if I remember rightly, you were sixteen when you found out you were pregnant with me. So, Mother, does that make you a slut?" Stefan's voice was not faltering at all.

My eyes widened, Knight choked, and my dad just stood, arms across his chest with a proud as punch look over his face.

"I... I..." his mum stammered.

"You can choose to be in our baby's life, or you can go back to your big house and live your lonely life." He shrugged.

"You're going to ruin your life," his dad replied, letting out a bated breath, his shoulders dropping. His eyes softening, his face not as red now.

"Was your life ruined once you had Stefan?" I couldn't help but ask.

"It was hard work, that's what it was," his dad boomed.

"That's not what I asked. I asked, was your life ruined when you had Stefan?" I asked sternly, my eyes volleying back and forth to theirs. Stefan's mum's hand rested on her husband's upper arm, squeezing it gently.

"No," his mum breathed out, dropping her head.

"Mum, Dad..." Stefan stopped for a moment, his head turning to look in the doorway where Poppy was being comforted by my mum. "Our baby has already lost one set of biological grandparents, don't make it two..." His eyes fell to his shoes, and I could see his shoulders sag. He looked completely broken.

"Son..." Stefan's dad mumbled, moving towards his son and wrapping his arms around him and squeezing him tightly, kissing his mop of dirty blonde hair.

I stepped back, my dad holding his arm out for me to stand under, a kiss being placed on top of my head. "Proud of you kid," he muttered.

I quickly looked over at Knight, his eyes were dark, hooded and burning with something I had never seen before. I moved my eyes away, focusing on Stefan when he broke away from his parent's embrace, his arm reaching out, his hand open for Poppy to take. She smiled, running down the steps, sniffling and palming her tears away as she grabbed Stefan's hand.

I smiled, moving aside and walking back into the house. I needed a moment. My mum was still standing on the doorstep, her eyes welling.

"You okay, Mum?" I stopped just before the stairs.

"Yeah," she muttered, her eyes locked on Stefan, Poppy and his parents.

"Good," I mumbled as I started climbing the stairs.

I walked sluggishly over to my bed, dropping my phone on it as I continued to the window and pulled back the curtain. My heart warmed seeing Stefan's family accepting their relationship. I just wish Poppy's mum and dad would come around. They wouldn't let her bring Champ with her either. I am hoping that once the baby is here, they'll change their minds.

Sighing, I let the curtain fall, turning on my heel when I saw Knight standing there. His head was low, his eyes ablaze as he devoured me.

"Hi," I breathed. Kicking the door behind him, he let it close. I couldn't help but jump from the noise. He didn't say anything.

"How was tea with your nan?" My breath hitched.

"Stop talking," he growled. "I am so fucking hard for

you right now, those fucking leggings..." He bit his bottom lip, pulling it between his teeth, holding it for a moment then letting it release slowly.

My chest rose up and down quickly. I walked towards him, I needed his hands on mine, his lips all over my body.

He started moving towards me, and I jumped into his open arms and wrapped my legs around his waist.

"Fuck, Pey," he whispered against my lips, his hands running under my bum cheeks.

My mouth covered his, my tongue stroking his slowly, teasing. His tongue danced with mine as he walked towards the back of my room, hitting my back against the wall. I gasped, pulling away from him for a second, my eyes on his plump lips before I kissed him again. He put me down gently, my feet just touching the floor when he fell to his knees, his fingers wrapping around the band of my leggings and tugging them down in one swift move.

I heard the rumble in his throat, his long fingers wrapping around my thong as he moved it to the side, exposing me. His other hand pressed the inside of my thighs, pushing into them with his fingers so I opened my legs more.

"Perfect."

His finger trailed up and down my inner thigh, stopping as he got close to my pussy. Each time he did, I felt myself tighten. I couldn't help but watch. I was so turned on.

His fingers dug into my thigh, lifting one of my legs over his shoulder before his mouth was over me. My breath caught, a moan escaping through my lips as his tongue flicked across my clit. My fingers ran through his hair, tugging, but being mindful I didn't catch the cut, as his tongue continued to stroke me.

"Knight," I moaned.

"Baby, you taste so good, fuck." He groaned, his tongue gliding slowly between my folds before flicking over my clit again. His finger teased at my opening, my hips rotated slightly, silently begging for him to push his finger into me.

I whimpered when his mouth left me, his hazel eyes meeting mine, his lips glistening with my arousal.

"How much do you want my fingers?" he whispered, his lips pressing on the inside of my thigh, his index finger still teasing at my opening, the tip circling in my wetness.

"Please," I begged through ragged breaths.

"Tell me, angel, how much do you want me to fuck you with my fingers?" His dirty mouth set off a fire deep inside of me.

"Knight..." I breathed as his finger stilled.

"Tell me." He smirked, his lips brushing across the most sensitive part of me.

"So bad," I whispered, my fingers wrapping around his hair and pulling harder now.

"Oh, baby," he moaned, slipping his index finger into me and filling me. My head fell back against the wall, and I couldn't stop the moan that echoed around the room. Knight stood slowly, his finger pulsing inside of me, rubbing slowly, his thumb brushing across my clit. His spare hand covered my mouth.

"Quiet, Cherry, your parents are downstairs. We wouldn't want them to hear you now, would we?" he whispered in my ear, nipping at my lobe as his finger continued to pump in and out of me. "So fucking tight."

His words only made me moan louder, his finger stilling inside of me then pulling out quickly as his finger rubbed faster across my sensitive clit, covering me in my own arousal.

"Fuck," I mouthed onto his hand, his eyes burning into mine.

He stopped suddenly, his T-shirt being ripped over his head, showing his toned body. His fingers fumbled with the button of his jeans, and he kicked them down his legs with his boxers. My eyes focused on his thick cock.

Nibbling on my bottom lip, I went to step forward. I wanted to do something for him. His hand moved to the base of my throat, pinning me back against the wall.

He shook his head. "I want to fuck you, angel."

His words made me ache. Lifting me up, my legs wrapped around his waist, my arms locking around his neck as one of his hands moved between us. Lining his cock up at my opening, slowly——so slowly——he rocked up into me. The breath was sucked from my lungs as the feeling intoxicated me, finally getting my hit and subsiding my craving.

His head tipped back as the ecstasy hit him. It felt so different today, the sting was only there slightly, but the feel of him inside me, stretching me and filling me felt amazing.

Pulling out slightly then pushing deeper into me, my back kept hitting the wall. His eyes widened, and he pulled out of me. I couldn't help the whimper that left me from the loss of him, my insides burning with want. My pussy clenched to stop the delicious ache.

"Shit, Pey, I don't have a condom." His head pressed against mine as he still held me in his arms.

"Knight, please. Just pull out. I need you," I begged, my eyes moving back and forth to his.

The animalistic growl that left the base of his throat was too much. Walking me to the bed and dropping me softly onto the covers, his hand cupped over my pussy, pushing me up the bed so I was sitting against the headboard. His hands gripped my thighs, pushing my legs wide, his eyes devouring me as I heard the sharp intake of breath that he sucked in.

"Fuuuuuck," he drawled out the word, kneeling in-between my legs, lining himself up and pushing into me slow, both his hands moving to my hips as he held me in place, his cock slipping out of me and pushing back into me deeper and harder each time. My eager eyes could see everything. His cock was pulling to the tip then pushing into me, and I had never been so turned on in all my life.

"Feel okay, baby?" he panted, his grip around my hips tightening.

"So good," I moaned, my eyes momentarily flicking up to his before they fell back to watch him bring me to an almighty high.

"Touch yourself," he groaned, his head tipping back as his hips moved faster now, his thrusts hitting that delicious spot, the sound of his skin hitting me. His hands glided to my legs, pressing harder into my skin as he spread my legs further.

My hand trembled as I glided my fingers down between my legs, my fingers rubbing gently over my swollen clit.

"That's it, angel," he whispered, his cock filling me fast and hard now, his teeth sinking into his bottom lip as my fingers continued circling over my clit.

I could feel the delicious build up, bubbling and tingling.

"Knight," I moaned out, his hand covering my mouth quickly.

"Quiet," he warned, his thrusts slow and hard now, pulling out to his tip then slamming back inside of me. My pussy clenched around him, my hips involuntary moving

LOVE ALWAYS, PEYTON

with him, my fingers circling faster now.

"I'm so close, baby." His voice low and he was trembling as he tried to control himself. "I want you to come all over my cock, I want to feel you tighten around me, baby."

He pulled his cock out, rubbing the head of it over my clit and covering himself in my wetness before slipping it back in so slowly. That's all it took.

My back arched off the headboard, my legs trembling as I came hard. I cried into his hand; my moans muffled.

"Oh fuck, Pey..." He groaned, spearing in and out of me faster now, his jaw clenched, his hand pushing my vest up round my neck, his fingers wrapping around the base of my throat and tightening slightly before he pulled out of me and came over my bare stomach. He shuddered, biting his lip to stop his moan. I couldn't help but stare, the warm, creamy liquid sitting on my skin.

His breathing was harsh, and my chest was heaving up and down, both of us covered in a sheen of sweat.

"Fuck," Knight whispered as he rolled onto his back next to me.

"Fuck, indeed." I giggled, not wanting to move.

"Shit, I'll be right back," he muttered, pulling his boxers up as he disappeared into the bathroom and returned with tissue. He knelt on the bed, wiping himself off my stomach and smirking before disappearing again.

Now I knew what Poppy meant about getting caught in the moment.

He laid next to me, his head resting on his propped elbow as he lay on his side, his other hand hovering over my body, waiting a moment as his fingertips moved up and down my over-sensitized skin.

"You feeling okay?" he asked, his voice quiet.

"I feel fine." I nodded. I was sore, but it wasn't too unbearable. It was just a delicious reminder that Knight Pierce had fucked me.

"Good," he muttered, his lips pressing to my bare shoulder.

"How many girls have you slept with?" I couldn't help but ask. I––all of a sudden––felt self-conscious, pulling my vest down to try and cover myself.

His fingertips continued stroking up and down my arm.

"Does it matter?" He smirked, his fingers stopping for a moment then continuing.

"No, but I just wanted to ask," I admitted, a blush spreading across my face.

"Just a few," he mumbled, his eyes pinned to mine. I couldn't look at him. I felt too embarrassed. "But trust me when I say that none of them have been like you. I have never felt like this with anyone but you." He sighed. "I can't explain it, but everything feels more heightened with you."

"I get it," I muttered, even though I didn't know how I got it when I was a virgin until this morning.

Now it was my turn to sigh.

"I need the loo," I whispered, slipping off the bed and walking towards the bathroom. Locking the door behind me, I let out the deep breath I felt like I had been holding. I sat on the toilet, my face in my hands.

How had I let myself fall so fast for him? A few days ago, I couldn't think of anyone else but Casanova, but now, Knight plagued me like he did when I first met him.

I hated the fact that he had been with other girls, but of course he had to have to be that good. No one was that good and a virgin.

I wanted to give him something in return, I wanted to take control of him. But I had to bide my time, he wouldn't give up control that easily.

Standing and walking to the sink, I turned the tap on and splashed my face with water. I needed to cool myself down. I felt hot.

I jumped when I heard a soft knock on the bathroom door.

"All okay, Cherry?" Knight's voice was hushed.

"Yeah, fine," I muttered, turning the tap off and patting my face dry with the towel.

I plastered a smile on my face and unlocked the door to see my handsome Knight standing there.

I felt his breath on my face, his hands cupping my cheeks as he brushed his lips over mine.

"I've fallen for you, Pey, and I don't think I'll ever be able to stand again," he whispered, his hands still cradling my face. "You're it for me."

Chapter
Twenty Four

The next week had flown round, and I still hadn't had the courage to open Casanova's letter, but tonight––the night before the pen pal fete––I had to.

Knight had been over every night, but we both agreed to spend Friday night alone. We hadn't made anything official, but the thought of him meeting his pen pal made me feel sick. As I am sure it made him feel the same.

He belonged to me. Now and forever.

Flipping the sealed envelope in my hand over and over, the nerves crashed through me.

I inhaled deeply, running my finger under the flap and opened the letter.

Dimples,

I can't believe this will be the last letter

that I write. I can't wait to see you next weekend, you have been on my mind constantly and I can't wait to put a face to a name. Or even a name to a nickname.

You'll know who I am as soon as you lay eyes on me. We're soulmates, somehow connected already.

I won't drag this letter out, but I hope your exams go well. Then it's into the adult world, as such, university and jobs.

I am counting down the days until I see you.

Love,

Casanova xx

I let out the breath I had been holding, folding the letter up and placing it in the box with the rest. I just didn't get the same feeling I did as before.

Knight had completely taken over any feelings I once had for Casanova.

Making my way downstairs, I saw Poppy sitting in the kitchen with a cup of tea. Stefan was nowhere to be seen.

"You okay? How you feeling?" I asked, her little belly starting to pop out.

"I'm so tired, how is it possible to be this tired?" she whined, her fingers wrapped around the mug.

"Oh, hun, just try and take it easy." I smiled at her, flicking the kettle on. "Another one?" I asked, and Poppy nodded as she finished what was in her cup then slid it across the breakfast bar.

"Where's Stefan?" I asked as I put two tea bags into the bottom of the mugs.

"With Knight."

Just the sound of his name covered my skin in goosebumps.

"Oh, really?" I tried to act not overly interested, I wasn't ready for this conversation yet.

"Yeah, Knight wanted to talk about this fete thing, think he is nervous. Stefan said he has never seen him like this before," she continued. "Maybe he is coming around to this soulmate thing? He told Stefan he really likes his pen pal and that he can't wait to meet her. Said he has never felt like this before."

I stilled, I felt the bile bubbling in my stomach, the burn scalding my throat from the apple-sized lump that sat there, tears threatening. It hurt, the thought that what

I thought we had was so special, but he obviously didn't feel the same. Maybe I read the whole situation wrong? Maybe I was just an easy target? Something to keep him occupied until it was time to meet his soulmate.

Pouring the burning water over the tea bag and stirring in the milk, I hit the teaspoon a little harder than intended on the side of the mugs.

"That's nice, I hope she is everything he wants." I pushed a fake smile across my face as I sat next to her.

"I hope so too, he deserves an epic love." She swooned, sighing happily. "Just like me and Stefan." She smiled as she turned to face me. "Are you excited about meeting Casanova, finally?"

"Yeah, I am. I can't wait to fall madly in love with him." My lips pouted before I took a mouthful of my tea.

"You gonna let him take your 'V' plates?" She wiggled her eyebrows, shuffling in her seat excitedly.

I choked on my mouthful, my eyes widening at her words.

Her eyes looked past me. "Hey, babe." She beamed. "Hi, Knight."

"Hey, baby," Stefan cooed as he walked towards her, his hand rubbing over her belly before he kissed her.

I felt Knight step behind me, his hand wrapping around the edge of the back of my chair, his fingertips teasing across my back.

"What were you talking about?" Stefan asked as he

re-filled the kettle then flicked it on.

"Just about how Pey is gonna give her innocence to Casanova."

I stilled. Knight's fingers stopped, his breath sucking in.

"I can't wait to hear all about it, wonder if he has a big co––"

"Oh my God, stop it!" I called out, placing my cup down and covering my ears.

I saw Poppy laugh, her eyes on Knight. I slowly removed my hands from my ears, my head turning slightly to look over my shoulder at Knight. His jaw was clenched tight.

"What's wrong, Knight? Don't want to hear that someone is gonna get to Pey before you do?" Poppy sniggered, licking her lips.

She was antagonizing him.

"Fuck off, Poppy," he hissed, his fingers back making small circles through my top. My breath hitched.

"Oh, Knighty, don't pout. Not like you haven't put it about before. Peyton needs someone a little less––"

"Enough," Stefan barked.

"I'm playing." Poppy rolled her eyes, crossing one leg over the other.

"How do you know I haven't already fucked Peyton?" Knight's voice was low and steady as he glared at Poppy, not taking his eyes off of her.

Poppy just glared, her eyes on me, not Knight.

My heart was jackhammering in my chest. I was sure you could see it pounding through my skin.

"Because she would have told me." She sat there, proud as punch.

I stayed mute.

"Isn't that right, Pey?" Her brow lifted slightly.

"Mmhmm," I hummed, my cup resting on my bottom lip before taking a mouthful.

"Or maybe she doesn't want to tell you shit. Maybe she doesn't want to tell you that she is mine." I could hear the smile in his voice. "Maybe she doesn't want to tell you just how good I make her feel, showing her what it's like. Casanova hasn't got shit on me."

I wanted the ground to swallow me up.

"Knight..." I whispered, the blush creeping on my face.

"What, angel?" He leant down, his lips by my ear, the whisper sending shivers up and down my spine.

"Peyton wouldn't be as stupid to let you take her innocence," Poppy spat, sliding off the chair and tucking it back under the breakfast bar as she placed her cup in the sink. Stefan said nothing, his eyes on Knight the whole time.

Had Knight told Stefan?

"Can we just stop now? Stop assuming I am going to sleep with Casanova, Knight, stop winding her up and,

Poppy, stop fucking antagonizing the situation," I hissed. Standing from my chair and putting my cup in the sink, I spun, walking out the room and leaving the three of them down there.

I wasn't in the mood.

Climbing the stairs, I slammed my bedroom door and threw myself into the covers.

I wanted tonight over with. I wanted tomorrow over with.

My anxiety crippled me at the thought of seeing Casanova and having to tell him I didn't feel for him like I did before. To tell him that I had fallen for someone else. My best friend.

But then it felt like a knife was pushed through my heart, the pain searing through me, an agonising pain burning through my gut. Knight was meeting his pen pal, and from what Poppy said, he felt things for her. What if he did? I didn't want him feeling anything for anyone else but me. But how could I be so selfish to think that when the whole time I was using him to make myself better for Casanova?

I threw my hands down, letting out a deep sigh as I stared at the plain white ceiling, jumping when I heard my bedroom door go. I propped up on my elbows to see Knight standing in the doorway, waiting to be invited in.

"Come in," I murmured. He took a step over the threshold. I could see how hesitant he was, as if he was walking on eggshells.

"Have I upset you?" he asked, his head dipping down, his eyes beating up to mine.

"No." I sighed, exasperated and falling back onto my bed.

"Then what's wrong?" His voice was getting closer now, my skin covering in goosebumps as I felt the bed dip from his weight.

"Just a little anxious for tomorrow." A laugh bubbled out of me as he laid on his side next to me. It wasn't a complete lie, but it also wasn't the truth. Far from it.

"It'll be fine, this is what you've wanted, isn't it?" His brows pinched; I could see the hurt etched onto his face.

"Yeah..." I muttered, even though my heart was lurching herself at my chest, screaming at me that I was a damn fool. She wasn't wrong.

"And you? I heard you're looking forward to meeting your pen pal as well."

I heard the deep sigh that he exhaled, his eyes widening a little. "Yeah," he breathed. His fingers hovered over my stomach, waiting for the go ahead.

But after tonight's conversations, I didn't feel like it was appropriate.

The room fell silent, a tension so thick you could feel it rock through to your core.

"Do you really think Casanova is your soulmate?" Knight's voice was shaky as he asked the question. My eyes moved from my ceiling and to his beautiful hazels.

"I don't know anymore." My heart raced, my stomach dropping at my small admission.

"Why is that?"

"Things have changed a little, haven't they...?" I trailed my voice off, turning away from him. His glare was too intense for me to handle. "How about you? Do you think your pen pal is your soulmate?"

"I do..." His hand splayed across my stomach now, his fingers setting my skin on fire. I felt the air being knocked from my lungs, a desperate gasp leaving me as my heart obliterated into a thousand pieces. His truth floored me. It felt like a steel pipe had been pushed into my windpipe, the agonizing burn rupturing in my throat as I tried to push the hard lump back down. I wouldn't cry in front of him.

"I think you should leave..." I managed, my voice barely audible. I pushed up from the bed and stood away from him, my arms crossing over my chest. I couldn't bear to be near him.

It was too much.

"Pey..." he muttered, his hand pushing through his curly, beautiful hair. His perfect, pink bow lips parted as the air escaped his lungs. Closing the space between us, his hands were on my waist, his fingers digging into my skin.

"This is what you wanted..." His minty breath was on

my face. "You made it very clear that I was just a fill gap, a little life experience to get you ripe and ready for *Casanova*," he spat his name as if it was venom lacing his tongue. "I did what you asked, angel. How can you be mad at me?"

It felt as if a baseball bat had just been beaten across my back, pulling any last bit of air I had out of me, and the pain that splintered through my heart was unbearable.

"You're right..." I managed, my eyes volleying back and forth to his. "I did want this." My eyes fluttered shut for a moment, my hands moving to his chest as my fingers grabbed onto the thin material that stopped me from feeling his warm skin under my fingertips.

"I'm mad at myself, not you..." My lip trembled, my eyes glassing over.

"I'm sorry, Pey..." he whispered, his lips pressing to my forehead. Dropping his hands from my waist, the swarming sensation left me as soon as his hands left my skin.

"I hope Casanova is all that you have wanted, Cherry." His voice cracked as he walked towards the bedroom door, not looking back as he left.

I felt myself go weak at the knees, my legs buckling underneath me as I broke into uncontrollable sobs.

And it was all my fault.

I had no one to blame but myself.

Chapter Twenty Five

To say I slept shit was an understatement. I spent most of the evening typing messages to Knight before deleting them. He hadn't contacted me either and that made me feel worse.

Rolling over in my bed, my mind whirled with a million thoughts.

I didn't want to go today. I wanted to bail. But how could I? I owed Casanova that much.

Sighing and ripping the covers from me, I padded to the bathroom, my shoulders slightly hunched.

My heart ached, the burden of Knight laying heavy on my shoulders.

Turning the shower on, I peeled my clothes off of me and discarded them to the floor before stepping under the shower, the warm water gently washing away my thoughts for a moment. Once all the suds were out of my hair, I turned the water off and wrapped myself in my towel. Looking in the mirror over the sink, I groaned. My eyes were dull, my bags heavy and dark. I didn't like wearing make-up, but I was going to need to try and cover these awful pouches under my eyes.

I felt like my glow had diminished when Knight walked out the door, not looking back. That hurt. I had never seen him so broken like I did when he walked away from me.

Sighing, I held my toothbrush under the running water then pushed it all around my mouth.

I stood in front of my wardrobe, looking for something basic to wear. I didn't feel like getting dressed up. It was out on Augustine's playing field.

The summer had really kicked in, the British air sticky. Grabbing a pair of light skinny jeans that were ripped at the knee and an off-the-shoulder yellow peplum top, I clung onto them while rummaging through my underwear drawer, my fingers gliding over the black lacy thong I wore the morning Knight made love to me.

My heart raced; my breathing hitched as flashbacks poured through my mind. The delicious dull ache spread through my body and thighs. Pinching the knickers and a strapless bra, I moved quickly into the bedroom. I stilled, Poppy was sitting on my bed, all dressed in a pretty tea dress that covered her small bump. Her long blonde hair sat in beach waves that tumbled down to her waist.

"Hey," I muttered, dropping my clothes on the bed.

"Hey." She beamed, her smile spreading across her face. "Excited for today?" she asked, clapping her hands together.

"Not sure if excited is the right word I would use." I laughed, slipping my thong up my long legs and under the towel.

"Why? You have been waiting for this for months, you finally get to meet him." I watched as her perfectly shaped brows pinched in the middle before she smoothed them out.

"I know, I am more nervous, I think." Doing my bra up and sliding it up, I let the towel fall away from me.

"That's understandable." She nodded, nibbling on her nails. "Me and Stefan will ride with you, if that's okay?"

"Yeah, fine. To be honest, I didn't think you were going to be coming." I shrugged my shoulders a little as I walked back into my bathroom and sprayed my deodorant.

"Why wouldn't we? We are still in the programme."

"I suppose," I mumbled, slipping my top over my head and re-adjusting the sleeves that sat at the top of my arms, making the top more like a bandeau. Pulling my jeans up, I looked in the full-length mirror and smiled, it actually was a cute little outfit. I finished it off with my black chunky-soled Doc Martens.

"You look lovely, boo," Poppy said as she stood from the bed. "Can I do your make-up and hair?"

I nodded, taking a seat on the chair that sat under

my dressing table. I didn't have a clue when it came to make-up, so I was grateful that Poppy offered.

"Just gonna go and grab my bag, won't be a moment," she muttered, her hands on my shoulders as she gave them a gentle squeeze before disappearing. I sat back in the chair, slouching slightly.

I just wanted today over with. I wanted nothing more than to crawl into my bed and sleep the rest of the day away.

But no such luck.

Poppy came strolling back in the room with two big bags full of make-up, followed by my mum holding a cup of tea.

"Morning, darling," she cooed, placing the tea down on the dressing table and then standing by my bed as she made it, fluffing the pillows up. I watched her intently in the mirror, a smile on her face the whole time before she turned and pulled back the curtains.

"Morning, Mum." I smiled at my reflection then inhaled deeply as I waited for Poppy to work her magic.

"Ready?" she asked.

"Ready." I nodded, even though inside I was far from ready. I was terrified.

An hour later and I looked like a different girl. My dark brown hair was in waves––similar to Poppy's–– falling down my back. My blue eyes popped against the light golden tones that were brushed across my eyelids. I fluttered my lashes, they were dark, thick and long. I couldn't stop staring. My glow was back, a shimmer over my face, and my lips were finished in a nude lip gloss.

"Oh wow," I muttered, standing from the chair. "Poppy, you are a genius." I laughed, pulling her in for a cuddle. "Thank you."

"It's nothing, couldn't have you looking all tired and shit for the day that you meet your soulmate." She winked, letting go of me and packing her things up off the dresser.

"That's true," I mumbled.

The nerves were prominent, the butterflies fluttering away in my tummy.

My mum re-appeared, an even bigger smile on her face now.

"Darling, you look beautiful." She stepped towards me and pulled me into an embrace. I heard Poppy tut from behind me, pulling my mum's arms from me.

"Careful, Cassie, her make-up will smudge, and her hair will fall... she's got to look perfect."

I rolled my eyes.

"We ready to go?" my mum asked, excitement lacing her voice.

"Yup!" Poppy chimed, holding her make-up bags. "Let me just go put this away and grab Stefan. I will meet you out on the driveway."

"Okay, cool," I said, searching the room for my phone. I saw it on the bedside unit, my mum must have moved it there when she made the bed.

Walking over and grabbing it, I slipped it into my back pocket.

"You not taking a bag?" my mum asked as she stood by the bedroom door.

"No, I don't need one." I shook my head from side to side.

"Okay, darling. Let's go, shall we? Don't want to be late now." Her arm extended as she waited for me to walk near her. "You're going to have an amazing day."

Sitting in the car, I twiddled my thumbs continuously. The drive was literally minutes, and my heart was jackhammering against my rib cage.

This was it.

The nerves crashed over me like a tidal wave, I couldn't seem to stop them. My palms were sweaty, and I felt nauseous.

"We're here," my mum chimed as she pulled into the large carpark. The field looked amazing. Massive balloon arches, flower walls and tepees.

"What are the tepees for?" I asked, looking at my mum.

"Just somewhere for you to have a little privacy to speak to your pen pal." She smiled at me in the rear-view mirror. "Consider yourself lucky, we had pop up tents when me and your father did this." She laughed loudly. "Now go and have fun, I can't wait to hear all about it."

LOVE ALWAYS, PEYTON

I leant forward, kissing her on her cheek before climbing out the car, Poppy and Stefan following.

"Have you heard from Knight?" Poppy asked Stefan as they walked hand-in-hand over to the check-in table.

"Nope, thought I would have though. Thought he might have rode with us." Stefan shrugged his shoulders before his eyes moved to me.

"What about you, Pey? Have you heard from him?" Stefan asked.

"Nope, not a peep," I whispered as we stood at the desk.

"Good morning kids, nick names?" This young boy sat behind the desk, pushing his round glasses up his nose.

"Dimples." I felt so silly.

"Ah, Peyton." He smiled at me, ticking the name off.

I walked forward, scanning the field for Knight, but I couldn't see him. Maybe he wasn't coming?

Poppy grabbed my hand as we walked towards where our name badges were. I saw mine, my heart slamming against my chest.

Dimples

Peyton Fallon.

Quickly grabbing it and pinning it through my top, I

drew in a deep breath. I waited for Poppy and Stefan to do theirs, not that they had to, they already knew they were each other's pen pals.

"Do you mind if me and Stefan go off for a bit?" Poppy asked as I looked out onto the filled school field.

"Of course not," I mumbled, but I did mind. But I was never going to tell her that. She smiled at me, her hand resting on the top of mine. "Have fun." She winked before clinging onto Stefan and walking into the crowds.

I wandered aimlessly around, my eyes on people's name badges as I tried to see if I could see Casanova's, but it was no use. There were just too many people. I walked towards this small aluminium caravan that was selling peach lemonade. Ordering one and taking it gently, I wandered back to an opening in the field, watching as couples found their pen pals, a small smile gracing my face.

"Peyton," I heard Mrs Tides voice, and in that moment, I was so grateful to hear a familiar voice.

"Hey, Mrs Tides," I muttered, the straw between my lips as I took a mouthful.

"Not seen Casanova yet?" she asked, her eyes on me as I continued to scan the field around me.

"Nope, not yet." I couldn't help the giddy laugh that escaped me.

"He is here, his name tag has gone. Just got to find him." She laughed. We stood in idle chit chat for a few moments before she disappeared to man one of the desks.

Sighing deeply, I was ready to give up. I just wanted to go home. I was so over it already.

Letting my arm fall down to my side, my fingers holding onto my empty plastic cup, I wandered over to the bin, chucking it away when I felt eyes burning into my back. I stilled, my breathing fast, my heart pounding as I slowly turned around.

My eyes were searching, when all of a sudden, they locked on him.

My lips parted, my eyes going wide.

"Casanova?" I whispered.

Chapter Twenty Six

I stood, frozen to the spot. I couldn't even move if I wanted to. I tried so hard to pull my eyes from the figure that was walking towards me, but I couldn't.

He stopped, leaving a gap between us as my eyes trailed down his body to see a white envelope that was pinched between his thumb and index finger. It took me a minute to register what it was. It was the letter that was intended for him that was missing from my bag the day we broke up from school.

"Surprised, *Dimples?*" My nickname slipped off his tongue, sounding like pure silk, making my knickers melt as he closed the gap between us.

"Yes," I whispered, my eyes focusing on his badge.

Casanova

Knight Pierce

I couldn't believe it. A mix of emotions stirred inside

of me, the blood pumping in my ears.

He cupped my cheek, pulling my lips towards his. His brown curly hair sat on his forehead.

"I can't believe it's you," I whispered, silently begging for his lips to be on mine.

"Did you not even have an inkling?" He smirked, his eyes on my parted lips.

"No," I breathed out. "Not even a little bit, did you?"

"Oh, angel... I have known it was you from our first date."

My eyes widened, the shock vibrating through me.

"No," I whispered.

"Yup." Cockiness laced his voice.

"And you didn't say anything..." I mumbled. "After everything I said, and when you walked out last night..."

"All part of the plan, Cherry." His lips brushed over mine. "Didn't want to ruin the surprise."

I couldn't help the silly smile that played across my lips, my arms linking around his neck, my heart singing as it beat for him.

"Oh. My. God." I heard Poppy's screech, making me wince. "No, fucking way!" She swatted Stefan as I dropped my arms from Knight's neck, his arm wrapping around my waist as we turned to face them.

"Yup." I laughed.

"What the actual?" She looked gobsmacked, turning to face Stefan.

"Did you know?" she asked him, her head back on me and Knight.

"Yeah, I did... known for quite a while." Stefan smiled at his best friend, a small nod firing his way. Knight nodded back.

"What about you, Pey? Did you?"

"Nope." I shook my head, my eyes closing for a moment. "Not a clue."

"Well, I'll be honest... I wasn't expecting that." Poppy side eyed Stefan before they were back on me.

"Neither was I." I turned my head up to look at Knight and smiled at him.

"Wanna get out of here?" he muttered into my hair.

"Yes," I whispered back.

My tummy fluttered as he slipped his hand into mine and walked me to the carpark. I furrowed my brow to see my mum sitting there, her eyes widening as she saw us approach, her mouth forming an 'O' shape.

"No way!" I heard her call out as she undid her window.

I couldn't help the blush that crept onto my cheeks, a silly smile spreading across my face.

"How about that..." she muttered, her eyes moving between me and Knight. "Well..." She shook her head, her own smile gracing her face now as her eyes faced ahead.

Climbing in the back of the car, Knight followed, his hand back on mine as soon as he was next to me. Poppy slipped in beside him and Stefan sat in the front with my mum.

"So, Knight." She looked at him in the rear-view mirror. "You're the famous *Casanova*."

Knight didn't reply, he just laughed.

"I am so happy for you both." She beamed as we pulled up on the drive.

My emotions were all over the place, I was excited, nervous, apprehensive and giddy. I couldn't believe that all this time, Knight was who I had been writing to.

I was sitting on the edge of my bed, my hands wrapped around a hot cup of tea. My eyes stayed fixed on the floor, my ankles crossed as they dangled off the high bed. I heard his footsteps before I saw him. My eyes moved slowly up to meet his as he leant against the doorframe of my bedroom.

"You okay, Cherry?" he asked, his arms folded across his chest, his head dipped down slightly.

"Yeah," I muttered, giving him a weak smile before my eyes fell back to the floor.

"What's wrong?" he whispered as he stepped towards me, sitting next to me.

"Nothing, as such... I just feel a little out of sorts," I admitted, a small laugh escaping me before taking a mouthful of my tea.

"How come?"

"I was going there today to tell Casanova I wanted

nothing more to do with him, to break it off as such, and then you came along like a wrecking ball." Nibbling on the inside of my lip, I sniffed. "I am so grateful it was you Knight; I haven't stopped thinking about you. I want to be with you every minute, of every second, of every day." I sighed.

"And we can." He nudged me softly, making me shift from my spot on the bed.

"Until you go to Uni..." My eyes finally moved to meet with his, my heart pounding in my chest as our souls intertwined.

"Then we do long distance, it's only a few hours. I am sure we can manage." A small smirk danced across his lips, his eyes not moving from mine. His hand came up to my face, cupping my cheek as I leant into him.

"I know," I whispered. "But what if you meet someone else?" The anxiety sliced through me at the thought of him being with someone else.

"I won't. You're it for me, angel... now, tomorrow, forever." He edged closer to me, his hand still cupping my face as his lips hovered over mine. "I promise."

I finally let out the breath I had been holding before his lips crashed to mine, his tongue slowly sweeping across mine as he claimed me. I felt myself melt into him, my whole body relaxing and sagging towards him. His arm wrapped around me, pulling me closer to him and supporting me.

LOVE ALWAYS, PEYTON

I never wanted to lose him.

"Be mine, completely, Pey. Be mine." Knight's voice was low, his breath on my face.

"Always," I whispered back, his mouth covering mine once more.

—

The last few weeks had merged into one. Me and Knight lived in each other's pockets, trying to see each other as much as we could before he left for university.

We found out our placements at the end of the week. I got back into Augustine's and Knight got Oxford, like he wanted. I would be lying if I said I was happy for him, I wasn't. My heart shattered right there. Most long-distance relationships didn't work, especially when you're a good-looking boy in university.

I couldn't shake the feeling that I was losing him before he had even left. He was out with Stefan getting bits he needed for his dorm room. He was so excited; I don't think I had ever seen him this happy. And that's what gutted me. How could I be upset that he was leaving? How could I express my sadness when it made him the happiest he has been?

"Pey, baby..." Knight's voice brought me back round from my daydream.

"Yeah?" I called out, turning round as I filled the glass I had been holding with water.

"You okay?" His brows pinched across his handsome face, his hazel eyes boring through me.

"Yeah, fine," I chirped back, turning the running tap off.

"Okay..." He trailed off, walking round to meet me and kissing me on the lips so softly. My insides lit with desire and want. "I'm off to pick my tux up, I'll be back to pick you up at seven, okay?" he muttered, both hands cradling my face.

"Okay, see you at seven." I smiled as his lips kissed the tip of my nose delicately.

"Love you, Cherry," he called out as he walked towards my front door.

"Love you more." I spoke to the empty room, sighing as I flopped down into the chair that sat overlooking the window of the drive. I watched Knight walk down the driveway and out of the gates before disappearing behind the trimmed green hedges.

I felt my heart sink, my palms clammy instantly. I hated being away from him. I wanted to be near him all the time.

"Darling." My mother made me jump. I sat up in the chair and turned to face her.

"Hey, Mum." I beamed at her, she looked as beautiful as ever. Her blonde hair was blow-dried and styled so it sat on her shoulders, and she was wearing a peplum white blouse and faux leather leggings.

"Ready for tonight? We have the salon in an hour, decided how you want your hair yet?" she asked as she flicked the kettle on.

"I think so." I nibbled on my bottom lip, sitting back in my chair and gazing out the window.

"Morning, beautiful ladies." Poppy's voice echoed around the large kitchen.

"Morning," I called out, not taking my eyes off the window.

"Morning, darling." My mum's voice was light and chirpy. "Tea?"

"Please," me and Poppy both said in unison as she sat down in the chair next to me, her feet resting on the windowsill as her hands sat under her small bump.

"You okay?" I asked, my voice low as I turned to face her.

"I am, thanks." She smiled. "How about you?"

"Yeah, I'm okay." I nodded, taking a mouthful of water.

"What time we at the salon, Cassie?" Poppy asked my mum, her head tipping back so her neck was resting on the top of the chair, her golden blonde hair hanging over.

"Leaving here at nine-thirty, that okay?" My mum's voice was closer to us now as she handed us a cup of tea each.

"Thanks," we both mumbled.

"Peyton, darling, why are you so down?" my mum

said as she perched herself on the windowsill opposite me and Poppy.

"I'm not," I lied.

"Don't lie. I am your mother; I know when you are upset, or something is bothering you."

I sighed, rolling my eyes.

"Just the Uni thing, I hate the thought of him going to Uni without me––and being so far."

"Oh, Peyton. It's not that far, plus a little bit of distance makes the heart grow fonder and all that." She winked. "Just see how it goes, and if you really can't be without each other that long then look at transferring. I'm sure Daddy can have a word with the board, I know he managed to get one of them out of a pretty hefty fine." She winked before raising her brows. "But I said nothing." Her finger moved to her lips as she pulled an imaginary zip across them.

"Now, cheer up. It's prom day, one of the most important days for young girls." She clapped her hands together so loudly that me and Poppy winced.

I liked that idea. See the first term out and if it is really as bad as I am imagining, I can transfer. A smile crept onto my face. Maybe we didn't have to be that far from each other after all?

Chapter Twenty Seven

Taking my appearance in, I couldn't believe it was me that was standing there. I never did my make-up, I just wasn't into it and had no clue what I was doing.

My mum had my make-up and hair done professionally. My long brown hair sat in loose curls down my back with two sections clipped away so it sat off my face.

My lips were a matte pillar-box red, my eyelids covered in a nude shade, my lashes flicked with a layer of black mascara. A dusting of bonzer was brushed across my cheek bones, followed by a small amount of highlighter. My look was finished off with diamond platinum earrings that my parents had bought for tonight.

I wore a pillar-box red dress that matched my lips perfectly, the spaghetti straps sitting over my shoulders, the neckline straight and not plunging. I didn't want my chest on show. The skirt came out slightly and sat on the floor. I was a bit worried about the slit that sat on the left leg, but it stopped mid-thigh. My mum assured me I looked classy, and not tarty at all. My feet sat in strappy sandals with a small heel. I had never felt so dressed up in my life.

My eyes were pulled from the mirror when I saw Poppy walk in. I couldn't stop my eyes from welling.

She looked stunning.

She wore a bandeau black dress. The top half was covered in crystals before the chiffon skirt flowed down to her feet. Her blonde hair was pulled into a neat bun on her head, and she finished the look off with small gold hoops. Her bump looked lovely sitting under the skirt.

"You look beautiful." I dabbed my eyes with my ring finger.

"As do you." She smiled before wrapping her arms around me, my arms around her neck as we hugged each other tight.

"Oh, girls." I heard my mum's voice, and we broke our embrace as we both turned to face her.

"You both look absolutely gorgeous." She beamed before snapping photos on her phone. My father appeared by her side, wrapping his arm around her and pulling her close as he wiped his own stray tear from his eyes.

"My two girls." He beamed.

"Thanks, Dad." I smiled a small smile back at him before linking my arm through Poppy's.

"Wait until you see the boys, they look so handsome." My mum winked which caused an eye roll from my father.

I couldn't help the little laugh that left me, dropping my head for a moment and inhaling deeply.

"Ready?" Poppy asked.

"Ready." I nodded as we walked out the room, side by side, my parents following behind us. We both held onto the handrail, my fingers skimming across the oak. Poppy let go of me and rushed to be with Stefan, and my eyes slowly moved to where Knight was.

I stilled, my heart skipping a beat, my breath catching in the back of my throat before the air was pulled from my lungs.

He looked so handsome. He stood with one hand over the other in front of him, his curly brown hair styled just how I liked it, a small bit of it falling forward and sitting on his forehead. He was wearing a skinny fitted tux, and a crisp white shirt sat underneath his jacket with a black bow tie sitting in his collar.

His eyes were on me, glued to me. I felt myself blush. I couldn't help the little laugh that tittered out me as my father sorted his bow tie out for him.

It felt like forever before my legs could move, my heart jackhammering in my chest, the butterflies swarming in my stomach. Knight moved to the bottom of the stairs, holding his hand out for me to take. As soon as my hand sat in his, I felt the current course through me.

I would never tire of how he made me feel.

He placed his lips on my cheek, his lips moving by my ear.

"You look fucking incredible, angel."

The hairs on the back of my neck stood, my arms covering in goosebumps at his words.

I felt the blush creep onto my face as he led me towards the door.

"Okay, my lovelies, turn around so I can take a photo of you all, please," my mum called out.

Knight wrapped his arm around my waist and pulled me to him as my mum snapped away on her phone.

"That's enough, Cassie, the limo is outside." My dad shook his head from side to side as my mum slipped her phone away. Stefan opened the door, letting me and Poppy walk out first as they followed behind to the black limo that sat on the driveway. Stefan opened the car door, and Poppy climbed in, followed by Stefan then myself and Knight.

Poppy and Stefan were in light chatter amongst themselves when I felt Knight's hand graze my bare thigh, giving it a squeeze before his fingertips circled over my exposed skin.

"You okay?" he asked, his eyes watching his fingers.

"Yeah, I am." I beamed, feeling lighter than I did this morning.

"Good." His eyes held my gaze. "I don't want you being upset about me going to Uni." He sighed.

LOVE ALWAYS, PEYTON

"I know…" I trailed off, I wanted to speak to him about it, but this wasn't the right time.

He smiled at me, his hand still firmly on my thigh when our attention was moved to Poppy.

Her face fell, her brows pinching as her eyes fell to her stomach, her hands over her bump.

"Ow," she cried out, her body jerking from the pain.

"Babe?" Stefan's voice was calm as his eyes moved from her face to her bump.

"Ow, Stefan," she whined, her hand reaching across and grabbing his wrist, tightening her grip. "Something's wrong." She panted, her breaths shallow. I could see the pain etched in her face.

"We will get you dropped to prom, then I'll get her to the hospital," Stefan muttered as he started shuffling up towards the driver.

"No!" I shook my head, moving towards Poppy and grabbing her hand. "We come with you." My eyes narrowed on Stefan; he gave me a silent nod before moving to talk to the driver.

"It's okay, Poppy, we are going to the hospital, everything will be okay," I reassured her, my finger stroking a bit of stray hair away from her face.

Stefan came back to her side, taking her other hand in his. "We're going to the hospital." He leant across and kissed her on the forehead. I could see the worry all over his face, but he was trying to put on a brave face for her.

I looked over my shoulder at Knight. He just sat there, he was just as worried, his eyes glassy. I gave him a small smile, and he smiled back at me.

I was relieved when we pulled up to the hospital. Stefan had already been on the phone to the maternity unit, so they were ready for us when we got there. Knight darted out the limo before it even stopped and ran to grab a wheelchair. Me and Stefan helped move Poppy to the wheelchair, and Knight took my hand and helped me out the limo then took Poppy from me as him and Stefan lifted her into the wheelchair. Stefan started walking towards the door, and I walked quickly behind him when I felt Knight's fingers slip through mine. "Are you okay?" he asked, clearly distressed.

"I will be, as soon as I know that Poppy and the baby are okay." I nodded, swallowing the hard lump that had formed in my throat back down. My throat burned; my eyes stung. But I wouldn't cry. I needed to be strong for Poppy.

"I know, I've called your mum. They're on their way," he muttered, his thumb stroking across the back of my hand as we walked into the hospital. The nurses were there, taking the wheelchair from Stefan and wheeling Poppy away. Stefan just stood, his shoulders sagging, his head dropping forward.

Knight rushed to his side, pulling him in for a hug,

his hand moving to his hair. Knight's eyes didn't move from mine.

"Come on, mate, let's take you to her," Knight said quietly, his arm wrapped around Stefan's shoulders as he walked him down the corridor of the brightly lit hospital. I ran quickly to be the other side of Stefan, to act as a pillar to hold him up.

He wasn't just a friend. He was family.

Stefan was shown where Poppy was as me and Knight sat outside the room while they did their checks. My heart was racing, my anxiety piercing through me. My thoughts invaded any peace that was once there.

What if there is a problem with the baby? What if she loses the baby? Oh my God, will she lose the baby? She will never get over this. Will Stefan stick around? What if there is an underlining issue that was missed on both of her scans? What if that's what is causing the pain. If she goes into early labour, will the baby survive?

All of this was crashing through me, and I couldn't shut it off, the same questions turning over and over. My racing heart turned into palpitations, my breathing fast. I forced my eyes shut, I needed to be brave for Poppy and Stefan. I couldn't let this happen. I couldn't let my anxiety win.

I felt Knight's hand over mine, my heart calming suddenly. I forced my eyes open and felt as if the sweat was running down my face.

"It's okay, I'm here." His voice was like a comfort blanket, helping me pull myself out of the anxiety attack I was in.

"Sorry," I muttered.

"Don't say sorry." He shook his head from side to side. "Never be sorry."

"I love you," I whispered as I leant into his side, his arm wrapping around my body.

"I love you." A kiss was placed on the top of my head before he sat back up.

Our moment of silence was soon over when I saw my frantic mum and dad, followed by Stefan's mum and dad. Knight looked just as confused as I did.

"Did you call them?" I whispered.

"No," he breathed out, his own voice a whisper.

"Any news?" my mum asked as she looked at the closed door then to us, then back to the closed door.

"Nothing yet." I shook my head as she sat next to me, her hand on mine as she squeezed it.

"Positive thinking, we all need to keep positive," my mum said, a little louder than she intended as she winced at her own voice.

"I'm going to grab us all a coffee. Jason?" Stefan's dad said, nodding his head down the corridor, insinuating for my dad to walk with him.

"Of course. Knight, Peyton? Drinks?" my dad asked, his hands in his pockets. I could see how much he was worrying, he loved Poppy and Stefan as if they were his own. This would be killing him.

"Coke, please, sir," Knight asked.

"Water for me." I smiled, my hand finding Knight's as our fingers interlinked.

"We will be back soon." My dad nodded before turning on his heel and following Stefan's father.

My eyes cast over to Stefan's mum. She stood, staring at the window which the blind was closed on. She held a napkin to her mouth as she just stared.

"Melinda, darling," my mum said. "Come and sit down, here." Moving her bag, she put it down by her feet.

Melinda turned around, her eyes red as she nodded, keeping quiet as she took a seat next to my mum. My mum patted her leg and gave her a smile. "It'll be okay, we've got to keep positive." She repeated her earlier comment.

"I know, and I am trying. I feel awful for the way I treated that poor girl and Stefan in the beginning, and Tom was so furious." She shook her head from side to side as she started crying. "I am just so glad we didn't lose them completely, and now here they are. I am just praying everything is going to be okay." She sniffed, wiping her eyes with her napkin.

"It will be, I promise you," my mum reassured her, wrapping her arm around her, pulling her in for a cuddle. "We're a family," she muttered.

It felt like hours had passed but we were allowed in

to see them. My parents had just come out, along with Melinda and Tom. Me and Knight stood, walking in hand-in-hand as we closed the door behind us.

"Oh, Poppy." I wept as I ran over to her, hugging her tightly. She was in a hospital gown with the monitor strapped up to her.

"I'm okay." She smiled, wiping one of my tears away. "The baby is fine. Listen, that's their heartbeat."

I stilled for a moment, the room falling quiet as we listened to the sound of galloping horses––that's what it sounded like.

"Wow," I whispered.

"I know, isn't it amazing?" she said, her smile growing.

"It is." I nodded as I took a seat next to her.

"Do we know anything yet?" Knight asked from across the room.

"Not yet." She sighed. "But the baby is okay, and that's the main thing." She rubbed her hand over her bump slowly, adoration all over her face.

Just as I went to speak, the door opened, and the doctor appeared.

"Poppy." He smiled as he closed the door behind him and took a seat on the edge of the bed. "How are you feeling? Is the pain still there?" he asked as he clutched her folder.

"I'm okay, and not as bad." She smiled, her hands

LOVE ALWAYS, PEYTON

still firmly on her bump.

"I'm glad to hear it." He smiled. "Okay, so we have your test results, most of it came back clear but it seems you have a small urine infection. Now, this isn't what would have caused the pain because it never got out of control, but I can give you some antibiotics to clear that up." He pulled his pen from the top pocket of his doctors coat and jotted some notes down on the paperwork inside her folder.

"Now"--he cleared his throat and leaned forward so he was closer to Poppy--"the pain you described when you came in, it's trapped wind. It's completely normal to get a little more gassy during pregnancy as things move around, and being nearly twenty-six weeks, things are still being pushed up. How have your bowel movements been?" I saw Poppy's eyes go wide, her face turning a crimson red before her eyes darted to Stefan, then Knight, then me.

I rubbed my lips together, pushing them into a thin line.

"I, erm..." She fidgeted uncomfortably. She was feeling awkward. "Well, I haven't been going that well..." Her face was still red from embarrassment.

"That's okay. Again, it's normal, but you need to let your midwife know so we can give you something to relieve you." The doctor was so kind, and his eyes didn't leave Poppy's.

"I'll get your prescription written up, then I'm sure your boyfriend will go and collect your meds for you." The doctor darted his gaze to Stefan before he stood from the bed. "But if you have any other issues, please, don't hesitate to come in. You did the right thing." He smiled at Poppy, nodding then walking out of the room when the parents came rushing in.

Me and Knight took that as our cue to leave.

He took my hand, bringing the back of it to his lips as he kissed it.

My heart swelled in my chest; he was it for me. Always.

—

We sat on my bed––in our comfy clothes––with a cup of tea and a plate of biscuits that my mum had brought up. It wasn't the prom night we had planned, but it was still perfect. I was with Knight; Poppy and the baby were okay and that's all that mattered.

"What you thinking about?" Knight asked, reaching for a digestive biscuit and dunking it in his tea.

"Just how this wasn't how we would spend our prom night," I admitted, blushing slightly.

"Oh, angel, don't worry... we've got plenty of time for that." He winked before taking a bite of his biscuit. I felt myself burn, the ache growing in-between my legs.

"I was thinking..." he muttered, leaning across and

placing his tea on the bedside unit. I couldn't help the panic that sliced through me, the overthinking starting.

"It's nothing bad before you start overthinking." He smirked, reaching for my hand and squeezing.

"Okay..." I muttered, a little apprehensive.

"The whole university thing. I know you're worried about the long distance, and you don't want to be away from me." He laughed, nibbling his bottom lip. "And I don't want to be away from you, but I need to do this, for me. I need to find my place in the world, and it isn't here, in this town, in Blossom Creek. I need out, I need to grow." I saw the pain flash across his eyes.

"I know," I whispered. It was my turn to squeeze his hand.

"It's three years, and I know it seems like a lifetime, but it won't take long. I will visit at every chance I get, and you can come to me for the weekends too. But we can also email each other, do a little pen pal lettering, just like old times. A little reminiscing. What do you think?"

I couldn't stop the smile that was growing. "I would like that, but I also was thinking..." I shuffled, moving onto my knees and closer to him. "If we didn't like being apart, I could transfer after the first term. My mum thinks I have a good chance of being accepted." I couldn't contain my excitement.

Knight's eyes widened; he smiled his best smile, showing his perfect teeth.

"Really?"

"Really." I squealed as he pulled me onto his lap, my legs either side of his as my arms wrapped around his neck, his head falling back slightly.

"That's amazing, Pey." He beamed. "But we can do the emails though, yeah? It'll keep me going, give me something to look forward to," he admitted as he tightened his grip around me.

"Definitely," I muttered against his lips.

"Good." He groaned, his voice slow and low. "And also, I was thinking, before we both leave for university, we should write each other an email to be opened in ten years' time... we will be together, and how awesome would it be to read together about what we think our future will be like? You'll be in midwife school, I'll be running my father's firm after buying him out and taking him for everything he's got." He sniggered before his lips pressed against my neck. I couldn't help the sigh that left me.

"What is it?" Knight asked.

"I still haven't told my dad I don't want to work for him..." My voice trailed off as I felt my heart shatter slightly at the thought of telling him.

"Baby, don't worry about that now. But when you do decide to do it, I'll be by your side, holding your hand. I promise," he whispered as his lips moved over mine.

"I fucking love you, Peyton Rose Fallon," he mumbled between kisses.

LOVE ALWAYS, PEYTON

"And I fucking love you, Knight Arlen Pierce."

His fingers traced down the side of my body, his fingers wrapping around my shorts and pulling them aside as I hungrily pulled his cotton shorts down, releasing him. He lifted me off him slightly, lining himself at my opening before filling me, completely owning me, mind, body and soul.

Epilogue *One*

Knight

I had just said my goodbye to Peyton. It was emotional, and my heart broke. Her sobs still soaked into my T-shirt. I kept seeing her make-up and tear-stained face. I knew this was the best thing for us, a little time apart for us both to find a small bit of independence.

Before I left Pey's, she told me that she had left me a letter on the blossom tree outside my nan's house.

My heart thumped as I got closer to the tree. My eyes focused on the branch, where I saw a small light-pink envelope. Picking it up, the scent of her perfume swarmed me. It made me feel some sort of comfort, and the thought that it would wear off soon made me feel sick. The thought of not being with her every day was agonising.

I smiled, turning the letter over and slipping my finger under the envelope flap and pulling it out.

LOVE ALWAYS, PEYTON

Casanova, sorry, I mean Knight. (just habit, I guess.)

I can't believe you are leaving me for three years; I know, I know that we will see each other at the weekends, but it just doesn't feel enough. How am I supposed to cope without you? You're my life, my breath, my reason for existence.

I just can't seem to see how I will get through this without you.

But just know one thing.

You will always be mine; I will always be yours.

I love you.

I would never be able to express just how much.

Love always, Peyton xx

—

Three Months Later

I was glad when Friday finally rolled around. I was in my last business and economics lesson of the day and then I was free. Peyton was coming down this weekend and I couldn't wait. We couldn't see each other last week as her classes overran and her professor gave her class a last-minute assignment. I knew she would be getting herself in a state because she wouldn't have had the time to plan and organise her studying.

The bell rang, my professor wishing us a good weekend. I packed my bag up and threw it over my shoulder when I heard Freddie's voice.

"Knight!" he called as I walked towards him. "You fancy a few beers tonight at the bar? I could really do with a couple of drinks after this week." He laughed softly as we walked out and into the rammed corridors.

"Ah, I would have loved to, man, but Peyton is coming down this evening so will have to give it a miss."

"No worries, mate. Well, if you fancy it, you know where we will be." He smiled, patting me on the shoulder as he walked towards his girlfriend, Lily, and her friend,

Autumn.

Autumn's eyes drawled up and down my body. She was pretty but not my type. No one was my type apart from Peyton.

I shook my head, ignoring her burning stare as I walked towards my dorms. I needed a shower.

Dropping my bag by the door as soon as I was in, I walked straight into the shower. I was grateful that my roommate had gone home for the weekend, so me and Peyton had the place to ourselves. Our dorm was pretty decent. We had our own bathroom––which not many did––and we also had our own kitchen area, seating area and lounge. The warm water washed the lessons off of me. This week had really been ramped up. We had our first set of exams next week, so we didn't have much space between lessons at the moment. If we weren't in class, we were studying.

Stepping from the shower and towel-drying my hair, I reached for my phone out of my bag and noticed two missed calls from Peyton and a voicemail. My heart raced. I hope it was to tell me that she was pulling in and not to cancel on me again.

No, she wouldn't do that. Not again.

I clicked on the voicemail, bringing it to my ear, smiling as soon as I heard her voice.

"Hey, it's me. I am actually grateful that you didn't answer..." Her voice trailed off, complete silence for a moment. "I've been thinking, Knight, and this, us being apart... I can't do it anymore. I can't be the girlfriend that sits at home every night, waiting for our scheduled video calls, our scheduled emails... I can't get into Oxford. My dad has exhausted every avenue and it can't happen." She stopped again. *Fuck, is she crying?* I could hear choked sobs. I wanted to cut it off and call her, but I needed to hear the rest of her message. "I'm sorry, Knight, but it's over." Then she cut off.

To listen to the message again, please press... I cut the phone off, pulling her number out and ringing. No answer. I did it again, and again, and again.

My heart shattered, the pieces falling away. My chest was heavy, tight. I felt like I had just had the air knocked out of my lungs, my eyes filling, my throat burning.

I called her again, but this time, she sent me straight to voicemail.

"Pey, baby... Please..." I didn't care that I was crying, my words coming out in stages through the broken, choked sobs. "You don't mean it, Cherry... don't do this...." I cut the phone off, I couldn't even finish my sentence. The hot tears rolled down my cheeks, my heart exploded and obliterated in my chest as I fell to my knees.

I scrolled to find Stefan's number.

No answer. I called again. And again until he answered.

"Knight?"

LOVE ALWAYS, PEYTON

"Did you know?" I screamed down the phone, my throat hurt, my voice hoarse.

"I've just found out from Poppy." His voice was cautious.

I fisted my hand into my hair, grabbing and tugging at it.

"What did she say? Why has she broken up with me?"

"I, er..." Stefan stammered.

"Fucking tell me!" I screamed at him, my heart jackhammering in my chest.

"Knight..."

"TELL ME!" My voice was loud and strained.

"She's met someone else... I am so sorry, man..."

I didn't listen to what he had to say next, I let the phone fall to the floor. My head tipped back as I roared into the empty room before falling forward and letting the tears flow.

She had broken me completely.

It didn't make sense.

I slowly sat back on my knees, the tears stopping, the pain seeping through my pours. I took a moment and welcomed the silence. Closing my eyes, I tried to still my heart from racing in my chest.

After what felt like a lifetime, I found my phone and punched Fred's number in, sniffing and palming my tears away.

"It's me, still going out?" I asked, my voice steady and low as I pushed all emotion away.

"Cool, I'll be there, and Freds, bring Autumn and a few others." Cutting the phone off, I threw it into the lounge area on the couch and walked into my bedroom, slamming it behind me.

How the fuck could she move on? I thought what we had was forever?

I felt my heart splinter again.

She didn't want me.

She didn't love me anymore.

If she could move on this quick, then so could I.

Epilogue Two

Knight

Ten Years Later

Looking at my watch, then back to the tool that was talking non-stop shit in front of me, I couldn't stop the roll of my eyes. I stood from behind my desk, buttoning my suit jacket up and walking in front of my desk before stopping. Clapping my hands and cocking my head to the side, I stopped the guy from talking.

"I've heard enough, thank you," I snarled at him. "Pierce Construction is not interested in trying to save your business, we build, we grow, we innovate. We're not a charity case," I snapped at him.

"But, Mr Pierce..."

I held my hand up. "Don't Mr Pierce me. You have already wasted enough of my time. I have to go." I didn't look at him as I walked past, heading straight to the elevator.

I had dinner with Amelie tonight, I needed a couple

of hours to unwind before we had to put on the show.

Waiting kerbside was my driver David, standing with the door open.

"Sir." He tipped his hat as he greeted me.

"David." I beamed at him as I slipped into the all-black Mercedes.

"Home, sir?" David asked as he started the car.

"Please."

We sat in silence on the short journey home when I saw my penthouse block in the distance. I built this building from scratch, and it was one of the tallest buildings in London, sitting like a giant along the city skylines and I had the best view of them all.

Kicking my shoes off and dropping my briefcase by the door, I padded through to the lounge of my open-plan home. Lifting the lid off of my crystal decanter, I poured myself a bourbon. It was Friday after all.

I heard my computer ping, and my brows furrowed as I turned to where I heard the noise coming from. My study. But this wasn't my work email, it was my personal.

Intrigued, I walked slowly into my study, placing my crystal glass on my desk and sitting in the chair as I clicked onto my email.

And there, an unread email sat at the top with a name I hadn't seen or heard in ten years.

Peyton Fallon.

LOVE ALWAYS, PEYTON

The End

Knight, Peyton, Poppy and Stefan will return for Way Back When Duet, Book Two.

Acknowledgements

Firstly, to my husband Daniel. Without you, none of this would have been possible. You support me in my dream, and push me when I feel like giving up. I couldn't do this without you by my side. I love you.

My amigos, thank you for being my ear when I have my moments of doubt, thank you for being my BETA readers. I am so glad I met you.

Lindsey, thank you for editing my book. I am so grateful to have met you.

Leanne, thank you for not only being an amazing, supportive friend but for also making my books go from boring word documents to an amazing finished product. I am so lucky I got to meet you two years ago.

Lea, thank you so much for not only being a wonderful friend, but for taking the time to read through my book not only once, but twice to make sure it all reads smoothly.

My bookstagram community, my last thanks goes to you. I will never be able to thank you enough for the amount of love and support you show me. Thank you.

If you would like to follow me on social media to keep up with my upcoming releases and teasers the links are below:

Instagram: http://bit.ly/38nen4b
Facebook: http://bit.ly/38qujyi
Reader group: https://bit.ly/3dkaxfa
Goodreads: http://bit.ly/2hmuxpz
Amazon: https://amzn.to/2hojupf
Bookbub: http://bit.ly/2ssvisd

If you loved my book, please leave a review.